THE UNDERWHARF

Gaby Naher was born in Sydney in 1967. She has studied in Sydney, Paris and Zurich and worked in New York and London as a book publicist. She has also worked in the fashion industry and as a disc jockey, a camera operator and a bookseller. She currently lives in Sydney.

THE UNDERWHARF

Gaby Naher

HAMISH HAMILTON · LONDON

06735882

HAMISH HAMILTON LTD

Published by the Penguin Group
Penguin Books Ltd, 27 Wrights Lane London W8 5TZ, England
Penguin Books USA Inc., 375 Hudson Street, New York, New York 10014, USA
Penguin Books Australia Ltd, Ringwood, Victoria, Australia
Penguin Books Canada Ltd, 10 Alcorn Avenue, Toronto, Ontario, Canada M4V 3B2
Penguin Books (N.Z.) Ltd, 182-190 Wairau Road, Auckland 10, New Zealand

Penguin Books Ltd, Registered Offices: Harmondsworth, Middlesex, England

First published by Penguin Books Australia, 1995

First published in Great Britain by Hamish Hamilton Ltd 1996
1 3 5 7 9 10 8 6 4 2

Copyright © Gaby Naher, 1995

The moral right of the author has been asserted

Printed in Australia by Australian Print Group

A CIP catalogue record for this book is available from the British Library

ISBN 0-241-13608-3

For their encouragement and support,
my thanks go to Katherine Bright-Holmes, Bryony Cosgrove,
Margo Daly, Justine Ettler, Jill Hickson, Kate Jones,
Jacqueline Naher, Tony Peake, Rosie Waitt and Adrian Weston.
For their inspiration: Anna Bubner, Gus Monette and
Liz Phair's lyrics. And for a different sort of support,
George Naher and Paul Watchman.

THE FOOL

I've read and re-read the cards, and still they won't tell me what to say to him. Or how he'll receive me, or if he'll receive me. I rehearse my story, the story of my life without him. Perhaps I should tell him nothing, leave him to ask, him to tell, him to explain.

Draw a card, any card from the pack on the floor by the bed. How many cards have I drawn this interminable, sweltering night?

And will it suffice for me to tell him whose daughter I am? He could not sentence me to a life as a guest in the families of others. He'll say, Sophia, what a beautiful name. Tell me everything. Tell me your whole life.

- What will I say? I ask Sam when I call her from the becalmed void of the Manhattan loft, where the breeze has yet

1

to stir the gauze curtains, where my hand sweats fear onto the black plastic of the telephone receiver.

- Tell him about the bush and how we were The Adventurers, she says, her voice high with the excitement that whirls around her. In the background, her son's wail announces another mealtime. Soph, what time is it there?

- Three. In the morning, I admit, fretful from sleeplessness now. Yeah, I'll tell him, Sammy. I'll tell him about the bush, and the harbour, and about always running away. I'll tell him I would have been a lousy daughter. That he was lucky.

- Soph, don't. Tell him he's the one who missed out, she says, and mid-sentence drops the phone. I can hear her cooing to her son – he's even needier than me.

- Sammy, better go. Better try to sleep. Give my love to that boy. Give him a kiss, no tongue, and tell him I miss him, I say, jumping at the staccato round of bottles being smashed on the pavement below. And thanks for everything Sam, in Sydney, I mean. I would have been so alone without you. I would have hidden from them all without you.

Weekends were for scavenging, seagull-like, on the harbour's shores. They were for Sam and me and the slip of sand and rock that held the land and sea apart. Of course it wasn't always able to keep the two apart: out at the point, the drowned sailor's crucifix was testament to the fact. Before a vast expanse of water, where winds crashed into each other from all points of the compass, a slab of sandstone had been buffeted by sea to form a natural grotto. Wrought iron, dark as coal, entwined to fashion a crude crucifix. No-one had said so, but Sammy and I just knew that there on our own shoreline, a metre from the shell-shaped rock, a blue-eyed, blond-haired sailor boy had met his death. He'd looked up at the limitless, luminous sky one last time before being dragged under, down and away. The cause of death varied, according to our mood: one day it was a simple drowning; the next a shark attack in knee-deep water; and the next a youth suicide, pockets filled with smooth harbour stones.

During the week, Sam and I barely saw each other, our schools on different sides of the city. Sometimes I caught a glimpse of the maroon school uniforms worn by her and her two sisters. When she was with them she belonged to them, and our world of the bush and the bay and the drowned sailor's crucifix couldn't possibly exist. From the bus window I waved to her, a small, secret gesture, as she and her sisters helped their mum with the shopping. Zelda and I never shopped together; she had her secretary telephone the order to the supermarket on Fridays, and I unpacked the delivery on Saturday mornings.

It grew so hot in November that the neighbourhood cats and dogs passed out under verandas and parked cars. I stopped twice at garden hoses on the way from the bus stop to turn the sun-warmed water on my fuzzball head. The first trickle from the tap was warm as piss running down my inside leg, but by the time I hosed my body the water had turned cool as deep earth and left my skin white with goose bumps. There were two regular shower stops on the way home, both in gardens with hoses near the footpath, a screen of wattle between the road and the house. The snake-spitting sound of garden sprinklers cannot but evoke a lifetime of walking home from school alone on those torpid Sydney Harbour afternoons. The closer to our house I got, the more the gum trees crowded in on the road and the breeze from the harbour nudged the afternoon heat haze.

In the lush darkness of my bedroom I dropped the sackcloth

of my school uniform and rolled the damp, blue regulation cottontails down my legs. My mother hated the Indian dresses I wore at home: long, flowing cheesecloth adorned with tiny glass mirrors and bells that filled the silent house with their laughter. Even more she hated my refusal to wear anything beneath them.

Freshly brewed Lapsang Souchong and great green and gold slices of chilled melon and pineapple. There by my grandmother Nella's Russian teapot, I recovered and steeled myself against the return of my mother. Just as Zelda and I were opposites, so too were Zelda and Nella. Nella didn't live with us there among the gum trees, but it was Nella who raised me. If I am anyone's daughter, I am hers.

My afternoon meandered. Day faded, and with it, the heat's hard edge. Alone, I listened to the relentless buzz of the cicadas as it rose to a brilliant crescendo towards dusk, the creatures smug in the knowledge that another day had passed without falling prey to the snapping blue-black beak of a kookaburra.

My body tensed as I heard the angry growl of my mother's car in the driveway. Before the car door slammed or the sound of stilettos on concrete travelled inside, I was gone. My Dunlop Volleys, soft, grippy shoes, stuck to the mossy rocks and water-engorged branches by the moonlit creek bed. Blue-tongued lizards scuttled into shadows at my approach.

Where the creek suddenly dropped down to the inlet, mangroves wallowed and mosquitoes swarmed. There I cut across towards the headland, passing beneath the row of cliff-top houses with my skirt bunched high around my waist, lithe as any nocturnal bush rodent, all eyes and curling, clasping tail. I plucked a stick from the ground near the creek and waved it maniacally before me to clear spider webs from the path. One night, when the stars were too arresting, too filled with my own dreams, I'd walked into a web that wrapped itself around my face like a warm cloth, lightly coated in sugar water. Spider-spun fairy floss in my mouth. Silent screams as I ran my fingers through my uncombed frizz, feeling gingerly for the spider. Frantic lest I should feel its velvet legs on my scalp. Imagining it crawling into my gaping singlet and down towards the bunched folds of my skirt.

I moved much faster through the bush then, less mindful of the possums I might frighten, and clambered onto my rock. Grateful for the familiar sensation of sandstone crumbling under my fingertips. In my own domain of three square metres, water before me, suburbia behind, I wrestled the singlet over my head and shook it so hard that no spider could cling to the weave. I ran my fingers across my breasts and back and shivered at the thought of furry legs, dancing on my skin.

With singlet for a pauper's pillow I lay on warm sandstone and imagined moonbeams on my breasts. The breeze soothed me, sweetened the night. I was a moon child, entranced by the glow of the lunar dawn, mapping the moon's trajectory that measured my days, divided segments of my life, and assured me that time was passing. That gentle presence removed me from the house, the mother, and the tiny voice that screamed, What else? What else?

The caramel-coloured sandstone held the sun's heat long into the close, whispering night. Grains of rock coated the backs of bare calves and shoulderblades, rubbing into elbows and adorning strands of damp hair. Cicadas, loud and shrill in the still darkness, provided a rhythm for my breathing. I focused on a single gum. Eyes straining through the black ink of night, I could make out, or perhaps dream, the white saucer eyes of a possum, staring at me with as much quiet intent as I myself was generating. And once, oh small miracle, there was the second set of tiny, white-ringed eyes of the possum pup clinging to the bristling back of its mother.

The wind rose and the song of the halyards, wire slapping against aluminium mast, floated up from the bay, reminding me of monastery bells. The prayer bells of the lost and lonely.

When I left Sydney for London at nineteen, my mother had her secretary, Jonathan, drive me to the airport. Despite the fact that I hadn't seen Zelda since the morning of the previous day, the plan didn't incorporate a stop at her office; she was working with an author. A young hopeful, someone who would redeem her reputation after a recent fiasco related to the company's purchase of a previous lover's fiction trilogy.

The Jonathan who arrived to pick me up was not the Jonathan I'd met at a party in our house a year earlier. The latest Jonathan informed me that in fact there'd been a Steven in between him and his namesake. It was around midday when he turned Zelda's car into the drive, and Sam and I ran through the house to find each other, both saying, He's here, he's here, oh no, oh no.

It was Sam who dragged herself to the door to let him in, wearing her best grunge: chunky black combat boots, ripped leggings, cut-off jeans that were tight enough to make me wonder whether she'd been wearing them since she was twelve, hair in what she told me were over fifty braids and black bra top under the inevitable black leather jacket. Grunge aside, she'd made a remarkable recovery from the previous night's farewell party. From my room I could hear Jonathan saying, But, I thought this was Zelda's house. You're not Sophia are you? I mean, are you?

A schizoid's laugh escaped her as she took Jonathan by the elbow and dragged him to an armchair. I heard her offering him a drink and him saying, Oh no, couldn't, got to drive. Zelda chose dull, servile assistants, or ground them down to this condition, but they were always male and I couldn't help approving of that touch.

- Are you sure, lovey? Sam asked. We're not ready to go yet.

- No, no, he said, clearing his throat in tortured embarrassment. You really don't look like Zelda.

- No-one looks like Zelda, she said, shrieking with laughter again. No, lovey, I'm Sam, but you can call me Samantha, seeing as you don't really know me.

I sat, desolate, on my suitcase, listening to the gush of vodka being poured straight into one of my mother's scotch tumblers. We were already two drinks past hair of the dog. The euphoria I kept trying to swallow at leaving Zelda's house was overwhelmed by the remorse I felt for leaving my oldest friend.

- Help, Sammy, I called, feeble. I can't do this alone.

- Want a voddy? she called back.

I said no but she poured regardless and fell into the room with a glass in each hand. She never spilled a drop.

- Oh Soph, she said, holding back the tears that threatened her forced delirium. You're gonna have to leave one of those boxes of photos behind. And I really think you should take out the kelim.

- But Sam, that's where—

- I know, I know. That's where you had your first fuck. But Soph, without this room it doesn't mean shit.

- Just come and plant yourself on this corner, I said in a sad, little girl voice.

- Oi, Jonathan, don't just sit there, screamed Sam, loud and dirty as the street itself. We need your muscle, boy. You do have muscles don't you, under that pretty blue blouse?

In the doorway Jonathan shifted from loafer-clad foot to loafer-clad foot as though entering that domain of chaos might interfere with his trouser pleats. He applied his beautiful, white manicured hands to the zipper, coyly negotiating his way around four booted legs.

On the deck I was reassured by a kookaburra's laugh; my last kookaburra, I thought. It's good to be able to mark such events, otherwise I'd be up all night in London, trying to remember exactly when I last heard one. Sam and I stood with arms around each other's waists, wet cheeks pressed together.

- I won't come back here Soph, once you're gone. I'll just stay in the city ... only think of the suburbs when I want to feel good about what I'm doing with my life.

- Your Mum'll start talking to you again, Sammy, don't worry, I said, squeezing the clump of leather jacket I held in my hand and pulling her closer. Time heals all wounds ... well, that's what Nella reckons.

- If Mum's not on my back about who I'm sleeping with, she'll find something. Y'know, the house I live in, the dole, the number of earrings I wear, the tattoo. And she'll never even know the real shit.

- Come on Sammy, we don't want to ruin our last day together talking about her, do we? I said, watching a tear that threatened to rearrange her mascara.

I left heaps of discarded clothing around my bedroom floor, provoking Zelda to break the only house rule and enter my room. Just like I'd gone into hers to take a black silk teddy to wear under my charcoal tube dress on the plane. Would she simply clear the room of my things, bundle them up and put them under the house in my empty darkroom? Or worse still, give them away? As I shut my bedroom door, it seemed I would never again sleep in a bed that felt quite so full of dreams as that canopied relic.

We drove along the leafy streets I'd walked so many times. I pulled my Pentax out of its case and turned around to snap Sam in the act of popping the cork from the bottle she'd pilfered from Zelda's fridge. As Madonna blasted from the two speakers at the front of the car and Sam and I sang along to 'Papa Don't Preach', small, sinister beads of sweat appeared on Jonathan's upper lip, on skin that looked as though it may never have known razors in its entire lip-hood.

- Sophia, he said, trying to make himself heard without going beyond his own natural boundaries of assertiveness, your mother asked me to get your keys from you.

- What? I said, choking on the fizzy stuff as I passed the bottle back to Sam.

- I'm sorry, he said, sweat now on his forehead. I thought she'd have told you. She asked me to get your house keys ... probably worried you'll lose them with all the travelling. You know?

Giggling great waves of vodka and champagne out of my body, I worked three keys off a ring with my thumbnail, hung my hand out the window and dropped them into a conveniently positioned drain.

- Oh, sorry Jonathan. I seem to have lost them.

Shrieks from the back seat as Jonathan eyed me in disbelief. He cut the engine and began to open the door before changing his mind as the traffic started moving again and drivers behind us honked their horns.

- Probably worried you'd give them to me, Soph, said Sam,

all concerned understanding, omitting to mention that she had her own set, anyway.

- Don't worry, Jonathan, Boy Wonder, I said, using Zelda's endearment. Just tell her I lost them. So long as you reassure her that I've really left the bloody country, you can be sure of staying in her good books for at least another six weeks or so ... depending on your performance of course.

On the Harbour Bridge, Sam and I shout-sang the words of 'Like a Virgin', exaggerating the camp Madonna sighs like we'd done when we first heard the song in an Oxford Street night-club. As we emerged from the curving tunnel, I braced myself for a last glimpse of the fingerwharf.

Fingerwharves? I asked, when I first heard Nella use the term. I imagined ship-sized, fleshy human fingers protruding into the bay, being slowly consumed by barnacles, periwinkles, oysters, mussels, congis and the occasional sick shark that didn't have the strength to fend for itself out where the swell was big as a house. Out there beyond the Heads.

The car powered through Sydney's streets of inner-city terraces, Woolloomooloo and Darlinghurst blurring in my bloodshot eyes, me gulping down the tennis ball that had lodged itself in my throat. Reliving parties that spilled from Surry Hills terraces through interminable, sultry nights, then moved on to one of the early opening pubs near the breweries around seven or eight in the morning.

As the car idled in the traffic below Taylor Square, Sam and I exchanged looks that said I dare you, I dare you. Before the car could turn onto the road for the airport, we were out and cutting through traffic and shouting to Jonathan to meet us at the Exchange in ten minutes. Without bothering to check whether he had heard, or even knew the Exchange, we hurtled around the corner and collided with the news-stand crammed with glossy boys' magazines. Sammy went down on her knees on top of those laid out on the ground, straddling ten hairless chests in one drunken tumble. Then we were black booting our way down Oxford Street, passing too fast the night-clubs, gay bars, Lebanese fast food joints, cafés and hipper than hip boutiques.

I ran with my tube dress up around my thighs, flashing Zelda's lace teddy, and Sam ran with her thumb over the bottle's opening, stopping to take a slug when the traffic permitted. Slowing at the sight of a ute on the other side of the road that looked like Jake's, I stopped completely on the corner of Crown and Oxford. A man in a shiny grey suit, scabby with cheap wine and miscellaneous bodily fluid, took two steps in one direction and said, Help, took two steps in another direction and said, Help, and then repeated the procedure. I was struck by his calm, by his absolute conviction. His tangle of grey hair belonged to someone much older than he, someone who'd spent years sleeping down at the Matthew Talbot, not just months. Help. Help. Help, he said after every second step, looking through people, calling to someone who was not there.

- You alright? I asked, easing my skirt down, putting a hot hand out to touch him and watching it left empty as he paced on. What's wrong?

- Help, he said, not looking at me.

- Tell me what you need, I whispered, convinced that both of our lives depended on this moment.

- Help, he repeated, looking through me, eyelids never dropping over those enormous pupils.

Around us, the pace slowed. People were stopping now, when before they hadn't; casual observers, watching me, not him. I was the spectacle, the idiot who thought she might make a difference. He was just regulation issue. As Sammy pulled me on towards the bar, little refugees from suburbia that we were, my heart beat in time with his pleas.

- Hey, it's The Adventurers! shrieked Tom from behind the counter, a fellow refugee from the harbour foreshores.

Sydney's like that – filled with people you went to school with or grew up next door to and whom, inevitably, you're trying to escape. Trying to erase. Tom, as a fellow escapee, didn't really count. He wasn't someone whose appearance on the street prompted me to dive into the nearest open doorway. I'd find myself in barber shops studying the girlie postcards around the mirrors, in shops that sold corsets and false limbs, in beauty parlours all sticky hot pink, and in the sort of pubs where men sit and drink all day without catching even a fleeting glimpse of a woman. I dreaded being approached by one of those girls from school who would say, Hi Sophie, we wondered what happened to you. Do you still read those crazy cards and fancy yourself a photographer? We got married and didn't finish university and now we're pregnant and living in the same street we grew up in. We've already booked a place at Star of Jesus and another at St Michael's for the child.

And they would press for details, for good gossip to trade. Ho, me, I'm just a tattooist, mainly, but sometimes, what with HIV and all, I strip to make more money. Y'know how it is?

- Quick, Tom, two double voddies, on the rocks. Plastic cups, we've got a plane to catch, barked Sam, her voice taut.

- Oh, Darls, you off to Melbourne again?

- Nah, Melbourne schmelbourne. London, Tommy, London. Piccadilly Circus. Leicester Square. Punk. London, Sammy said, in a wistful, crummy cockney accent. Well, Soph's going to London. I'm going to the airport.

Ever so subtly a crack had formed in her voice and threatened to engulf her. In an instant, Tommy was on our side of the bar with his arms around us both, all cigarettes, amyl and Eternity.

- What will Marlborough Street do without you? he said, alluding to Sam's group house that I all but lived in. You can do it. Live apart. You'll both be just fine; think of the homecoming party, think of the presents you'll score from London, Sam! Think of the piss we'll take when she comes into the Sexchange with a pom in her mouth!

- Yeah. The bitch. Going away and leaving us in this big, old country town, said Sam through her sobs, turning herself into Pierrot le Fou in two swipes at her eyes with the back of one hand.

My gaze kept snagging on these tiny details, things I'd seen a hundred times and ignored: the tiers of the empty dance floor, ledges I'd stumbled from while dancing, a mirror ball looking grey and tarnished in the daylight, the smoked mirrors on the walls that dulled my reflection when they were wet with the breath of the whole heaving dance floor. That corner nearest to the stairs where I'd first sniffed amyl, that alcove on the back wall where I'd first seen two women pashing, the steps leading downstairs to a second dance floor that you had to reach by running past a row of urinals.

When Sam and I stumbled onto the pavement, clutching a bottle of Seaspew champagne that Tom had slipped under the counter, Jonathan was pacing the footpath in some white-rabbit-without-a-pocket-watch impersonation. Looking harassed but resolved in his powerlessness. It was unthinkable that a guy like him would set foot in the Exchange ... he never knew how many men were in there, just waiting to get a handful of ripe buttock. As Sam and I fell into the back seat, tangled in each other's limbs, Jonathan swung out into the traffic with a panache that made me look again. I kept catching his eyes on us in the rear-view mirror as we necked the second bottle.

- What're you looking at? Think you're going to see some lesbian sex that you can tell the boys in the office about? Tell them that Zelda's daughter's a convent school dyke? I shrieked, setting Sam off on a great show of groping my tits and poking her tongue in my ear.

- I don't care what you do, he said, opting for the worldly tone. It just seems to me that you're drinking an awful lot for someone about to embark on a twenty-eight-hour flight. I mean, last time I did it I was a wreck when I got to London, and that was without the booze.

- That was the missing ingredient, I quipped, thinking that maybe Sam and I looked pathetic to him, thinking that he must just know that neither of us had ever been overseas. With any luck I'll sleep all the way to London. Wake up when I reach Piccadilly Circus. Have my very own neon revelation.

We drove in silence, watching the last of the inner-city pubs fly by before hitting the industrial wasteland that had breathed its blight into that part of the city. The extended mix of 'Blue Monday' was the only thing that kept us from hearing each other's thoughts clanging around in our heads. The only thing that stopped me from hearing the man saying Help. I climbed into the front seat, forcing Jonathan to press himself against the door as my bottom invaded his driving space. It was a brilliant, late spring afternoon. The sky so blue that it penetrated my alcohol daze like the wet tongue of the most brutal lover.

- So, Jonathan, I said, turning the music down low and moving my whole body side on to face his. Have you fucked her yet?

- I beg your pardon! Jonathan almost swerved into a car in the inside lane. What are you talking about?

- Oh, don't play dumb, Boy Wonder, you don't have to protect her reputation on our account. We've both grown up with her lovers. With her one-night stands.

- Tell us where you did it, said Sam from the back seat, her tongue sounding thick, dry in her mouth.

- Don't be ridiculous, said Jonathan, frowning in concentration before the intersection ahead.

- Don't take it personally. Zelda fucks all her assistants. That's why she only employs men. Young men. I know because one of them was my lover for a while, I added, watching like a vulture for his undoing. Shame we didn't meet earlier.

As we drove around the perimeter of the airport, past the hangars and the cargo jets, I felt mean, ugly and unwashed. Part of me wouldn't permit myself to even attempt to recall the number of times I'd put her down in front of her colleagues. I never meant to, but somehow I'd glimpse her vulnerability and have to sink my teeth in until I drew blood. My mother, the angry feminist, just couldn't stop seducing men: young boys, business associates, authors, even the fathers of girls I went to school with.

The car swung into the unloading bay and Sam and I stepped into the sobering world of porters and taxis and families of vast suitcases. I welcomed the sense of purpose that came to me, and I became efficient, taking control through the champagne dusk. Poor Boy Wonder was told to wait around and drive Sam back to the city, and then we were fussing with trolleys and tickets and passports and departure taxes. Sammy knew the Qantas guy at the desk from some club, and he delighted in bumping me up to first class, winking when I asked about free drinks. He told me he had a surprise for me, and asked how did I feel about wealthy middle-aged men?

Sammy was reluctant to leave the check-in area and kept looking towards the clear sliding doors that led to the street.

- Come on, Sammy.

- But Jake ...

- He's not coming, I said, feeling in my pocket, panic rising until I felt the cool, stone carving he'd given me the night before.

- Of course he'll come, she said, brave but giving me a wet-eyed smile.

- He walked out on me last night while you were out of it. I already told you.

She hung her head for a moment then started rooting around in her woven shoulder bag, almost as an afterthought.

- Here lovey, you won't find these in Pom, she said, pressing five Violet Crumble bars into my hand in a gesture that was our undoing.

- Sammy, I said, through a tightening throat. If I don't go now I never will.

We glided like deep sleep victims to the point of no return, both eyeing the Passengers Only sign and identifying it as the enemy.

- You look after yourself, Sammy, y'hear? I'll be really angry if you let yourself get all fucked up, I said, my mouth close to her ear and my free arm clamped tightly around her neck.

- Oh, Soph, don't worry about me. You're the one going night swimming alone. Go Sophie, go, she said, putting all my pieces in place and pushing me away. And don't you forget to tell your father about me and how maybe he knew my Mum as well. How maybe he's got two daughters ...

On the other side of the panel I could still hear Sammy

calling, Bye Soph, bye Soph, bye Soph; and at that moment, in a room filled with teary fellow travellers, I felt as though I'd been clobbered with my own aloneness. What am I doing? I kept asking myself, rushing the words of my new mantra.

- Travelling alone? the man at the desk asked as he tried to reconcile my blotchy face with my prim passport photo.

Behind me, an Englishwoman said, I just don't know why they all go to London, they've so much more than we do right here, at home. I was filled with scornful disbelief. It wasn't that I was an anglophile, more that I was convinced Sydney couldn't contain me. A lover that I'd outgrown.

Before boarding, I spent twenty minutes sitting in a moulded plastic chair, feeding myself Violet Crumble after Violet Crumble. Only when I finished all five and deposited the purple wrappers did a great wave of nausea send me scrambling for the cool, porcelain relief of a toilet bowl. With my body convulsing in the tiny cubicle I thought, Help, help, help, but knew there was no helping myself.

I walked back and forth along the departure strip, watching the shadow and light cross the faces that floated by. Watching the great conveyor belt of tourism and displacement. I wandered into a bar, but before I reached the counter I turned away. How could I sit in a bar and drink without Sam? And anyway, it seemed halfway smart to try to embark on my new life on legs that didn't shake and with breath that didn't smell like my mother's. But finally, in my first-class window seat and getting my last eyeful of *Terra australis tarmaccus*, I knew that I hadn't even begun to leave my mother behind.

Zelda accuses me of misremembering everything, but I know

that, in my first years of school, it was Nella who came each day to collect me at the gate and take me on the train over the Harbour Bridge. We sat on the top floor of the old double-decker carriages, and from my position by the window I described the arrangement and rearrangement of the container ships in the west harbour. There was nothing finer than the sight of a Russian cargo vessel moving towards the silos at White Bay to fill its hold with wheat.

In the subterranean warren of Wynyard station we changed onto the Eastern Suburbs line, direction Bondi Junction, Nella gripping me tightly at the elbow lest we be separated by the crowds brewing before rush hour. She lived in what was once Sydney's most cosmopolitan enclave, prior to its descent into a briny, tourist-infested red-light district. Kings Cross was an education that began to distance me from the girls at school, anaesthetised as they were by the niceties of Sydney's leafy harbour suburbs.

We rode up the escalators from the platform and I caught random glimpses of angry or vacant people; Nella called them hookers and junkies. She told me that hookers were products of a patriarchal, capitalist society, labouring to explain her words. We, as their sisters, needed to understand and sympathise with the way they lived. She insisted that economics had forced them into this role in society, and that she and I were in no way better people than they were.

In religion, our sixth-grade teacher, Mrs Powell, asked us to write an essay on our favourite biblical figure. I chose Mary Magdalen. On the morning the essays were returned, with a voice unnaturally high, Mrs Powell asked me if I knew what a prostitute was.

I stood up.

- A prostitute is just a woman, like you or my grandmother, who has been forced by the patriarchal capitalist society to charge men money for doing things to their dicks, I said, confident in the belief that I knew something no-one else did. It's not that they're any better or worse than you, Mrs Powell, though usually they're quite pretty to begin with; it's just that society has forced them into this role.

The class was silent for a moment, and then girls began to whisper to each other and squirm in their seats with ill-contained, embarrassed laughter. Mrs Powell opened and closed her mouth like a goldfish trawling for food, then turned on her wedge heel and with great clunking steps ran from the room.

- Is your grandmother a prostitute, Soph? Maria asked, her voice cracking with excitement.

- Na, but she lives in Kings Cross where the prostitutes work. She knows a few of them. Drinks coffee with them sometimes.

- What do they do with the men's dicks, Soph? screamed Katie, burying her face in her hands at the broken taboo of her own utterance of the dick word, which was really nothing compared to cock or schlong or penis.

- I think they mainly rub them, but sometimes they put them between their legs or in their mouths, I told them with suave nonchalance as Mrs Powell and Sister Superior entered the room.

Sister's cane pointer quivered. A sudden dryness came to my mouth as the cane was pointed in my direction and Sister gestured for me to come forward. As she began to tell the silent room that prostitutes were sinners, fallen women who had to ask God for forgiveness, I forced my body to do as it had been told, wondering what they'd fallen off, those women, by way of distraction more than anything else.

Then came blurred, bright flashes of pain. I don't remember

what Sister said to me or what I thought when she made me bend over her desk with my dress up and my cottontails down. Nor do I remember who carried me to the sick bay, where Nella found me an hour later. Face down on a narrow bed with my tear-swollen cheek on the blue terry cotton spread, I worried about my school uniform staining where it was sticking to my bottom and the backs of my thighs. I fretted about my underpants and where they might be. Zelda would be livid if I caught the train all the way to Nella's bare-bottomed.

We didn't take the train that day. Nella swept in and ushered me slowly, gravely, into a taxi waiting outside the school gate like Cinderella's carriage. I remember seeing Sister trying to stop Nella as she stepped into the taxi and Nella saying in her biggest, most scary voice that she would indeed be speaking to her. In the presence of the family lawyer after a visit to the GP.

- Why did she take my underpants, Nella? I asked, drowsy from something the doctor had cajoled me into drinking.

- Never you mind, Sophie, my sweet. Nella enfolded me in her musky embrace as though I were as frail as a ladybird on her sleeve, kissing my curly head. She just became very angry and took her anger out on you.

I saw we were driving through gum trees, not city streets.

- She's an unhappy woman, Nella said. What she did this afternoon has nothing to do with anything you said or did.

As the taxi pulled up outside Zelda's, confused, I registered the black car's presence.

- But do you think she'll do it again, Nella?

- You don't ever have to see her again, she said. I promise you don't.

It was Nella who settled me in my oversized wooden boat of a bed, making a fortress for me among the brightly coloured pillows, opening two windows so I could sleep to the sound of the Japanese bell and wind chimes, just outside. It was she who sat stroking my hair and singing in a low, sad voice.

Later, I was woken by the sound of them screaming at each other. Nella's voice had turned big and frightening again, while my mother's voice was just a pitch higher than usual.

- How can you send an intelligent, sensitive child to a convent school, Zelda? They're for primitives. Oh, for her sake, take her out before you succeed in ruining her life.

I could hear the tap tap of my mother's heels on the Tasmanian hardwood floor in the lounge room, the thump of a glass, probably gin and tonic, on one of the low Nepalese coffee tables.

- Why don't you keep the hell out of my daughter's life? And then came Nella's ridiculing laugh, reassuring me that her presence was irrevocable. I'm not moving her. She needs the discipline and you know she's getting a top-notch education for a fraction of the price father forked out for me.

- Oh, that's right, you just go right ahead and rely on them to discipline your child. I suppose that's a prime concern for you as you're never here to do it yourself.

- What would you have me do, Nella? Quit my job? Spend a few years as full-time mother to a child that resents me? Watch her leave home as soon as she possibly can?

More clacking of heels on hardwood, ice-cubes against crystal. I tried to remain very still as I listened with dread for Nella to tell her, Yes.

- If she's as smart as you say she is, then the religion won't make any bloody difference, Nella. She'll make her own decisions.

- Well, religion made a difference today ... if that's your idea of discipline I'm appalled! I know you don't want to think about it, but you're going to have to face those welts of hers. She'll never forgive you if you don't deal with this.

- I'm not in fucking oil, Mother, shouted Zelda, her voice beginning to lower in spite of herself. I can't afford to send her to one of the private schools near you, and give her holidays, and God knows what else she'll need as she gets older.

One of the few things I knew they agreed about was not asking my father, whoever or wherever he was, for money. Mother had told me from the earliest that he didn't know I existed and that was how she wanted it. Nella backed her on this point: women should raise their daughters.

- Alright then, Zelda, she'll stay where she is, but you and Rob are going to pay a visit to the head of the Order with the doctor's report, said Nella, resolute. The woman's a psychopathic bitch. We'll go right over her haloed head and get *her* disciplined – threaten to go to the *Herald*, the *Australian*, the *Sun* . . . wherever.

I took my mother's silence for assent, an agreement that must have hurt her because it necessitated calling on Rob for a favour. Rob, the son of Nella's lover, Charlie, was a solicitor with one of Sydney's biggest firms. Nella and I had been to his office several times to plan a surprise party for Charlie on his seventy-fifth birthday. I was so taken by the view from the glass tower, encompassing Circular Quay and its frantic, darting ferries cutting strips through the teal-coloured water, that I told Rob he could be my lawyer. Sometimes a liner was berthing or departing, and I'd see ropes of coloured streamers that seemed to anchor the ship to the wharf, then threaten to drag those teary and left behind in the terminal to Fiji or New Caledonia in the wake of the SS *Arcadia* or *Oriana*.

When Zelda finally came to me, I could smell the gin on her

breath. It was not yet hot enough for her to be sweating it as she did over Christmas and New Year.

- Zelda? I began, before she had a chance to say all the mushy things she probably felt she ought to. Can we go to Rob's office tomorrow to watch the ferries before you go and see Sister and her halo?

- Sophie! Zelda tried to control the irritation in her voice. How many times have I told you about eavesdropping?

- But I wasn't eavesdropping, Mummy, I replied, calling her that because I knew she hated it. I was just lying here in bed and you and Nella were shouting. I couldn't help hearing what you said. It's not as if it wasn't my business; you were talking about me.

- Go on, love, show me what Sister did to you, she said, pulling back my sheet.

Again, I was worried about the underwear situation. Nella had put me to bed wearing only a muslin camisole. I couldn't tell if the sharp intake of breath was because of my bandaged bottom or the weals that were crusting on the sheet.

- Does it hurt, Soph? she asked, trying to make her voice sound kind, like Nella's.

- No, I lied, frightened of her sympathy. Nella took care of me.

- Good, she said, flicking the sheet up to my waist and striding back to the doorway. Well, if you need anything I'll be in my study, reading. Thomas has just finished his new novel and if I like it, he'll give it to me to publish instead of those incompetents who made such a dog's breakfast of his last one. Isn't that exciting, Soph?

- Yes, Zelda, I said, then mumbled into my pillow, and it's probably a load of horse shit.

Nella and I had competitions to see who could come up with

the foulest smelling item in any category. In the shit category, I decided it was horse shit, for healthy animals at least. In cheese it was Stilton, which we both loved. She told me how my grandfather had once brought some Harrod's Stilton into the country after a trip to London. The wax that sealed the cheese had cracked, and for days his underwear gave off a full-bodied Stilton stench. She said that he really had smelt good enough to eat.

When Zelda said she'd be in her study reading a manuscript, I knew that meant only to disturb her if the house was burning down, and then not to expect her to react immediately. From behind the study's closed door at the far end of the lounge room, I'd hear a sudden peel of laughter, or agonised groans, or sometimes she'd swear and I'd hear her saying the author's name. Other times she'd come out of her study with her skin flushed and her clothes dishevelled, as if she'd been in there with a man. Sometimes she'd stride into my room, maybe turn the light on if I was asleep, and tell me she'd made a brilliant discovery. Mostly, her brilliant discoveries were men I'd met at the breakfast table a few days before; sometimes I'd even get to know them by name and by how they liked their coffee.

Down the aisle of the jumbo came the promised, wealthy middle-aged man – late forties, early fifties – but one who worked out. And as far as rich went, I assumed that anyone who flew first class, aside from real scumbags like me, had to either be very wealthy or have some top-notch executive job, which wasn't the same thing in my opinion.

He took one look at me, huddled against the moulded vinyl around the window, and let out a long, low chuckle. Diabolic, I thought. Great! I'm spending the next day and a bit of my life with a serial killer. Though for a serial killer, he dressed alright – immaculate khaki gabardine trousers, expensively cut, and a simple white t-shirt without the tragic chains and chunky jewellery that the most unlikely men were wearing those days. He wore Doc Marten combat boots just like mine.

- Well, hello, he said, in a mid-western drawl, not quite in my direction. So, will you be joining me in champagne, or will you be doing that black coffee thing?

I looked around slowly, just to be sure he was speaking to me and not to some flight attendant, or to his own id.

- I drink champagne, I said, reaching into the bag under my legs and pulling out my shades.

- The champagne will be much more therapeutic than the dark glasses, he said. Trust me, I know.

I gave him my most withering stare, lost on him on account of the shades. Through the window I watched men in Stubbies and long socks loading suitcases into the hold. I watched toy cars without roofs on them buzz around like worker bees feeding their queen. Across lawns the size of three football fields I watched the smaller, domestic planes load up for flights to my childhood holiday destinations – Surfers Paradise, Hobart, Melbourne.

As the jet engines forced us backward, I pressed myself into the seat and squashed my knees together. Take-off was the best of all, the real start of the journey, that surge of power that evoked the mixed blessings of freedom and anonymity. We flew out over the ocean and the dunes of the Kurnell Refinery and then my breath came slow and shallow as the jumbo banked to its left and we flew over the harbour. And over the bay where my mother's house was barely visible among the gum trees. Was that Sam down there on the point, near the crucifix on its sandstone pedestal? No, she was in Surry Hills seducing Zelda's secretary if I knew my Sammy.

- This is your captain speaking. You're all a bunch of arseholes to be leaving Sydney on such a gorgeous day, but as you felt compelled, I want to thank you for choosing to fly Qantas.

He couldn't have called us a bunch of arseholes; none of the other passengers were reacting.

- The first leg of our journey takes us across the New England Tablelands and then out over the desert. The desert's awash with its own blood because you wankers don't appreciate your own country.

I began to wonder whether Sam had slipped a trip, Blue Pyramid or Purple Dusk, into one of the morning's vodkas. Maybe the captain was tripping. You'd have some pretty disturbing hallucinations in the cockpit of a jumbo jet.

I relished the sensation of my body pressing into the sumptuous blue velvet of the seat and wiggled around, pulling my tube dress down so it didn't bunch around my middle, loosening the laces of my boots, standing to remove my leather jacket, stashing it in the overhead locker with my camera case, then sitting down and doing the whole settling into the seat procedure again.

- How do you feel about wearing other people's undergarments? I asked my neighbour once we were sipping our first glass of champagne. My name's Sophia.

To his credit, he didn't choke. I liked him for that. A slow smile crept over his tanned, puffy face. Fucken great, I thought. A serial killer and a fetishist. Probably wearing lace knickers himself.

- I'm wearing my mother's silk teddy, you see, I said, confessional. It feels weird. I've never done it before.

- You could just take it off, he said with that same 'trust me' tone as he slid his cold blue eyes over the length of my harbour swimmer's body.

- Maybe later, I said, ignoring the runny, olive oil feel of his eyes. It's just that, well think about it, my mother's tits were once draped with this very silk. The same breasts that fed me. And now that silk is touching me in those intimate places ... reminds me of sharing a man with her.

- And how was that? he asked, voice smooth as bush honey.

- Not so bad, I shrugged, staring out the window, watching the rough scar on the land, the Great Dividing Range, as it mellowed into the checker-board order of New England. And then the earth seemed to dry and crack as we flew over it. Out the window, lush green turned to pale green turned to brown and I supposed the red was out there somewhere. I hardly knew my own country and was just buggering off.

- Fucken great, I repeated under my breath as I turned to see my neighbour scribbling in a spiral-bound notebook with a greenish tinge to its pages. A fetishist, a serial killer and a writer, too.

- You're not a writer are you? I asked, prepared to give him the benefit of the doubt in case the notebook was a diary.

- Well, actually I am, Sophia, he drawled, pen still moving across paper. What do you like to read?

- Nothing, I said. All I read is tarot cards.

- That's odd. You strike me as the sort of woman who would be a passionate reader.

- Nope, I said after waiting a few moments for him to elaborate. You must have me confused with someone else.

He stopped writing to hold out his glass to the flight attendant and gestured that she should refill mine as well. The attendant sneered down her nose at me. I decided that not only did she know I wasn't a real first class passenger, but that she knew I was wearing a black teddy stolen from my mother.

- What do you do, Sophia, if you don't read? he asked, holding his glass at eye level.

- I get by. Even before I said it I knew he wouldn't believe me. Sometimes I work as a stripper, but mostly I'm a tattoo artist.

- Oh, how nice. Don't you believe in supporting your own profession? I don't see any tattoos on those lily-white arms of yours.

I didn't flinch as he peered down the loose cowl neck of the dress, getting an eyeful of black lace. As I stood to inch the skirt up my legs, the thought that this guy could be the one, the father, flashed in my head like football results at the bottom of a TV screen. The first revelation was a serpent chasing its own tail around the bottom half of my calf. The tattoo was in a rare, dark jade ink, a treat to myself on the day I had finished school.

- Hey, I said, as he traced the curve of the snake around my leg, I don't even know your name, buddy . . . you're being mighty intimate there.

- Richard, he said, not lifting his finger from my skin. People who know me call me Dick. People who know me even better call me Dickhead.

As he chuckled to himself at his favourite introductory quip, I hiked my skirt up higher, again exposing the teddy, then I edged the silk up over my hip-bone to reveal a pentagram.

- Beautiful, he said, leaning forward to block the view of the bored businessman in the seat across the aisle.

- That was my first, I said, shimmying the skirt back down over my thighs. You're supposed to be able to draw pentagrams with one stroke of the pen, but my tattooist couldn't manage it. It's a very primitive sign that dates back beyond written characters. Celtic priests called it the witch's foot, I continued, hoping to sound threatening. It can also represent the five senses ... even the male and female principles. Y'know, the way the five points mesh?

- Mm, he said, raising an eyebrow as I tried to show him with my fingers.

- People once saw it as protection against demons. A safety symbol, I said, more for my own reassurance than for the telling. Worn as an amulet it's supposed to promise a happy homecoming. Kinda hard to see that applying to me.

- Mm, he repeated.

- The Star became my card when I was growing up – y'know, in the Higher Arcana. I knew if I followed the Star it would lead me somewhere else, somewhere better. I've always known I'd go away.

- If you wanted to follow the star, why hide it on your hip? he chuckled.

- I only put it there because of Sam. Couldn't let her parents see. Breasts were out, and somehow hip-bones got voted in. Sam's my best and oldest friend. She got the Sun and I got the Star.

He took a long, luxurious sip from his glass and scribbled quickly in his notebook. I wasn't going to ask him what he was writing. That's what they were always dying for. If I asked, I'd be trapped, listening to him jabber about his genius all the way to Heathrow.

- Was that Sam who saw you off at the airport? he asked, jiggling the foot he'd hoisted onto his knee.

- Yep, I said, swallowing hard. You saw us?

- Saw you? The whole airport was ogling you two clinging to each other. Quite a sight. She your lover?

- Na, I said, rolling my eyes. We're just close. Orphan sisters, sort of.

Down below, I saw the shadow of the plane on the lunar landscape and felt a chill of premonition. But I was unsure where the danger lay. I searched the desert floor for some sign, some clue, but all I found were roads that ran off at crazy angles and faded to nothing.

- What will you do in London, Dick? I asked, trying his name for size.

- Got a book coming out. Know anything about how that works?

- Nope, I said quickly.

- Guess that figures, seeing you don't read. I'll be going to parties, doing readings, interviews, that sort of shit.

- And will you enjoy that shit? I asked, slinging him one of my favourite questions for authors.

- Yeah, sure I like it, that circus. I like playing Mr Enigma. I never tell 'em the truth, those smart-assed journalists. But I sure give them something to write about.

I had to know who published him, was desperate to know whether there was a trail leading back to Zelda. Not that there was a physical resemblance between us ... And anyway, I'd never seriously entertained the thought that my father could be anything but British because Zelda had been in London when she got pregnant.

- Dick, let's get a bottle, I said, trying a seductive pout. We'll toast enigma and your new book.

I gave his arm a little squeeze as I waited for him to jump in and say first book. As I waited for him to knock himself out of the paternity field.

- So, what's it called? What are we drinking to? I asked, once we'd persuaded the flight attendant to let us open the bottle ourselves.

- *The Search*, he said, as we slammed our glasses together. It's about a man searching for his daughter. He has a fetish for red-haired women like his daughter's mother. The narrative tension hinges on the fact that he doesn't know what his daughter looks like. The reader knows that he'll meet her and won't recognise her as his own.

The falling sensation I'd been trying to arrest intensified. I realised that we were over the sea, and I had not even bid the desert good-bye. The hairs on my arms and on the back of my neck stood on end. I watched my hot palm frost the cold, empty glass and then stared into Dick's washed-out blue eyes. There was no doubt in our minds that we'd get off the plane and go straight to a hotel room together.

THE FALLING TOWER

I get up out of the sweat bed and turn the covers back so the sheets might dry before I try, again, to sleep. Naked, I stand at the window where the air is just as still, where there is no indication of morning's approach, where there is no sign that the city still breathes. Even the lights in the World Trade Centre have gone out. Am I the only person awake in this city?

I prowl the loft, bumping into the low table, unused to the layout of another woman's life. Her cat comes lumbering into me, unable to suppress its need for human reassurance. And for a moment I see myself pressing against a man to whom I am, in effect, no-one, in the same pleading, vaguely pathetic way. I see myself hindering his stride, as the cat does mine. I see myself opening my mouth, and closing it again lest the *torrent of long-stored words comes screeching out as mournful as the cat's miaow.*

I kneel by the window and the cat rolls onto its back, offering me its great downy belly. But when I stroke its fur, the cat sinks its claws into my wrist, its teeth into my hand.

Dark beads of blood glisten in the night. At the sink I wait for the water to run cold, and wait, imagining his hands that might look like my own. Imagining his big man's hand that might dwarf my own. I imagine this man whose face, whose body, I will appraise as I've never appraised a man before.

The white gauze bandages on my thighs and buttocks had to be changed every day. The morning after my thrashing, Zelda placed me on the front seat of her car, frightened, it seemed, to touch me lest she be tainted with my suffering. We swung off the Harbour Bridge, took the expressway that ran beside the street where Rob's building was, and where I glimpsed the international liner terminal, the ferry wharves and Opera House, before we dived into the darkness of the curving tunnel in which I practised holding my breath. Catapulted then into the other-world of Woolloomooloo Bay, we drove past the derelict grey shell of the fingerwharf and the pubs for thirsty sailors.

Following the curve of the bay we passed aircraft-carriers, battleships, destroyers, crawled over by pertly suited sailors. Zelda's car snaked all the way to the top of the winding road to the Cross without losing speed.

When we pulled up opposite Nella's building, Uncle Jerry was out the front, hosing the black tarred pavement until it shone like the patent leather shoes other girls in my class wore to special masses and school plays. He wasn't really my uncle, but he maintained that his family name, Jaruzelski, was too much for me to get my tongue around. Uncle Jerry tended his building until it gleamed in all its art deco splendour. He kept the taps from dripping, the windows from jamming, the foyer from filling up with junk mail that no-one wanted and the lift from behaving as though it had a will of its own.

He rushed to turn off his hose and darted across the road to help me out of the car. Zelda silently placed my suitcase on the footpath and was gone. With a gentle laugh he swung me into his arms as though I weighed no more than the oversized arrangements of gladioli he carried home from the florist once a week to position beside the lift. Nella was one of his favourites; nothing was too much for her. Once a week they hunkered down on her overstuffed sofas to discuss the world and, more importantly, what they were both reading, over rich pastries and bitter black coffee.

Before the War, Uncle Jerry had been a philosophy lecturer at Kracków University, who, with his mother, had been forced to flee to Italy and board a liner in Genoa bound for Australia. His mother was spared the trauma of the New World by dying quietly of shipboard pneumonia. Spared the tragedy of watching her brilliant son, her only son, train as a plumber. She died of the loss of home, Jerry told Nella.

The smell of toast filled the lift as the doors opened on the eighth floor and the British-sounding voice of the ABC's news announcer came in disjointed snatches from Nella's flat. The breakfast ritual involved toasted brioche or black rye bread, stewed apples and cups of aromatic Russian Caravan tea. Charlie was there, and that meant the toast was thicker and the tea stronger. He took charge of breakfast and liked to make omelettes with theatrical gusto, flipping the perfect half-moons in the air instead of just turning them with an egg-lift, as other people did.

After breakfast, Charlie took the bus to Circular Quay and then rode the ferry under the bridge to Balmain to tend the lush garden behind his federation cottage. I lay on my tummy on Nella's high bed, facing straight out the window to the harbour, and she gently tended my wounds. Once she had removed the dressings I lay there for an hour, letting the lacerations breathe, soothed by Nella's Chinese herbal ointment.

I was to stay with Nella until I was better. It was in those days of waiting for my skin to grow back, waiting for the flexibility to return to my legs, that Nella told me of the world out there beyond the Heads, beyond the Pacific – about the part of the world we Australians had every right to call antipodes. It was Nella who explained to me the restlessness in my own bones, juggling words to form a family tableau. Explaining away the generations of transience. Even then, all I wanted to do when I grew up was to go overseas. Abroad, as Nella liked to say.

The only daughter of a British ambassador, Nella had been born at the end of her father's stay in Rome and christened Antonella as a tribute to Rome's pre-eminent cellist. Her early childhood was supervised by nannies in Athens and Helsinki. Just when she was old enough to begin to appreciate the wonders of the latest posting to Paris, she was 'sent home' to boarding school.

- That, my dear Sophie, was the greatest betrayal of my childhood. Don't think it was by any means the norm for diplomats' daughters to be sent away to school ... even then, there were international schools in the European capitals.

- But why did they make you go?

I pictured her my own age, with a battered brown suitcase and a bag of apples, travelling by boat train, alone. And then there was a brief flash, an old photo of another child going to boarding school, but this time a boy. Her son, Randolphe, whom I knew, in the context of our conversation, not to mention.

- It was my mother's wish. We weren't close, you see, even less so than you and your mother. I was brought up by nannies while she was off playing Ambassador's wife in Paris drawing rooms.

Nella paused, and I watched her dark profile against the electric blue of the sky beyond the window. Her gaze, I knew, took her beyond the Heads clean to the other side of the world.

- I spent more time with my father, if you can imagine that.

- What was he like? I asked, unable to grasp the concept of such a person in our family.

- He was a bear of a man, Sophie, but gentle and warm and generous. Her eyes closed in a half-smile, a child's smile. He was my hero, my dark knight, my protector, my secret love.

Her voice trailed off and she was in some world that I was no part of.

- He had me finely dressed and paraded me before anyone invited to our home. No matter how important they were, she said, plucking at her purple cotton slacks. He took me with him to concerts and plays and parks and zoos.

She held her arms close, across her body, guarding the warmth of memory.

- Even though I didn't accompany him to his official evening engagements, I spent more time with him than my mother did.

- Why did he let you go? Why did she make him? I asked, on the brink of tears for her loss, and for my own.

- Don't think it was that my mother was especially interested in my father ... in being his companion ... it wasn't that. It was jealousy, Nella said, in a voice tinged with bitterness. She took lovers all the time, but especially in Paris. The city made her wild.

This was familiar territory. I could imagine a different, softer version of Zelda and the lovers with whom she decorated her life.

- She liked to circulate with the bohemians ... played quite the benefactress. Spending Embassy money, lavishing vodka and caviar on penniless artistes. She was quite striking, auburn-haired like you, skin as translucent as eggshell when you hold it up high.

- Was he terribly in love with her? I asked, staring at the cut glass surface of the harbour until it blurred into a screen where my exotic ancestors stood and glared at each other. Did he know about her lovers?

- He knew. Nella moved her hand to stroke one of my upturned feet. She wanted him to know ... to see him diminished.

She paused again to open the window. Outside, the flock of cockatoos that spent their mornings in the Potts Point trees had settled across the road.

- He loved her, regardless. Perhaps even more fiercely, for her cruelty.

Although I couldn't see the cockatoos from the bed, I could hear their commotion, their bickering. Nella delighted in living in such a built-up area, but in having the cockatoos and the harbour itself just outside her windows. And I, spoilt child of Sydney's harbour foreshores, took it all for granted.

The sound of the cockatoos reminded me of another of Nella's Paris stories about spending whole mornings moving from pet shop to pet shop on one of the city's quays. Surrounding herself with the smell and otherness of the exotic birds and animals.

Dreaming, already, perhaps, of a place like Sydney Harbour.

- In Paris, things suddenly changed, Nella said, returning to her chair. She took a woman for her lover. A young American who moved with some of the most famous of the Modernists. I saw her a few times. She wore her hair cropped, sometimes under a dark turban. And loose, flowing trousers – the first I'd ever seen on a woman. She jammed her cigarettes into long ivory holders and drank gin from a silver hip-flask. I thought she was wonderful, but I was too frightened to go anywhere near her.

I could see her vividly, my great grandmother's lover. Could almost hear her reckless, mannish laugh and smell the cigarettes and spice of her clothes.

- Finally, he put his foot down. Enough of parading these lovers before the world and the innocent child. Nella's voice grew softer, as though tired. They struck a bargain. She agreed on discretion, he agreed that I be banished.

- But Nella, why? How could he agree? Your lovely, wonderful father . . .

- Darling Sophie, he believed it was best for me. That was his way of protecting me.

- Was she like Zelda, your mother?

- Perhaps, Nella said, weighing the word, making the comparison herself as though for the first time. In some ways they were similar. Their attitude to their daughters.

- To you and me.

- Like you, I felt she had no time for me, she said, beginning to cut white gauze into strips. I felt like the item at the bottom of the shopping list . . . the one that usually got forgotten. I learnt never to ask a damn thing of her. Then she couldn't hurt me by saying no.

Nella concentrated on getting the gauze into position and I lay there, breathing in the frangipani scent of her perfume. Diorissimo. There was a frangipani tree in one of the parks down by the water, and when we went there after school I'd fill the skirt of my uniform with those little white flowers, making sure not to bruise their delicate petals. After carrying them all the way up the hill in this awkward fashion, I'd empty the terracotta fruit bowl, fill it with water and launch each of the flowers on the water's surface until they formed an unbroken mat. A pool of pale wishes.

- There's a fundamental difference between your mother and mine, Nella said, putting away the tape and scissors and surveying her work once more. Zelda's consumed by her work, her need to make her mark in the world. All my mother felt compelled to do was hurt my father.

- They both had lovers, I added, though unable to imagine Zelda with a woman who wore a turban and smoked cigarettes in long holders like Cruella Deville in *101 Dalmatians*. I couldn't imagine my mother with any woman, even an important writer. Although she called herself a feminist, Zelda didn't seem to like women at all. She tolerated Nella and me, but never asked for our opinions on anything. She had one close woman friend – another powerful publishing type – but they weren't real friends like Sam and me. They never talked on the phone late at night, or stayed over at each other's places.

- You'll have lovers, Sophie, said Nella. Don't think you're so very different. Monogamy is no friend to the women of this line.

We spent the rest of the morning on schoolwork, although it wasn't half as interesting as talking about my mother and great grandmother. Zelda made us promise we'd do at least three hours a day. At least! I would only miss a couple of weeks of school before term ended. The summer holiday glimmered before me. Had I known it would be my last summer with Nella, perhaps I would have behaved differently.

That summer she began talking to me as an adult. Telling me more and more about the world and its secrets as December raged into January, January wilted into February, and February was washed away by the warm, late summer rains.

Dick and I checked into his swish Mayfair hotel, opened a bottle of plonk, bathed, and then fell upon each other, glass in one hand, flesh in the other. Oh, Daddy, tell me what to do 'cause I'm so lost. My Mummy tried to tell me, but I was so frightened of turning out like her that I rammed my hands over my ears and swayed my hips all the more.

There in that unknown city, so far from anything I could call my own, I wanted him to tell me what to do. When Dick said turn over and show me your arse, that's exactly what I did. When he said suck my cock, rub your tits, bite my arsehole, lie there and play dead, I was a picture of mute obedience.

And when I told him that he was a bad Daddy, that Daddies didn't fuck their daughters raw, he cried and kissed each of my toes in turn. This little piggy went to market, this little piggy stayed home. He held me in his arms and told me I was safe, so safe, then turned me over and imprinted his belt buckle on my moon-pale buttocks. When I told him it was story-time or bath-time or dinner time, whether it was three in the morning or not, I was his darling daughter to be loved and served. And after he'd slipped the last mouthful of ice-cream between my red and swollen lips he pulled out his cock and fucked my mouth till the taste of chocolate became tainted by the vegetable taste of sperm.

It took me eighteen hours to realise that I was to become a prop for Dick's publicity campaign. His publicist took one discreet look at us over breakfast and knew she'd hit the bloody jackpot. She was imagining her call to some tabloid journalist, at the *Evening Standard* or the *Sun* ... Yes, really, he's here with a red-haired woman young enough to be his daughter and really I wonder whether we shouldn't have him apprehended up front before he has a chance to, well ... you know. Yes, they met on the plane from Sydney and she doesn't read books so she won't know ... that she's *it* so to speak. And when I asked her why she was in London she said she was looking for her father. Simple as that. Oh Lord, how exciting. Maybe the *Mirror or Private Eye* ...

Dick bought me a purple, mini Azzedine Alaiia frock that clashed shamelessly, gleefully, with my hair and begged me to wear it to his launch party. We decided that we'd both wear our combat boots and tread on as many toes as possible. Secretly, I wished it was a launch party that my mother was throwing, so Dick and I could turn up and out-sleaze even her.

It all seemed too easy, though, to turn up at this party, reveal myself and see who came sniffing. I had established that Dick had never been published by my mother's old firm, and instead of feeling relief that I wasn't fucking my father, I tasted, once again, the immense futility of my search. We'd been at a dinner in north London where he and an old school friend sat drinking whisky and I'd watched a video of *Barbarella*. He told me his publishing history in a taxi on the way back to the hotel while I oozed boredom. At Camden Town I looked out through the window to see a bunch of clubbers festooning the pavement in front of a rambling, grubby, mothball joint called The Palace. I told the cabbie to stop and turned to Dick who still held my hand as I was halfway out the door.

- I'm going dancing, I said as he tried to follow. Piss off you old fart. I want to go alone. Gotta clear my head.

He backed into the seat, wounded, clasping both arms to his chest and shifting his gaze to the line of traffic as it moved, sludge-like, towards the West End.

I turned my back on the cab and stood on the pavement, shivering in my leggings and tunic. I started to turn back, but knew he would be sitting there, staring, clutching my leather jacket, all wronged.

I dived into the warm familiarity of queuing bodies, digging cold hands into my empty pockets. Where was Sam when I wanted to get into my first London club for nothing? Pushing past the crowd, all politely waiting for their turn to pay, I grabbed the doorman's arm and moved in close.

- Excuse me sir, you've got to let me in, I said, leaning into his body, trying to make my cold lips tremble as Dick's had. I've just had a terrible fight with my boyfriend ... he's driven off with my coat, money and keys.

I stood back and fluttered my eyelids for a moment.

- My flat-mate's inside ... if you don't let me go in and find her I'll have to sleep down by the river tonight, I sighed. On my own.

- Well, let's see. I might be able to help you, he said, running his hand over my back and down to my arse. You're not from here, are you? New Zealand, right?

- No, Australia, I said, giving him my most inane, Haven't you seen this one on *Neighbours*? smile. I've only been here for a little while ... barely know a soul.

- G'awn, he said, once his hand had done its exploring. In

you go, but make sure you don't get into any more trouble tonight. If you do, you tell them you're Syd's friend, awright? Everybody knows Syd from da Palace.

- Thanks Syd, I said, scraping his hand from my bottom and running towards the warmth and oblivion, accidentally striking his ankle bone with the steel cap of my boot.

Within minutes I'd discovered a home from home. I heard the music that Sam and I had danced to in Sydney's Oxford Street clubs pounding away in north London. It was English music, after all. In the loo I took off my black skivvy and tied it around my waist so I could really boogie. The flash of a black lace bra was *de rigeur* – of that and only that was I certain. With the strobe for a pulse, I danced the twenty-eight-hour flight from my limbs and began to sweat out the alcohol. I gyrated till I didn't know I was alone, till I stopped straining to see a familiar face through the shifting forest of bodies. When my tunic began sticking to my skin, I went to lean on the bar beside a guy who was looking for someone just like me. His sleeveless t-shirt said 'Oi! Fuck the Pigs!'. On account of my being foreign and all, he wanted to make sure I knew that pigs were coppers and that he wasn't into kinky sex.

Stanley and I stood around nodding our heads at each other out of sync with the music, drinking lemonade from plastic cups. On the dance floor he tried to hold my body close, but every girl has her limit and I'd already reached mine. Instead, I danced for him, danced around him and danced right up close, while he stood with both feet planted on the ground and swayed in my direction. Like a palm tree in a gale, I told him and he claimed it wasn't cool for guys to jump around too much, unless you were gay, and then you were allowed to *vogue*. Forgiven for camping it up and acting out the words to the songs. Everyone *vogued* on Sydney's Oxford Street, but I didn't tell him. I wasn't going to be one of those ex-pats who talked about home all the time with a nasal drawl and a wistful look in their eyes.

Stanley paid and we sat on top, right up the very front of the night bus. It was my first red bus ride, and driving through the sleeping city, coated as it was in a phlegm-coloured fog, I decided I'd be London's night bus queen. By the time we walked from Trafalgar Square to Westminster Bridge, Big Ben had almost finished chiming five. Not that I would have recognised Big Ben's voice, or even Trafalgar Square, without Stanley to inform me. I wore his Air Force coat like armour over my damp clothes and stood on the bridge as the dance-induced sweat turned cold.

The river flowed silent and sulphurous beneath us. A black cab growled by, not slowing down for the two dregs on the bridge.

- So, are ye comin' back to Brixton with us for a fry-up? he asked, in what he said was pure Scouser, making me think Beatles and *Letter to Brezhnev*, not squalor, blight and poverty. There's a great place down Acre Lane. My shout. Awright?

- Na, thanks anyway, I said, swallowing a yawn and feeling the cold deep in my bones. Gotta sleep. I'm not speeding like some people.

- Y'can sleep at my place, he said hopefully. Spare room 'n all? Only a forty-minute walk.

- No Stanley, really, I said through chattering teeth, trying to get numb toes moving in my boots. My father'll be worried about me. Should really get back to the hotel.

- Thought y'said you were fightin' with your bloke, he said, his voice taking on a hard edge as he stared at the shit-brown water. Fucken sewer this.

- Well, no, my Dad actually, I said, feeling the colour creeping into my icy cheeks. I didn't want to mention my father 'cause I thought you'd take me for a bit of a dag.

- What's a dag then? he asked, brave, not hurt.

- Oh, y'know, a moron or a reject or something, I said, not bothering to go into detail about the shit-matted wool that hung around a sheep's arsehole. It's uncool to hang out with your father isn't it?

- So what's this hotel then? he asked, watching the way I was shifting from foot to numb foot.

- Some big white number in Mayfair, near The Green Park. Jesus, I can't remember its name ... must really be buggered, I said, breathing in short, sharp panic breaths. Do you know where The Green Park is?

- It's just Green Park, Sophie, all our parks are green, y'know? C'mon then, he said, grabbing my arm and hauling me, block-footed, behind him. I won't sleep for hours yet so I might as well escort you. Awright?

In the narrow streets between the Thames and Piccadilly, my mind hummed with disorientation. The fog-heavy city was foreign to me. Stanley gave me a potted history of the area's violent crimes, offering me similar tours of any other part of London, while I concentrated on my eyelashes, which seemed suddenly big with condensation. Walking the still, enveloping streets with their squat buildings, tall windows and corner pubs, Sydney's great, wind-swept, canyonesque roads seemed an impossibility.

Stanley insisted on disturbing the night porter for a pen. He wanted to write his phone number on my arm, though I didn't think this would help restore Dick's affection for me. Scornful at the attendant's squint-eyed gaze, Stanley enfolded me in his arms and lifted me from the ketchup-red carpet three times in a rough gesture of affection.

In the bronze-rimmed, smoked mirrors of the lift I looked like someone who'd spent most of the night sleeping in a cardboard box by the river, not gazing into it philosophically. I willed Dick to have left the door unlocked.

Dick's sardonic laugh sounded in my head and I recalled my first impression of him as a fetishist serial killer. I tried the door, turning the handle from side to side, all shaking stealth. To no avail. For a moment I contemplated spending the rest of the night in one of the comfy chairs in the foyer but before my weary mind could formulate a plan, the door was flung open and Dick grabbed my arm and wrenched me inside.

- Slut! he spat, shoving me onto the bed. Whore!

- Calm down, Dick, I said, face into the pillow, imagining him pacing the room and moving to the door every few minutes to fling it open, just in case. I'm tired and I want to sleep.

- You know what happens to bad girls, he said with a voice cracking, splintering near the realm of incoherence.

I heard him unbuckling his belt and pulling it through the loops in his jeans. Numb with fatigue, my reaction was slow, very slow, and I'd barely managed to haul myself onto my hands and knees when the first hot leather rod burnt my thighs. His hand fumbled at the elastic waist-band of my leggings, and with a sudden surge of anger-inspired energy, I turned and hit him a solid thwack across his jaw. Not stopping to enjoy his shocked child's expression, I bolted for the bathroom.

In a panic-sweat against the locked door, I had visions of his anger demolishing the wall between us. Huffing, and puffing and blowing the door down. I ran myself a bath and methodically rubbed cleanser into the chalk-white skin of my face. Funny how one resorts to the most routine of actions in a crisis. Zelda had once told me that people who cling to routines are essentially very lonely. Smoothing circles of cream around my eyes, I stared at their green and gold flecks, gum leaves and sand, and re-imagined how it would feel to see the same dark, almond-shaped eyes returning my gaze.

In the tub I lolled beneath mounds of bubbles, snow-capped peaks, compliments of the management. I couldn't help but marvel that I'd done something so bloody naive as checking into a hotel with a stranger on the basis that he was a writer of a certain age. If he went on acting tough, I'd just throw my things together and leave. Find a room of my own. Oh such rich promise.

- Sophie, Sophie darling, are you alright? What are you doing? I'm worried about you.

His voice was wetter than my bath and I guessed he'd been crying, drinking or both. I was bone tired and fed up with the game. I wouldn't tolerate someone trying to whip me in anger. Even I had some standards.

- What's an abnormal upbringing, Zelda? I asked her on my return from Sam's place one Saturday afternoon.

She was getting ready to go out, naturally. I was hanging around the doorway of her bedroom, watching her drawing kohl outlines to her eyes, watcing her turn her pale lashes into dark, stiff combs.

- Why do you ask? she said, her hands freezing halfway between her face and dressing table, and the sharp glint in her eye making me change my mind about going to stand beside her chair.

- Sam's mum was talking to the lady next door ... Sam and I were listening through the kitchen window, I said, frowning at the prospect of being reprimanded, again, for eavesdropping.

- Go on, she said, fiddling with the catch of her black bra.

- Well, Mrs Molloy said something about being owed the male point of view as a balance and then the lady next door said, It's like a witches' coven down there ... a thoroughly abnormal upbringing.

- A witches' coven! A witches' coven! I love it, she said, stamping her bare foot on the floorboards under the dressing table. Wait until I tell Nella!

I forced myself to chuckle, thinking it must be OK if she could tell Nella. I watched my mother rise from the chair, go to the chest of drawers and remove some dark, lacy things. I loved to watch her pointing her toes and rolling her fine black stockings up her pale legs.

- Do I look like a witch? she asked as she leaned down to clip the top of a stocking to the suspender belt. I'm not nearly warty enough!

When she caught me looking at her, as though checking to make sure, the laughter fell from her face.

- Alright Soph, she said, bending to the other stocking top. She's right, that cow who lives beside the Molloys. Your upbringing is abnormal, but all that means is that it differs from what they perceive as normal.

- I can give you something different and better, Soph, she said, slipping on a dress of fitted emerald silk before stepping into high, black heels. You won't have to grow up kow-towing to some man who claims he knows best for you. Who makes your ambitions and your feelings secondary to his.

- But my father wouldn't have been like that ...

- Your father? she said, turning her back on me and going to the mirror, tube of red lipstick poised. Your father was just like the rest of them ...

I scowled at her back, wanting to run and shove her as she was applying her lipstick so it would smear and she would say Bugger! and have to start again. What I wanted most, though, was to disbelieve her.

At school I was intrigued by the talk of fathers and brothers. There were no men in our family. The writers who sat at breakfast often enough for me to get some sense of their lives just didn't seem to do what the men in other families did. They didn't go to the office, they didn't play football, they didn't wash the car on Sunday morning, they didn't fix the burnt out fuse or put the garbage out. They didn't seem to have *mates*.

Charlie was the man of our family, but even he seemed to belong to some other species. He was the one who made the tea and spent most of his time growing flowers. What kind of man did this make him? What rare and gentle creature that I felt disinclined to discuss at school for fear of cruel ridicule. None of the other girls ever described their fathers giving their mothers complicated foot massages, with oils and essences, as Charlie gave Nella. Charlie was to be protected from mean, knowing school-girl laughter. And the writers could simply not be mentioned. Life was hard enough without being deemed out of bounds by other mothers.

With skin puckered to the texture of tripe, I slunk from the bathroom without a glance in Dick's direction. Wrapped in a white, fluffy hotel bathrobe, coarse against my nipples, I went to the refrigerator for a soda water and drank it straight from the bottle while standing at the window. For a few moments I was drawn beyond the room by the slender pink fingers of light in the sky and I wanted to cry for the Sydney Harbour dawns lost to me. I finished the soda, burped quietly, with dignity, and whipped the curtains closed, shunning the sky.

In the dark hotel room, Dick lay his head on my stomach and whimpered. Begging my forgiveness. Pleading with me to let Daddy make love to his baby. I shoved him away, curling into a foetal ball with my back to him.

Sometime late in the morning when the daylight had become intense enough to penetrate the tomb I had created for myself, Dick tried to revive me with hot, wet kisses applied lavishly to my inert body. Even a fetishist has a boredom threshold and after nearly half an hour of trying to raise a corpse, he left me to go and do some bookish thing. I heard him telling his publicist that I wouldn't be going to the interview with him, that if they bloody well wanted to photograph both of us they'd just have to wait for the launch.

On the borders of sleep, I lay in the hotel-stiff sheets that now felt dirty and contemplated taking a vow of celibacy and giving up alcohol.

When Dick got back with only an hour to spare before the launch party, I was sitting on the carpeted ledge by the window, reading tarot cards and drinking from a bottle. Down in the street the wind from the North Sea blew umbrellas inside out and sent hats skittering along rain-slick pavements. I didn't take my eyes from the cards as Dick moved to the window and expelled a low, animal groan. I didn't need to look at him to know that he was running his eyes over my fishnet covered legs, and letting them rest above my stocking tops. The way I was sitting gave him a partial view of my naked, newly shaved pussy, under the clinging purple fabric.

- Oh, Sophie, he said, his voice thick as sleep. Did you do that for me?

- Yeah, sure I did Dick, I said, still not looking up from the cards, not telling him that it was my own punishment.

Sometimes it was just easier to lie. And when he got down on his knees and turned my hips to him and rolled the purple fabric up around my suspender belt, it was just easier to let him have his way.

I painted on the eyes, lips and lashes of the writer's moll, and stood at the basin to wash between my legs. Dick made a point of telling me that he wasn't going to wash his face so that when he got bored at the launch he could ease his tongue out of his mouth and taste me on his skin. I pictured him going to kiss his publicist, a woman who wore floral skirts and velvet headbands, and leaving some trace of passion spent on her cheek.

In the lift on the way to the foyer Dick tried to feel me through the clinging fabric around my arse. I kicked him hard in the shin with my boot, but never to be outdone, he kicked back. As the doors opened, his bespectacled publisher got an eyeful of Dick's boot connecting with my calf and of my open hand stinging his cheek. Of course the fellow was very British about it, and pretended not to notice, but I know he was thinking, Oh how ghastly!, and counting the hours until he could go home to his portly but constant wife in Wimbledon.

I took along my camera for protection. Dick was touched, fool that he was, imagining I wanted to photograph him in his moment of glory. I wouldn't admit it to Dick, but I was excited at the prospect of attending a book launch; all those years I'd watched Zelda come home pissed from launches, either euphoric at her success or scowling because she felt she or her author had been somehow slighted. All of those dozens of parties and she'd never once invited me.

When Dick introduced me to his publisher, he stunned me by

using my full name. I'd never told him, but it would have been a cinch for him to check my passport or baggage tags. So much for controlled anonymity. The publisher scrutinised me from the dingy corner of the black cab we were riding in. I was sitting on what Nella would have called the dickie seat, the fold-down flap behind the driver's compartment that faced where we'd been. Conscious of trying to sit in a ladylike position so as not to offend the old bugger, I pressed my knees together and kept plucking at my dress's upwardly mobile hemline.

- I know another Australian woman of your name. She's a publisher, a very fine publisher. We called her the publisher from hell. Which is no slur on your fair country my dear, he said cheerily, patronising. I knew her when she was young, just starting out. She suddenly up and went back to the antipodes leaving a trail of broken hearts behind her ... none of us could understand it ... still see her at Frankfurt from time to time.

- Zelda's my mother, I said, surprising myself more than either of them. She's still the publisher from hell.

There was a roaring silence as the two men tried to reconcile themselves with my sudden change in status. One moment I was nobody, the writer's tart, and the next I was somebody's daughter, which is a few rungs up the ladder from nobody, but still a whole lot of rungs below somebody.

- Oh, I say, said the older man, taking off his glasses to wipe them clean so he could think before he spoke. Well, won't we have fun tonight? I shall introduce you to some of your mother's former colleagues ... they'll be delighted. And of course Randolphe will be there, he said, making me think of my uncle for the first time since I'd reached London. He never misses one of my parties. Oh, I'm not saying he's a lush, but he certainly likes the odd party he does.

The taxi moved haltingly through Soho's hard, neon-lit streets that reminded me of the mixture of froth and darkness in a glass of Black Velvet. Umbrellas hovered outside the plate-glass facades of bars, girlie joints, restaurants and boutiques, and I was reminded of a muted version of the Cross, back home. Pedestrians braved the elements for only as long as it took them to dive from one dank interior to the next.

- What did you say you did Sophia? the publisher asked me as we rose in unison to clamber from our taxi into the gutter.

- Most of the time I strip, I told him, ignoring Dick's pleading look. But really I'm a tattoo artist. It's just with HIV and shit, there hasn't been too much work around.

The publisher let out a tremendous belly laugh and then spent nearly a minute trying to regulate his breathing again as we three stood in the rain.

- Just like your mother, he said, gripping my elbow and propelling me into the foyer of the Groucho Club. She used to tell us she was really a belly-dancer.

We checked our coats and I got an eyeful of a smoky bar where well-dressed thirty-somethings sat huddled in cliques on low sofas. For a moment, I contemplated shoving my way into the cloakroom, retrieving my jacket and hurtling through those doors to regain the anonymity that was rushing away from me.

Upstairs in the function room we were handed flutes of champagne by a waiter and ushered into a room with tall, beckoning sash windows. I didn't expect a dramatic entrance for Dick, trumpet flare and blinding staccato of camera flashes, but I did expect him to walk into a room in which the guests would somehow acknowledge his presence. There were about forty people already in attendance, but we were greeted only by their backs, their attention being focused on the buffet that ran along the opposite wall.

- Most of them have come straight from their offices, said Dick's publisher, unapologetic, matter-of-fact. Come on then Richard, I'll do the introductions. I imagine you'll want to catch up with Randolphe, Sophia.

He had gestured towards a besuited knot of men defying convention by hovering near the bar rather than the buffet. One of them was my errant uncle, but having only seen photos of him as a young man I was at rather a loss. I stood there alone, the frock, Dick's gift to me, revealing more than I possibly could in a whole evening's discourse on my own character. Through the fishnet, the dark shadow of the serpent was visible, curling around my leg just there above my boot, trying to disappear into the soft, worn leather. My hair was wild, frizzy from the rain as though I'd come on foot through the bush rather than in a taxi through the streets. I counted six women wearing velvet headbands. I pulled out my camera and started zooming in on people's hands. Easier to tell what was on someone's mind by watching their hands, rather than the masks of their faces.

All too easily I could imagine Zelda, charged with some demon energy, flitting from one cluster of suits to the next. *Working The Room* was what she'd call it when she spoke to her weary publicist on the telephone before she drove into the office the next morning. It pleased her to take the liberty of ringing the poor woman at any hour of the day or night to pass on some comment, some scheme she'd just hatched. Or to chastise her for not having spent quite enough time with that magazine editor the night before.

For those without cameras, the only thing to do was drink. Surely even the worst paid publisher's dogsbodies would soon tire of popping sweating cubes of cheddar cheese or mayonnaise-smeared biscuits into their ever smiling mouths. Dick was being propelled from one sweetly sipping group to the next, flanked on the right by his publisher and on the left by his publicist. That evening she was swathed in black velvet, more drawn spinster than merry widow or chic vamp. The velvet headband had been replaced by a diamanté clip that held her thick brown hair off her face, emphasising her ultra-defined, anorexic's cheek bones. I wondered which of those powdered cheeks bore the trace of my own sex? I wondered whether, if I hadn't materialised, Dick would have offered her his tongue.

As I swanned past the gaggle of grey-suited guzzlers by the bar their conversation halted. And then as I turned the men made a great, unified show of throat-clearing and plunged back into their discussion. I sensed that none of them had read Dick's book and for a wonderful moment imagined telling him, in a voice that would sting like a lashing leather belt.

With my back to the window, buttocks resting on the sill, I became a voyeur, every now and then raising the camera to my eye and framing shots around the room. Visual excitement was exceedingly low. The women air-kissed and the men greeted each other with limp handshakes or strange gestures of elbow-clasping. Young women in modest, knee-length skirts stood talking to men with receding hairlines and florid complexions, staring off into space mostly, but occasionally making eye-contact and nodding their bobbed heads in earnest assent. I wondered what strange patriarchy I'd come to.

The party ebbed and flowed before my camera lens. The pitch only really rising when another group burst through the doors with a chorus of Hello Darlings, when all eyes would fasten on the new-comers in search of someone famous or infamous, preferably the latter. With a shock of glum resignation I realised that Dick was the most attractive man in the room.

On my swaying, second trip to the bar, I searched the cluster of staunch boozers for someone bearing a resemblance to either Nella or Zelda. God forbid that anyone in that room could have resembled me. The truth was that all the men had started to look the same, with only mild variations in complexion and hairstyle. Where was the music? I wanted to dance, wanted to find myself again, or lose myself more completely.

The muted clink of a silver spoon against a half-filled glass announced some moment of official business. I heard one woman express relief, she was dying for a pizza, as I was suddenly, too. I only half turned back to face the room as Dick's publisher told us how proud he was to be launching a novel the calibre of *The Search*. How delighted he was that Dick had come all the way from Los Angeles, via Sydney, to 'be with us' and how he predicted a rash of dazzling reviews ... an early film option.

A series of Here, Here, Heres rose from the group, and with a beautifully orchestrated sweep, everyone in the room emptied their glasses. For one ridiculous moment, I felt sad for Dick, sorry that I couldn't care for him and that there was no-one else in the room that would. Wasn't the launch of a book supposed to be one of the greatest moments in an author's life? And there was Dick, in the company of a bitch like me.

And then Randolphe was there at my side, staring into the night just like me. He said, Well, well, well, and I said I like it, referring to the night view of London, at just the same time, so we both had to stop.

- She called me, you know, he said obliquely, forcing me to turn and face him.

Tall, maybe six foot one or two with salt and pepper hair in unruly curls, full, ruddy cheeks and those sensuous, cherry red lips of Nella's. His eyes were the colour of old gum leaves, before they turn brown, much paler than mine, faded with age perhaps, or lack of exposure to any real colour. Striped grey suit, pink shirt, white collar and red bow tie. Highly polished brogues.

- Who called you? I asked, for form's sake.

- Zelda called me to say that you were coming. Said you were a decent enough type, though I suppose that means she doesn't entirely approve of you.

I turned back to the window.

- Also said I should get a lock for my liquor cabinet, he said, a smoker's laugh erupting from somewhere deep within his broad chest. We haven't spoken since she left London, you know.

- She just wanted to check up on me ... fulfil her motherly duty but not get involved.

- Hmf, he said, smirking. You don't get on with her either.

- Who does? I said, restraining myself as a matter of course, not loyalty.

- You know there's a room for you at my place, he said. You don't have to subject yourself to *his* charity.

The room with Dick in it and the literary gaggle receded, and there was just the Soho night and Randolphe and me. The notion of family that didn't comprise Nella or Zelda was so alien that it took more than an offer of hospitality to believe in it. And there was Randolphe, doing that benevolent patriarch thing that my mother and grandmother had taught me to scorn, and there I was, ready to embrace it.

- It's a fine arrival Sophia, he said. For what it's worth. I assume you've read his novel?

- I make a point of not reading, I said, noticing people drifting away from the ravaged buffet and out into the night.

- Hmf, he snorted again. I haven't read it, but I've been told it's the story of a middle-aged man who discovers that unbeknown to him he once fathered a child. He becomes determined to find her, but can't quash his diabolic obsession for women with long, luscious red locks, he said, raising a hand to my hair and then dropping it.

- Oh really? I said, thinking that I hadn't been tripping on the plane after all, more's the pity.

- His determination becomes perverse obsession and in his frustration he finds himself seducing and murdering, in the most unspeakable manner, a series of young red-headed women.

- I see, I said, with a wet cement feeling in my stomach. So does he find his daughter?

- Of course, said my uncle, tossing back the last of his drink and patting his full lips with the back of his hand. He finds her, seduces her, kills her and only later learns her identity.

A cold silence rushed between us as we continued our scrutiny of the night.

- You can read about yourself in tomorrow's *Londoner's Diary*, he continued. Can't stop the piece going to press I'm afraid. Tried already, once I knew it was you. Of course they'll name names ... people here remember your mother.

I pondered the prospect of instant notoriety and realised I was none too bothered by it. In fact, I had to struggle to keep my delight from jumping through my skin and hitting Randolphe square on the chin. But then, there was Dick and the story that had left the flesh all over my body bumpy.

- I don't mind being gossiped about, I said, affecting an over-worldly tone. In fact, a little exposure might serve me very well.

- My dear, I imagine you're more like your mother than you

know, he said, a hint of provocation in his voice. And in what way will publicity serve you?

- To announce my arrival, of course, I said, tossing my hair from my face in a gesture that made Randolphe's nose twitch. You never know who might like to meet the novelist's whore.

Randolphe smiled at me with a look of great fondness, as though I'd just told him that my favourite colour was pink and I liked to eat toast before bedtime. I felt stupid, mean-spirited, for trying to shock him and immediately raised the camera to cover the smudge of remorse.

- I look forward to hearing your plans for London, he said, with a diplomacy that I would come to see simply as a certain type of Englishness.

- My short-term plan is to leave this party, I said, pronouncing the word 'party' with a mixture of contempt and disbelief. No wonder Zelda always gets pissed at book launches. If she stayed sober the boredom threshold would force her to unleash the full and terrifying extent of her sarcasm, I said.

- Ah yes, that family affliction. Ruined many a romance made in heaven, or someplace near there, like Paris.

- Paris, I sighed, and without my affectation of worldliness I felt clumsy and naive – my boots were too big and too heavy, my jacket too battered, my accent too hick, my hair too tangled ...

Randolphe and I left the room quietly and separately, as though popping out for fresh air with every intention of returning. We rode in a purring black cab in complicit silence. Nella's son and I, I kept thinking; she would have liked this.

Randolphe waited in the foyer as I undertook the business of disentangling my life from Dick's. Instead of leaving behind the purple dress, as I had intended, it was the black silk teddy that would remain the only testament to our brief cohabitation.

I deemed any real farewell to Dick superfluous. Good-byes are only meant for the likes of Sam, I told myself, as yet another black cab wove north through West End streets towards Regent's Park.

During the school term Sam was allowed to stay the night on Fridays and Saturdays. Mrs Molloy felt sorry for me, on my own so much or sharing the evening with bored babysitters who asked me to paint their toenails for them while they ate all the chocolate biscuits. On Friday afternoons I'd hurry home, rushing past the garden hoses, ignoring the tea.

When my mother wasn't there to play style police I wore flowing Indian skirts, bikini tops and basketball boots. At the Molloys', Mary and Kate in their orange and purple nylon slacks stared at me nervously and ran away, giggling. Sam was into cut-off jeans that strained to contain her bum and knitted tank tops in purple and green. Some had matching caps that she gave me, an incredulous expression on her face when I actually wore them. The boys in the local boy-gang, who skateboarded maniacally up and down a steep hill near Sam's house, would shout 'Boobs!' when they saw us coming. Not that we had anything more than nipples, or that our clothes ever actually revealed them, but our gear sure gave the boys more to think about than did the get-up worn by Sam's sisters.

Fridays it was pikelets at Sam's with butter and jam, hot and moist, straight from the old Sunbeam electric fry-pan. There was a law against food like pikelets, pancakes, hamburgers and pizza in my house; the second point that my mother and Nella agreed upon. Their kitchens were filled with vegetables and pulses and tabouleh salads. When Nella made me hummous and watercress sandwiches the girls at school taunted me, told me I was eating something that had gone right off.

After pikelets and pretend coffee, loaded with milk and sugar, Sam and I slunk off to her room and locked the door before her sisters could wheedle in on the act. Sam and I were every bit as cruel to Mary and Kate as the cool kids at school were to me. Sam liked to play Abba records on her plastic, portable record player and mimed to 'Mamma Mia' and 'When I Kissed the Teacher'. 'Ring Ring' demanded the most active involvement; in sync with each other and occasionally with the music, we dialled that big telephone on the wall, fingers aquiver with anticipation. Then it was hands on bony hips and pacing the room, waiting all alone impatiently ... They were purges, our disco sessions, means of marking the end of the school week and the beginning of a weekend of infinite possibility.

The baby-blue vanity case lay on the bed with a crack in its mirror, covered and re-covered by sticky tape that always browned and buckled. Sam packed her gingham baby doll pyjamas, her toothbrush and her plastic Betty-Boop zipper purse bulging with all of five dollars after saving her week's pocket money. Finally, she slung in her cossie, just in case Zelda felt like getting rid of us and drove us around to Balmoral Beach for a day out of her hair.

Upstairs, Mrs Molloy, reclining on the brown velour lounge, laid down the law as she did each week. When we got to my place Sam had to call her mother to let her know that we'd arrived safely. Really. And then the babysitter would have to get on the telephone to prove that she was really there as well. She also had to run through the tedium of telling Mrs Molloy exactly what she was going to give us for dinner and after that, they discussed what we wouldn't be permitted to watch on television that night.

A hazy orange sunset sent the cicadas into a frenzy. Up on the power lines two kookaburras laughed as Sam and I scrambled into one of the best cicada trees between our two houses. It was a tree I'd fallen out of once, so I was always holding my breath when I climbed it, waiting for one of my feet to slip. Despite being a few rungs behind Sam, it was me that spotted the first cicada ... a big, fat Yellow Monday whose body quivered with the strength of its own song. With feet on two separate branches, my weight was distributed evenly and for a moment I was aware of nothing but air between my naked legs and the path below, where anyone walking underneath might conceivably look up into a young girl's skirt. I carefully opened the jar tucked into my waistband and, balancing the lid on a nearby branch, reached out with a sloth-slow movement to cup the cicada in my sweaty palm. The worst bit was lifting it off the branch, as I imagined I was either breaking its legs or crushing its wings with my clumsy, banana fingers.

As that old Yellow Monday started to shriek my whole hand vibrated, but before it could completely unnerve me, tiny creature that it was, I shoved it into the jar. The moment the perforated lid was secured the creature assumed dead insect mode.

- I got a Green Grocer, shouted Sam, shaking her own jar for me to see before jamming it in her hip pocket.

- So what? I said. Guess what I got?

- Um, Black Prince? she asked, coming alongside and grabbing my waistband. Wow. Yellow Monday.

Sam dropped from branch to branch with the grace of a forest primate, one hand clutching my Yellow Monday and the other moving easily between safe branches. I followed in flustered pursuit, intent on regaining my trophy. As I dropped from the lowest branch my skirt snagged and I struggled to cover myself while my best friend hooted. Across the road, Alex Watson sat in the gutter with his feet on his skateboard and laughed a great, dirty-old-man-in-raincoat laugh.

- I'm not wearing anything under my Billabongs, Sophie. Do you want me to show you? he taunted, standing and putting his hand to his crotch. My parents are out. You can come too, Sam.

I looked at my friend and rolled my eyes, but Sam nodded. Probably wanted a ride on his board. We shoved both our jars in her vanity case and took off after him as he turned the road into his own slalom.

The Watsons' place was one of the most bitched-about houses in the neighbourhood; labyrinthine, ostentatious and testament to unselfconscious wealth. It was in the row of cliff houses that overlooked my nocturnal pathway, set off on its own, closest to the point and the mouth of the bay. Alex stood leaning against the heavy, oxidised copper door, waiting for us to catch up. As I walked by he accidentally bumped my hip with the hand that was still holding the front of his shorts, in the same way that Sammy would accidentally pull her little sister's pony tail.

Sam and I padded down the long, marble entrance hall that led straight to a wall of windows overlooking the bay. With a mixture of shock and delight, I could just make out my rock through the trees below the house. One of the cicadas began a frantic morse code of screeches, an unheeded warning, and Sam opened the vanity case in the hope of calming the perpetrator. The Yellow Monday fell silent as I slipped the jar back into my waistband.

We followed Alex down a curving marble staircase to another

glassed walkway that ran parallel to the cliff. Again my rock was visible, enigmatic, alluring. On the other side of a games room with a billiard table, a drinks cabinet and some black leather lounges, Alex revealed his private domain. The room was dominated by a queen-sized bed covered in a tangle of black sheets that had a just slept-in look to them. Black! Sam and I mouthed to each other in disgust. In fascination.

- Come and meet Johnnie, he said, diverting our attention from the bed to a glass tank that ran the length of one wall.

Again Sam and I exchanged shrugs as Alex turned his back to us and reached into the green foliage of the tank. In one fluid movement designed to shock, Alex pulled a mottled brown snake out of the tank and turned to thrust it towards us. In less than a second, Sam had screamed, jumped backwards and dropped her jar, setting the Green Grocer free amid shards of broken glass. Afraid even to breathe, I didn't know whether to watch the snake or watch the cicada as it flew at a window pane and dropped to the floor to adopt dead insect mode.

- Dinner, said Alex, as he moved to the glass and placed the supine Johnnie on the floor a foot from the insect.

One moment the cicada was there and the next it simply wasn't, with Johnnie there instead, half his scaly body pressed to the glass.

- Ugh, was all Sam managed to say, though she was doing better than me.

As if programmed to react in such a manner, we both jumped onto the bed and knelt, clinging to each other's elbows. Our gaze never left Johnnie's for even a moment.

- Isn't he great? asked Alex, his hand back on his shorts again. You want to touch him?

Sam shook her head, but without my knowing it, I was

nodding yes. My hand crept towards Johnnie. I willed myself not to recoil from the lifeless texture of his scales. Alex let out a moan as I started stroking Johnnie's head. I ran my fingers along the paper-dry length of his body, all the while locked in a deadly clinch with his dark eyes, glistening like beads of newly spilled blood.

In a feat of devious contortion, Alex got his free hand into his pants and pulled out a dick that had the look of a pale, squashed aubergine about it. If it hadn't been for Johnnie, Sam and I would have probably been panic-stricken, neither of us having ever been confronted by a cock before.

- Sam, Sam, Alex growled. If you won't stroke Big Johnnie, you've got to stroke Little Johnnie. If you're not nice to Little Johnnie, I don't know what Big Johnnie'll do.

And there we were, the three of us, linked by this near lifeless snake, who might have been drugged for all we knew. The last thing I was about to do was disobey Alex or break the gaze I was hypnotising Big Johnnie with. Just on the edge of my vision, I could see Sam's hand on the reddening Little Johnnie. What Alex's facial contortions meant I didn't know. Perhaps Sam was hurting him, and the snake would strike out suddenly in defence of his master. It all made me feel so very strange, gave me an odd, warm feeling in my tummy.

Yes Sam, Yes Sam, Alex was saying, making a clumsy, fumbling attempt to press his fingers inside the cut-off inside leg of her jeans, into her undies. As soon as his fingers got to the place they wanted to be, this white yoghurt came dribbling out of Little Johnnie's single eye. Alex stopped breathing so hard and the crisis seemed to pass. We watched the sperm soak into the crumpled black bed sheet. As gracelessly as it had begun, Alex removed his hand from Sam's shorts and stepped over to the glass tank, putting away both Johnnies with a businesslike formality. It was all over, that was obvious, but both Sam and I were immobile, left kneeling on the mattress, watching Alex for some sign, some gesture that would release us.

- Don't tell your parents, he said, ushering us into the games room where he opened a bottle of beer and poured us each a glass.

I sat on the black leather lounge imagining the cold dry skin of snakes on my thighs, as subtle as air itself beneath my skirt. Sam snorted as she inhaled the beer's thick, frothy head.

- Aren't you supposed to kiss us? Sam posed, white foam moustache on her upper lip and the voice of a coquette.

- Next time, Alex said, staring at her tank top. Next time I'll kiss you, but you'll both have to try a bit harder.

Without warning, I was overcome by a fit of laughter at the notion that such a weird event could repeat itself. I kept having flashes of the patchy black sheets, the speckled back of Big Johnnie and the oily hair clinging to the base of Alex's dick.

When we arrived at my place, after a second glass of beer, the babysitter was leaning against the front door with her face hidden by a Mae West biography. She barely looked our way and failed to register our flushed disarray. Inside, Sam and I went straight to my bedroom and, with the door shut, played Kate Bush so loud we didn't hear the phone when Sam's mother called. The babysitter assured Mrs Molloy that we'd been home for hours.

- Do you think you can get pregnant from a man putting his hand between your legs, Soph? I mean, maybe he had sperm on his fingers?

- Don't be stupid Sammy. The sperm went onto the bed, not up your shorts.

- But how do people get pregnant then? she asked, wide-eyed with fear.

- The man does it to her. He fucks the woman so the sperm goes right inside her and then he says that she belongs to him.

- Do I belong to Alex now? Do you? she asked.

- I don't know Sam. Maybe we all three belong to each other.

It was the sort of still, humid night that would normally see me basking on my rock in the moonlight. Since the afternoon's happening though, I felt different about the rock, mildly protective of it. Sharing it with Sam suddenly seemed impossible, despite the fact that I'd shared it with her before.

Without remorse, we launched the Yellow Monday from the deck. When I tapped it out of the jar into the still night air it faltered, as though faced with some cruel deception. Where was Big Johnnie? And then, hesitantly, reluctantly, it opened its wings and rose to find its own oblivion. Long after the speck that was the Yellow Monday had faded, we sat wordless, staring into the fringe of trees just out there in the darkness.

The full moon was cream and translucent white and butter gold, all swirling, merging. Seemingly crossed by four or five of its own vague horizons. The water stole what it could of the moon's splendour, as water will. I liked to see water reflecting the sky: brilliant blue in the sunshine, grey and ominous before a storm, and tar and pitch at night. There in the bay, running from its darkest, most secret end point to its mouth with all its promise of the ocean and adventure, ran the moon's very own yellow brick road.

At the sound of the car turning into the carport, Sam and I were on our feet and climbing through my bedroom window in a rehearsed manoeuvre. Dumping most of our clothes on the floor in the middle of the darkened room, we crawled into the girl dream-world of my canopied bed and clouds of fine, magenta silk.

We lay in darkness, listening to my mother thank the babysitter and usher her quickly out of the house. And then a man's voice saying Zelda's name again and again, and her low laugh that I'd begun to associate with late night guests. Clinking of ice-cubes in thick crystal and the glug glug glug of scotch being poured. Then the changing click clack of her heels moving from the wooden floor of the lounge room to the slats of the deck. She liked it out there in the dark almost as much as I did. And then coming straight through my window the sound of her breathing as he did secret, silent things to her.

- Mm, Thomas, get up, get up, she said. Let's go to bed.

Her bedroom door cracked shut leaving the night to itself again and Sam and I restless, agitated. Left hanging. Wondering what Thomas had been doing, kneeling, lying or sitting out there that made her utter those strange, animal sounds.

- My parents never make those sounds at each other, or even say each other's names unless they're screaming. Do you think that means they never have sex? Sam asked, both of us giggling, then breaking off into long sighs.

There again, between my legs, was that uncomfortable, swollen feeling. And somehow I just knew it wasn't about wanting to go to the toilet. I knew it was something much more secret, perhaps even more intimate than that. And when I touched myself there, small charges of heat and energy went straight from my fingertips inside me, making me squirm and drawing Sam back from the edge of sleep.

- What are you doing, Soph? she asked, her voice knowing.

- I've got this funny, hot feeling between my legs. When I

put my hand there it sort of burns, I said, experimenting again.

- Let me try, she said, sitting up in the darkness and fumbling with her bitten-nailed hand between my legs.

- Oh, I said, wriggling and drawing both my knees together.

- Do you feel like that, Sam?

- I do feel sort of strange, she said, holding her hand there between her own legs and squirming as I'd done.

- Let me feel, I said, leaning over and putting my whole hand down there for a few moments. It's hot Sam, and sort of damp. Did you wee?

- No, she said shrilly, and then in a quieter, more serious voice. It feels good Soph, with your hand there. Do it again.

We lay there, hands squashed between each other's legs. Squirming, silent, almost daring each other to break the next taboo. But suddenly I could stand it no longer and jumped to run to the bathroom.

THE EMPRESS

And when this night does appear to have an end to it, how I cling to the darkness, burrow under the pillows and sheets and curse the wondrous light of morning. Clouds sail pink above the World Trade Centre and the blue of the sky is something so fresh that I must marvel at its defiance of the city's grit and squalor. The cat has left me, finally, to my twist of bedclothes, damp hair and ankles dressed in a fine lace of scratches.

He must be awake now, too, my father. Must be performing his early morning rituals, and marvelling as I am at the blueness and pinkness and freshness of the sky. He must sense my approach.

And if he asks me what I want, can there be a single answer? I want a father, I'll tell him. I want to know who you are and *so know myself. Someone I can look at to get a sense of who I might one day be.*

And how will I explain Zelda to him? This woman whom he once loved. The way I looked at her and cringed, felt cold with fear at the thought of growing up to look like her, to be bitter like her, to be alone like her.

I sit on the edge of the bed, waiting for my sense of the day to settle. My foot lands on the mass of tarot cards, familiar territory, fallen from the edge of the bed as I nodded off just that once in the early morning. Missing the shift from night to day. Missing the very first light. For the first time I think that he'll find me completely unlovely. So devoid of charm, so tainted by the spite and sleaze I've known that he simply will not claim me as his own. I fear what he'll see in my soul. That its turmoil will repulse him.

Dried bullet food for the cat, a smell that stays on my hands and will reassure me on the journey by train along the Hudson. The river of which he has written, and on which today he will become a father.

During her last summer, Nella gave me a camera. My first camera. A Canon with a zoom lens that the man in the shop warned her against giving to a child. There were cheaper models that would be far more suitable. In the end, he was glad of Nella's insistence; we became his best customers, shooting whole rolls in a day.

His name was Manni and his shop was just beside Nella's favourite patisserie. The Snappy Sisters, he called us, sending me into fits of girlish laughter. Of course, he was flirting with Nella, despite the fact that she was twenty years his senior, and not for a moment did she take offence. Once, when I went next door to buy *millefeuille* for afternoon tea, and came back into the shop, Manni had his hand on her bottom as he pointed to a lens in a cabinet.

On the street I was silent until we were beyond the shops. Nella, I said, on the verge of tears. Manni had his hand on your bottom.

- Sophie. She drew me to her side so we walked in step, joined at the hip. He wasn't hurting me. Don't think he was doing anything I didn't want him to.

- But why was he touching you like that? I asked.

- He was touching me because he thinks I'm attractive and wanted me to know that. Her voice was soft, and she spoke close to my ear as though conspiring, as though she were my best friend whispering to me behind a locker. He wanted to show me that he thinks I'm beautiful ... that he appreciates me.

- But what about Charlie? I asked, fretful.

- What Charlie doesn't know doesn't hurt him. Charlie and I love each other. Manni was just flirting.

- The men who touch Zelda's bottom do other things too, I said, gripping Nella's waist fiercely, determined not to let her return to the camera shop. They make growling sounds ... she wrestles with them, and when she gets loose she runs to the bedroom but never closes the door fast enough to keep them out.

- Now, Sophie, Nella said, choosing her words as I had yet to learn to do. Zelda likes men ... courtship and seduction are her releases. Don't think that they're making her do something she doesn't want.

We walked on, me resting my head against Nella's breast, mournful. An old purple Valiant came towards us from

73

Woolloomooloo Bay, burning rubber along Macleay Street. Fucken dykes, screamed a teenage boy from the back seat.

- She has most of them wrapped around her little finger, said Nella, never even looking towards the car and pretending not to notice the way I snarled back, finger raised.

In London, winter's long fingers stroked my breasts and left my nipples standing erect. Cherry red like the Doc Marten boots that all the right people were wearing. The skin on my face dried out and threatened to tear when I laughed or smiled. My hair was wiry with static or dense with ringlets, according to the moisture in the air. I consistently wore either too many or too few clothes, sweltering in the hot-house carriages of the Northern Line, or hopping from foot to foot, teeth chattering, waiting in Trafalgar Square for the night bus.

After our initial *tête à tête* at Dick's launch, Randolphe made no further enquiries of me. It wasn't that we didn't converse, in fact, conversation was one of his great pleasures. It was more that we conversed on a certain level. He was as enigmatic to me as the city itself. Initially I interpreted his reserve as a coolness, such was my inexperience of the English.

For a sixty-two-year-old retired journalist, Dolphi, as I called him at his sufferance, led a vigorous life. Early morning would find him striding up Parliament Hill, casting a condescending glance at the beet-faced runners and Barboured men with their defecating dogs. Regardless of weather conditions, Dolphi would tackle those heath paths with a wry determination to take in the view of the capital afforded him by Parliament Hill's elevation.

- But Dolphi, what are you looking for out there? I'd ask,

shivering and forlorn as the wind whipped through my leggings and left my fingers brittle as ice.

- What are you looking for in your clubs? he asked, never commenting on the hours I kept.

On the rare occasions I accompanied him onto the heath in the early morning, I only did so because I'd just got in from an all-night clubbing session and was still too wired to sleep.

- I'm not *looking* for anything. I'm not into this youth solidarity shit, or salvation through the joy of dance. I'm just out to have fun and dance some life back into my body, I said, but feeling crusty as an old boot.

- Perhaps our excursions are more similar than you imagine, he countered. I'm out here for diversion myself. I'm not up here to see London ... usually so obscured by cloud or haze it'd be a futile expedition. I'm here for a sense of perspective. To position myself in the world.

- But why every morning? Surely the perspective won't shift if you only come out once a week for this, I said, gesturing expansively from the Telecom Tower to Carnary Wharf.

- Nothing here'll change, but by staying away for a week, I'd change ... become a little old man hidden from the world in his rooms ... sitting by the fire in his slippers with a perpetual sense of dislocation, Randolphe said, suddenly raising both arms above his head in salute to his city.

- You're being a bit dramatic, don't you think? I said as he took my arm and started walking me away from the view, towards the hilly heart of the heath.

- Me? Dramatic? No, but you're blinded by youth, he said, squeezing my hand. This ritual gives me a sense of time passing. You're not the only one with a future!

- I used to watch the moon when I was a kid. I was so

desperate for time to pass ... desperate to move on, get out, get away. Here I am now in my own future ... and I can't work out what I believed would be so wonderful.

- So young and so jaded. So disaffected, he said, and grimaced.

- I'm not young Dolphi. I'm a very old twenty. You can't imagine how living with someone like Zelda has aged me before my time.

- Come on, you old thing, he said, vaguely steering us towards home on a path with a mild downward gradient. I'm going to cook some scrambled eggs to warm your blue lips. I take it they're not painted blue this morning?

He never asked where I disappeared to or with whom I passed my time when I overdosed on the clean streets of Dartmouth Park and fled to Brixton for a few days. Nor did I question him about his 'lady friends'; women with names like Marjorie, Cecilia and Penelope who left dignified messages on the machine and whose voices made me think of finely sifted icing sugar. When the smoky scent of his aftershave wafted down from the bathroom and Dolphi came out in his tuxedo and cashmere overcoat, again I didn't enquire, though I always told him how dashing he looked, how sexy. Often-times he too would arrive home in the wee small hours, looking considerably less dishevelled than I at that time. Within fifteen minutes he'd be out there on Parliament Hill in his autumnal tweed and corduroy, putting the world in its place.

Occasionally he'd mention a 'wretched' play he'd been to see, or an exceptionally good claret imbibed, but I never knew with whom he shared his moments of indulgence. To my knowledge, he'd never married, or lived with a lover, or even been in love. Like both Zelda and myself, he seemed completely untouched by romance. What had gone wrong in the wake of Nella's warmth and affection? I wondered why one of us didn't 'meet someone' and live in a neat little unit, like other people did.

Already I felt a greater kinship with Dolphi than I ever had with Zelda. My uncle and I were as close to direct opposites in lifestyle and appearance as any two people could be, or as my mother and I were. Yet, I doted on him as quietly and as secretly as he doted on me.

Whenever I asked Nella about my father, I could always anticipate her response. She knew nothing. My mother had been doing grand things in London that Nella wasn't privy to. Zelda had returned to Sydney unannounced to take a coveted publishing position. It was only a few weeks after her return, when she started talking about buying a house, that Nella discovered her daughter was pregnant.

- She told me nothing, Sophia, Nella said, treating my questions with indulgent patience. All I know is that he was very special.

- You're just saying that to make me feel good, I said, slowing my pace so Nella could hold my arm as we climbed down the steep sandstone steps to Woolloomooloo Bay. How do you know he was special if she didn't tell you anything?

We crossed a busy road so we could walk on the baking pavement by the water, shunning the late afternoon shade offered by the pub awnings. Nella liked to walk with her long, white, cotton wool hair in a wild cloud around her shoulders and had the air of someone whose joy alone would carry them through the world.

I stopped to gaze at the bulk of the derelict fingerwharf, jutting out into the bay, seemingly in competition with the headlands on either side. The whole storm-coloured structure haunted me. A fingerwharf was more than just a jetty sticking out from the shore, it was a great, shuddering beast of a warehouse, built out over the bay. It was the underwharf itself, though, that really stirred me; the waters of Sydney Harbour licked insidiously at its hundreds of wooden piles, and in my mind the dark, oily water beneath the wharf concealed sinister secrets.

Once, I'd watched two young boys in a small tin boat with an outboard motor navigate between the piles and disappear in the gloom. I demanded that we wait and watch for their safe return to the sunlit land of the living. After half an hour, Nella wanted to head home; a southerly was brewing. I insisted we go to the police, convinced that the boys had been trapped by the underwharf, or, more terrifying still, had found a way up into the building's ramshackle cavern and disappeared. Nella assured me that they'd simply gone in under one side of the wharf and emerged on the other. For days afterwards, I scoured the *Sydney Morning Herald* for a story about the boys' disappearance, or the discovery of their water-engorged bodies. At night, I'd wake suddenly, my head filled with visions of myself swimming around, mute with fear, in the inky darkness of the underwharf.

I let Nella pull me away from the fence that kept me from exploring the fingerwharf and we walked in silence around the bay, heading for the parkland of Mrs Macquarie's Chair and the Botanical Gardens, out of which the higher buildings of the city seemed to sprout like unlopped trees. We walked past the small sewerage plant where a bag lady's meagre possessions were clustered on the roof-top; Nella pointed out the cardboard boxes the woman used as a bed. Even the tough cops of Woolloomooloo Bay left her alone.

Once we were on the tarred path that ran around the headland

and along the curve of the next bay to the Opera House, Nella took my arm in hers again and drew me to her side. Right at the tip of the headland, where the second governor's wife once sat and waited for the fleet come in, we chose the bench closest to the water and sat awaiting no-one.

- Perhaps it's not my place to tell you this, Sophie, she said, clutching my left hand between both of hers. The veins under her skin looked like twists of blue silk cord, and I noticed for the first time how swollen her joints had become. It was just the heat. My Nella couldn't age.

- Come on Nella, I said, squeezing her hand, recoiling at the way she winced at the pressure.

- She was pregnant twice before you. The first time I had to give her the money for the operation.

It was harder for Nella than me, Zelda's story. She could picture Zelda then, less bluster, less ferocity, more a person who could feel and be hurt.

- It was the end of her first year in London and it was costing her all her pathetic salary just to pay the rent. She was proud ... wouldn't ask me for money. As far as Randolphe knew, she was living somewhere smart and doing just fine. Working in a very good company, thank you very much.

- So, what happened? I asked, staring at a ferry moving low in the water. Commuters fleeing their offices for the harbourside suburbs.

I was trying to picture Zelda at twenty. Dry-eyed and aloof at the airport, in the face of her mother's distress. Treating a trip across the globe as though it were little more than a peak-hour drive across the bridge.

- She told me she'd started seeing a poet they published ... he became too attached. In *those* days she worried about her reputation, Nella told me, as though I might not be able to conceive of such a thing. In a drunken stupor, he poured out his heart to his editor. The bastard made it too difficult for her to stay.

I was fascinated by the prospect of Zelda having been almost, but not quite, sacked. Tantalised by the thought that there was a time when she had not been absolutely vital to the world of publishing.

- She didn't have any trouble finding a new job ... got herself promoted in the process, Nella said, with the pride that changed her voice sometimes when she spoke of her daughter. She wouldn't hear of my flying to London to be with her.

Nella put the tips of her fingers to her right temple and winced. She was always there when I was ill. No matter how trivial, Nella had to see to me herself.

- She spent three days in bed afterwards, and on the fourth went into the office, so weak she could barely carry the manuscripts she'd been working on at home.

- She makes her *boys* carry manuscripts now, I said, remembering her announcing at a dinner that she could hardly be expected to lug half the Ecuadorian rain forest around herself!

- The second time it was some big journalist ... boasted about his seduction as though it was some kind of political coup. He was married to some novelist and wanted to leave her for Zelda.

Nella wasn't one to pronounce judgement, particularly on Zelda or me. Sometimes, she'd make a tight line of her lips and gently shake her head as though trying to deny what she was being faced with.

- Of course, by then she was tough enough to look after things herself. Put the bill in as a company expense, she told me. .... as though it was part of her job to go around sleeping with influential journalists.

What Nella said about my mother didn't surprise me. Zelda's succession of lovers was as constant in my life as the absence of my father. What I wasn't used to was Nella's openness. It made me uncomfortable; it was a dull, empty premonition of loss.

- You see, Sophie, she didn't really care for either of those men ... the concept of having a child by them was unthinkable.

- So, if my father was such a great guy, I said, bitter, watching the harbour turn shades of tangerine as the sun slid into the desert somewhere west of Sydney, why didn't she stay with him? Why did he let her come home, pregnant and alone?

- Oh Sophie, darling. Nella threw her arm around my shoulders and drew me close. She said he didn't know she was pregnant. She was full of her own independence ... terrified to bring someone into her life whom she couldn't control. She wasn't going to let herself be hurt, or let anyone keep her from what she wanted to do. She watched as your grandfather stayed away, took lovers in other countries, Nella said, pausing again, unsure how much I knew. Zelda was consumed by my hurt.

- I would have been, too, I said, giving her an adult look of understanding that made her smile.

- Irrevocable compromise was the term she used, Nella said, plucking absently at her white hair as the wind made it dance. She became so angry. She took upon herself the anger that I never expressed.

On the same path along which we'd come, I was chilled by the sudden shade and the insidious presence of the underwharf. The Woolloomooloo Bay Hotel and The Bells were already expanding in the cool of dusk to absorb the punters, ready to get down to the serious business of drinking. The climb back up to Victoria Street took a long time; it made the contrast between the bay with its dark pubs and darker wharves and the tree-lined, wrought-iron elegance of Victoria Street even more pronounced.

When we walked down that street at the beginning of summer and the jacaranda trees were bursting forth in billows of purple, the harbour glinting seductively at the end of the road, Nella would tell me that this was the most beautiful street in the world.

In her flat, she lit four candles around the room, so the last of the dusk wouldn't be consumed by electric light, and made a pot of jasmine tea. I was still feeling sorry for myself and reached for a shoe-box of photos, feigning absorption. Nella opened a deep, carved chest where I knew she kept her private things.

- Sophie, don't fret over what you haven't got. Concentrate on what you have ... on making your world a place you like to live in. If you start now, you might have learnt how to by the time you're really alone in this world.

I refused to look at her, refused to think of a time when she would no longer be there.

- I was going to save these for your birthday, she said, more gently. But I think you should have them now.

She took the shoe-box from me and replaced it with another, smaller box of worn cardboard that was a little too big to fit neatly into my right hand. I still didn't look at her.

- They were my mother's, Nella said, as she poured the tea and sniffed at my silence. Those cards were probably the only thing about her that I liked.

She came and crouched beside me to open the box in my hands, fingering the oversized, battered cards as if they were so fragile they might crumble in her fingers. She selected one bearing an illustration of a woman standing on a seashell, against a backdrop of blue water and rich, golden night sky: The Queen of Cups. For me that card became Nella's card. The card representing a cherished person, a friend and mother. A person of love, honesty and intelligence. Someone of great vision.

- They're tarot cards ... cards to divine the future ... to help understand the past ... see the world in a different light, she said. My mother let me watch when she read them for strangers in Paris. You should have seen the awe on their faces when she told them intimate, secret things about their lives ... some of them were shaken beyond speech.

I imagined Nella, at her mother's elbow, waiting for that wisdom, that warm solicitousness to be turned towards her.

- Their faces would just cave in ... the way faces do when a stranger understands more about you more than anyone else does.

- They're beautiful, Nella, I said, balling fists into my eyes. But don't you use them? Don't you tell people's fortunes with them?

- Not for years. Not since I met your grandfather, she said, sitting back in her chair so I could wander through the world of the cards myself. He talked me out of my faith ... I regret that. This is all I have of hers ... all I wanted.

- Why didn't you give them to Zelda?

- Intuition. I didn't think she'd be interested, my dear. She always had such a sense of purpose ... one was afraid to distract her ... important things to achieve out there in the world.

- Don't I have important things to achieve?

- You're not consumed with ambition, said Nella, closing her eyes and seeing a future that I couldn't. It'll take years for you to know your real purpose. Along the way you'll stray down all sorts of delicious paths until you find one that's irresistible.

Clutching my treasure, I closed my eyes and saw myself wandering alone, and at age twelve, I was not afraid.

In another city I travelled south, under the Thames, waiting for the tunnel to crack outside the windows of the slow-moving tube train. Waiting for the murky waters to penetrate. The syncopated hiss of a dozen Walkmen, playing a dozen different tunes, combined to form a mess of white noise. At the end of the line, the whole train emptied onto the platform and made a rush for the single up escalator.

The wide staircase from the underground ticket hall to the street was lined with grime-encrusted teenagers and their dogs. Hands, in gloves with cut-off fingers revealing bluish flesh, waited for coins to land in them. Twenty pence for some dog food please, luv. M'dog's hungry, miss. I gave fifty to a young woman with her right arm clamped around the neck of a spotty dog with a black patch over his left eye.

Outside the station's entrance, Brixton High Street thronged with shoppers and street vendors selling anything from cigarette lighters, five for a pound, to cheap plastic umbrellas and narrow sticks of incense. A group of well-dressed, shiny-faced Jamaicans sang of love and hope and faith. Pasty-faced young men in khaki fatigues with Jesus Army printed across their shoulders pushed pieces of paper at me. Up above, a train roared across an overpass sporting a jaunty sign against a faded backdrop of cracked, dried blood: We're Backing Brixton.

As I stood tapping my foot beside the singers, a pair of arms encircled me from behind and I was lifted off the pavement three times before Stanley spun me around to face him. The ritual shaking disoriented me, yet I was heartened by the sight of him. In my memory, Stanley was paler and slighter, much more a creature of the night than the tall, ruddy-cheeked skinhead who stood in front of me, grinning.

- Hungry? he said, dragging me off by the elbow before I could nod yes.

We plunged into a chaotic row of market stalls. Barrows displayed fruit, vegetables, cheap sweets, bolts of garish fabric, belts, shampoo, hair pieces and shoes. Clothing threaded through with gold lurex fluttered from unstable racks. Broad-hipped women with bulging plastic shopping bags stood waiting at the stall with the best okra and plantain. Children in padded coats and high-topped white sneakers chased each other around the barrows, falling over empty boxes and toppling carefully erected golden fruit pyramids. Teenage boys walked among the shoppers, oblivious to all but the volume level on their ghetto blasters. The clammy odour of raw meat washed over me as I passed the exposed flesh outside the butcher shop. A rank scent clinging to my skin like clubbers' sweat turned cold.

Off Electric Avenue, Stanley guided me through an archway and into a covered market, its glass roof dull with soot. The smell of uncooked mussels from the fishmonger mingled with the doughy, garlic aroma of cooking pizza. Outside the restaurant, the queue we joined was a hungry one. Franco's clientele, huddled over outdoor tables, looked hung-over regardless of how smartly or scuzzily dressed they were: an eclectic mix of film and advertising types in flawless black leather jackets, white shirts, blue Levis and chunky soled shoes; and the grunge set dressed all in black with Mad Max boots, biker jackets and extreme hair.

- Stanley, I can see the attraction of this place, but is any pizza worth queueing for?

- It's not the bloody pizza we're here for, he said, appalled at my ignorance. This is the place, that's all. Best scene, best coffee, and the pizza's OK, too.

- Oh, I said, relieved that indeed the world was such a simple place.

Inside, six or eight tables were squeezed together, and the room was so filled with cooking fumes and smoke that the customers appeared to inhabit a twilight.

- Especially on a Saturday, he continued. But then, I'm not usually here on Saturdays. Camden's a good place to catch up with the north London crew, but.

Stanley was nodding, and giving these cool, hip-level waves to anyone whose eye he caught.

- See that guy over there, leather vest and dreads? He's one of the doormen at the club down the road ... the Fridge ... he's someone to know, y'know? You just don't want to have to pay to get into a club.

- You're talking my language there.

We were at the front of the queue now and I was trying to keep my hands off the garlic bread on a table beside me.

- That woman inside's a photographer ... got a tiny shop-front gallery below her studio. It's just around the corner from M & S, he said, playing the local with an easy grace.

- Maybe I'll go and look at her stuff someday, I said, non-committal. Is it any good?

- Yeah. It's radical. Art-house, y'know, lots of superimposure and all that shit, he said, taking a moment out to order for both of us. You into photography?

- A little, I said, wary of a forced introduction. I take a few photos every now and then.

- You any good in black and white? he asked, suddenly more animated than cool.

- I like black and white. Why?

- Well, he said, pulling off his gloves to reveal discoloured hands, fingernails caked in black that left its trace on the plate when he picked up olives. I design t-shirts. Make 'em myself for the Camden Market scene ... I want to do some with photos. Local street photos. You interested?

- I'll have to think about it, I stammered. I've never sold any of my photos before. I mean, I've never really shown them or anything.

- But with the t-shirts, he said, still holding the same handful of olives, you probably wouldn't even recognise the photos in the end product.

- That's even worse, I countered, tense at the thought of losing control.

- I don't get it, he said, finally pushing four olives into his mouth at once and spitting the pips out in a neat little sequence.

Painstakingly, through mouthfuls of garlic bread wet with oil, I tried to explain the dilemma of my photos. About how they were so intimate that doing anything other than keeping the prints close seemed an impossibility. I told him that for me, taking photos had become a memory substitute. It wasn't that my memory was poor, more that I didn't trust it to remain unprejudiced.

- So what do you photograph?

- Well, things that are intimate, real images from a particular world, or from a friend or lover's life. My best friend lived in this house with three other people ... I used to spend a lot of time there myself. I used to photograph them.

- Doing what?

- Oh, y'know, anything ... getting out of it, hanging out, waking up, making love, whatever. Jessie and Lila liked to play at being leather dykes ... Jake did these sexy, sensuous sculptures ...

- Does that mean you're into porn? he asked, a watermelon grin of delight cracking his face.

- I dunno, I said, watching his eyes. It would've been porn if I wanted to turn someone on with it. When I was at school I did night classes in photography once a week ... built a dark-room under the house.

- Cool, he said.

- In this really subtle way, my mother started taking control ... guiding me in what I photographed. It was only when she went so far as actually inviting the art director from her firm 'round for dinner that I realised she was trying to build a career for me. I guess that's when I stopped photographing landscape and started on people ...

Our pizzas arrived along with the bravado of pepper being ground from a gargantuan mill, parmesan being scattered and salad being dressed. I was glad to change the subject, pronto, to mozzarella and tomato, and to garlic, the universal leveller.

Eating with the concentration of the ravenous, I let Stanley rattle on about clubs and markets and drugs and fads and Crusties, the people at the tube station asking for money to feed their dogs. Stanley had a way of placing himself within each of these narratives; he couldn't just tell me about the Crusties, he had to tell me about his own interaction with them. About the time he had taken one of the Crusties' dogs to the vet, and about how the vet had accused him of gross neglect. The dog belonged to an alcoholic who never seemed to have any change left after his trip to the off-licence.

With pizza bellies and greasy fingers, Stanley and I strolled through the covered market as though touring a rose garden. I stopped at a West Indian shop displaying baskets of salted fish and enormous tins of the custard-coloured vegetable called ackee. In a darkened corner of the tiny shop-front was a basket of writhing snails with shells as big as my open hand. Aghast, I stood and watched the brown, leathery flesh of the creatures ooze from their shells. A woman with skin puckered like a date's called from behind a simmering pot of something brown and green. How many?

- Oh, I'll come back later, I said, backing away. We've just had lunch.

- They make soup out of 'em, Stanley whispered, keen to provoke nausea. I've tried it and it's bloody good.

Delighted by my squeamishness, Stanley guided me to the window of a greasy spoon café specialising in jellied eel and mushy peas. Both sat in the window in great stainless steel basins, similar shades of green, and similarly liquid.

- We could have lunch in there on Monday, said Stanley with relish, making me think he was the sort of person who liked watching people vomit. If you wanted to stay the weekend . . . or will your father be angry again?

- Oh, it's a long story Stanley. I'd need the whole weekend to tell it. Maybe I'll have to stay . . . just so we know where we're both coming from.

- I know where you're coming from, and it's nothing like my street, he said, leading me away from the din and colour of the markets.

It wasn't that Stanley's street was threatening, more that it was unwelcoming. Two rows of identical Victorian brick houses, each two storeys high with bay windows at the front, all with doors either on the right or left, never the middle. Low brick walls enclosed yards where bins overflowed to reveal the nature of a household. They looked good and solid, the houses, and must have offered a degree of comfort between their walls. Small and ill-kempt compared to the houses on Randolphe's street, they were still individual residences rather than tower blocks built of concrete and glass. The absence of trees, grass and leaves was absolute.

Walking down that bleak street, crunching broken glass beneath my boots and pulling the sleeves of my leather jacket down over my blue, cracking fingers, I thought of the gum-lined streets where I had grown up; streets where you could barely see the houses for the trees. Mostly I'd walked alone on those streets, a place where you're treated like a freak for being alone. Then came a sudden flash of myself as part of this Brixton street, and of row upon row of identical streets, and suburbs. I suddenly felt it keenly, that I'd come to a place where nobody knew who the hell I was, and nobody cared. I liked it.

- How do you remember which one's yours? I asked, half serious, as we turned into one of the houses.

- They're all different, he said, looking at me sideways as though questioning my integrity, as though my street was further from his than he first imagined.

Don't let him think I'm a dumb bitch, I said to myself as we got caught in a tangle of bicycles in the front hall. My initial reaction to the house was a great, uncontrollable shiver. The temperature dropped a good ten degrees once we were inside with the door shut, and the light, pale grey outside, had simply turned to gloom.

- Have to watch the bills, Stanley apologised, squatting beside the coal fire to turn the knob, lighting the gas with a whoosh. It's a great summer house.

- Yeah, I said, through chattering teeth. I forgot about summer.

- Tea or coffee? he asked as he clattered down a short flight of hollow wooden stairs onto the kitchen tiles. We've got Tesco's own brand and instant coffee. We're not posh here.

- Tea please, I said, my eyes locked on the coals as they changed from dull black to a liquid orange traced with patches of blue like deep bruises beneath skin.

I wondered if he saw me as 'posh', and if he did, whether he despised me for it. I didn't have the energy to cope with being despised.

The front room was a gloomy avocado green and the tattered velvet moss curtains had obviously been chosen to match. The scratched floorboards were covered with a soft layer of dust and a heavy, blood-coloured Persian rug. Above the fireplace hung a red and gold circular design that I later learnt was a Buddhist mandala. On either side of the fireplace were rows of shelves, attached to the wall and sagging in the middle under the weight of hundreds of books. Half of the room was taken up by a scratched wooden dining table, with candle wax mounds of red and white haphazardly punctuating its surface. The room had such a lived-in feel that, despite its gloom, there was a warmth to it.

When Stanley returned from the kitchen – taking painfully small steps, his eyes on the heavy tray crammed with teapot, cups, milk and chocolate biscuits – I was reminded of Nella. The few people I'd ever been close to had approached me in just the same way, tray heavily laden, preparing for a long session of tea drinking and the exchange of life's intimacies. When Zelda made me tea, those very few times, she always summoned me to the kitchen to collect it, and rarely made a pot, favouring the tea bag in the mug.

- This could be the beginning of a beautiful friendship, I said, lying on my side in front of the glowing coals like some woman from a chocolate advertisement.

Stanley poured the tea with one hand on the pot's lid. He frowned at me.

- I mean it, I said, reaching over to touch his foot, now without its boot but clad in a lint-covered, red woolly sock. Anyone who makes a pot of tea for me, even if it is Tesco's own brand, soars in my esteem.

- Well, I'm relieved, he said, sitting back on his haunches and taking my hand in his. I thought you might be the type who only drank champagne, vodka and the occasional cappuccino.

- Who's been telling you stories? I asked, feeling got at.

- I heard you talking to some guy who offered you a drink at The Palace, he said. He offered to buy you a beer and you told him you only drank champagne and vodka.

- I've got a terrible repertoire of smart-arsed one-liners. I hate them, I said.

- Try one on me?

- You have to ask me what I do, you know? I said, in spite of myself. There are certain types of people who'll ask you what you do even before they know what you're drinking.

- Well, what do you do? he asked, affecting a public school accent.

- Oh, y'know, mostly I'm a tattoo artist, but what with HIV and all, I strip to supplement my income.

Stanley snorted his tea out through his nose. Then he rocked back and forth and wheezed.

- What the fuck was so funny about that? I asked, inexplicably offended.

- That might impress the toffs who've never been to a tattoo parlour or a strip joint, but to someone who isn't exactly – ah, well – a *stranger* to the underbelly, it's a right laugh, he said. You're hardly a girl from the wrong side of the tracks ... even with your accent, that's obvious.

- Dumbfuck! I spat. You're not supposed to believe it. It sorts the world into two categories: those who look alarmed and take a large step back, and those who laugh and say that's a good one ... we're all tattoo artists and strippers.

- Soph, he said, sipping tea more carefully. It's just, well, I can't imagine anyone believing that story ... look at you. You're hardly the sort of girl who looks as though she's been around, if you know what I mean.

- Oh yeah? I said, standing up, never to be outdone.

Stanley looked alarmed as I started to swing my hips and unzip my jacket. I thrust each booted foot at him so he could deal with the laces. Of course, it wasn't possible to be particularly sexy while taking off a jumper or unbuttoning a shirt to reveal a long-sleeved vest underneath, but I certainly had his attention. At least I was wearing a black lace bra under the vest, and high-cut black knickers. In the gradual shedding of my jeans, not only did I reveal two tattoos, but some devastatingly professional moves.

- So, I said to Stanley, hands on my hips, trying not to shiver in my underwear. Do I still not look like the type?

- I, I take it all back, he stammered. I think you should get dressed before I, before you catch cold.

Stanley poured more tea, trying not to look at me. He cleared his throat and looked as though he'd walked in on his parents having sex.

- Where can I get dressed? I asked, gathering my clothes.

In the bathroom on the first-floor landing I sat on the toilet with chattering teeth, feeling rotten to the core. I traced an icy finger over my pentagram, let down by its promise of protection, of wisdom. I wondered what I would stoop to in order to impress the man I was searching for. Or to repel him, as I was sure I'd done with Stanley.

In the lounge room, Stanley sat huddled over a spread of cards; for a moment I faltered. I hadn't known he was a reader. My delight turned to quick, cold rage just as fast.

- What do you think you're doing?

- They fell out of your jacket, he said, pushing the cards into a rough pile and trying to force them into the box. I haven't seen any like these before ... they're beautiful.

- Here, I said, taking the cards and trying not to look so annoyed. I get nervous when someone else plays with them. Sorry.

- No, I'm sorry, he said, neither of us knowing how to dispel the wet blanket of unease that had chilled the room.

February was a wet, heavy month, and although the heat remained I mourned the brilliance of summer and its irrevocable loss. January in Sydney was a month that seemed unending. A month not sullied by a single day of school as February and December were.

It had been a summer of long, slow walks by the harbour with Nella, of talks that started in the afternoon down by the bay and meandered sweetly into the still of early evening. A summer of late, adult dinners in cafés on Victoria Street, when I ate pizza Napoli and Nella and Charlie had 'something light' – a pasta with pesto sauce or a grilled lemon sole. A time of journeys between Potts Point and Balmain, of sitting on the bus that snaked down into the bay, wove around the back of the art gallery and cathedral, careened through the city, and wound up at Circular Quay. Of exquisite rides on ferries, sitting always on the front deck, of pulling away from the Quay so the city rose before me, actually grew as I moved away from it. Of gliding under the Harbour Bridge with the odd, distant sound of traffic overhead and a wide band of shadow on the water below that made me shiver as we cut through it. And suddenly, after the chrome and glass glitz of the skyscrapers came the bulk and texture of the cargo vessels. Where men were dwarfed by the whale's belly of a ship and I imagined I could smell the lingering residue of spices and grains.

Another world again when the ferry pulled into the Darling Street wharf at the end of a street with its slopes and dives, its antique shops and church markets and pubs. There was an ease about Balmain, a casual, dress down and sit under a frangipani tree feel to the place that distanced it from the high-rise, espresso style of Potts Point and the serious business of family life that marked the suburb where Zelda lived.

On the way up the hill I was allowed to buy a Splice or a Golden Gaytime at one of the milk bars that still sported pale green Formica counters and stainless steel fridges and milkshake makers. By the time Nella and I had worked up a sweat climbing the lanes contained by the grey of fence palings, I'd be licking the ice-cream from my fingers and chewing the wooden stick between my molars.

The journey itself was the best thing about going to Charlie's place; the spectacle of viewing the city from the water and cruising past the west harbour suburbs with such grace, such ease. Past the isolated tower block on the tip of Blues Point, where prostitutes lived and worked. Later, in London, I'd dream of that barren block with water and yachts on three sides. After the dream I saw a tiny article in a London paper about an Englishman who'd jumped from the top of the building with a parachute strapped to his back. It failed to open.

Nella and I took our shoes off and walked up Darling Street barefoot, just because we could. Just because it was such a good feeling, the heat from the pavement going right into your soul. I'd run across the scorching expanses of black tar as if crossing a patch of bindi eyes, trying to make as little contact with the ground as possible. One day, Nella wouldn't run with me. She paused to put her shoes on before crossing the road and stopped again on the other side to take them off. She had become frail, and any jolting movement caused her pain.

In the creamy shade of a frangipani tree, Nella and I lay on a threadbare blanket like the ladies of leisure we were. Snatches of conversations between Charlie and one of his silent orchids would waft across to us through the thick green of his garden. Or perhaps it was his marmalade cat, Myrrh, that he was addressing as he trained a passionfruit vine along the fence. The back part of Charlie's garden was intensively cultivated, dense with flowers, vines and shrubs, because it was from here he could work and watch the harbour at the same time. A different, industrial part of the harbour with grain elevators and railway sidings along the shore. Fewer of the frou frou sailing dinghies that I watched from my rock, and none of the luxurious bushland.

As the hollow, otherworldly sound of wind-chimes wafted to us over a wooden fence, Nella read the cards for me. She saw my plans for flight, my intention to find my father, something we had never discussed. She told me that the cards afforded the possibility of regarding an old ache from a myriad of different positions. They put the seeker in a position where odd, unutterable issues could be voiced, simply because they arose in the haphazard arranging and rearranging of the cards.

That summer I became obsessive about Nella, and she, knowing it couldn't last, indulged my obsession. Her hair seemed to have metamorphosed into a diaphanous shroud. I would pet it, stroke it in the same fondly distracted manner that a mother caresses a child. Her skin had become papery at the same time that the cards started to feel like skin.

Nella refused to allow me to read her cards for her. Unappeased by suggestions that I read for Charlie, I stomped off to the harbourside baths alone. Later, my wet Speedos soaking through my shorts, I dragged myself back to Charlie's, whispering, Nella and I don't fight; we don't fight.

From Charlie's kitchen, where he was preparing leaf-wrapped fish for our dinner, came the wondrous odours of garlic and coriander. Under the frangipani tree lay the crumpled rug, and beside it the abandoned cards and pairs of shoes. Nella's absence made me shiver. I walked into the kitchen and waited for Charlie to speak.

- She's lying down, he said to me, sliding a mug and a teapot across the table. It's jasmine.

- But she's been lying down most of the day, I said as though it was forbidden. Is she angry with me?

- I don't think she knows how to be angry with you, he said, lifting the lid from a pan on the stove and giving his face an aromatic steam bath.

- I don't believe what she told me about not being allowed to use those cards on her, I said.

I sipped from the mug and swung my feet beneath the bench: seeing Charlie in the kitchen cooking for Nella made me feel jealous; I imagined Charlie and Rob had a real family life, even with just the two of them.

- Sophie, I'm sure Nella has very good reasons for not wanting you to read her cards. Won't you just respect her wishes and let it lie? Charlie poured wild rice into a pot of boiling water. I'm the one who's offended. Why won't you give me a reading?

Humbled, I scampered out to the garden to fetch the cards, and returned by way of the bathroom, where I shed my wet Speedos. When Nella finally rose and came to join us, I was in the middle of telling Charlie I foresaw luxury and riches for him just around the corner.

- Not in this life! he snorted.

Their exchange of solemn glances wasn't lost on me, and I saw that Nella's eyes were rimmed red, like Zelda's when she'd been drinking. But my Nella didn't drink during the day.

- Nella, I said, going to hug her, to plunge my hands in her hair again. I'm sorry, I'm sorry. What's wrong? You look so sad.

- I'm not sad, she said, allowing herself to be led to the table and taking the mug offered her. I'm just contemplating change. Thinking that you're too old, now, to spend all this time with your decrepit grandmother and her hippie boyfriend.

- No, I said.

- You should be with your friends ... with Sam. She took my hands from her hair and held them. Going out and having fun ... the beach, the movies.

- No, I said, this time with such force that the other sounds in the room seemed to lack substance. I want to be with you, Nella. It's the best when I'm with you.

- Oh, child, she said, gripping my cold hands even harder. There's so much out there for you. I'm hindering you now.

- I don't want anything to change, Nella. I like it this way.

- Sophie, she said, as though talking to a child who keeps forgetting to shut the door after her, or to clean the sand from her feet. I've told you the only thing we can rely on is change.

On the last day of the holidays, Zelda sent Sam and me off to the movies, to Pitt Street, unaccompanied. We felt so very adult in our short skirts and halter-neck tops, going to see an American 'teen film' with Jodie Foster and Matt Dillon. A film, predictably, about the loss of virginity. Afterwards, we walked through Hyde Park, practising swinging our hips and spotting 'babes'.

At six we reached Nella's, where Zelda was to pick us up; we were disappointed to see her car already parked outside. The sight of that car, ready to take us both home to our newly covered schoolbooks and laundered, crisp school uniforms, symbolised the end of the summer as nothing else could.

Confused by the noise from within, Sam and I hesitated on the threshold before entering Nella's crowded living room to a chorus of Surprise, Surprise!

- We wanted to send you off to high school with a bang, not a whimper, said Nella, hugging first Sam and then me, and keeping both of us close to her.

Charlie handed us each a glass of pink champagne, and Uncle Jerry started cutting the thick poppy seed cake that was his speciality and sighing over the perfection of the chocolate eclairs. Zelda sat quiet and sober in a chair by the window. Although I could only see her in profile, I was struck by how deflated she looked. Rob emerged from the kitchen with a bowl of strawberries in one hand and freshly whipped cream in the other, his blue and white shirt spattered.

Unaccustomed to alcohol, Sam and I became silly, giggly. Over the summer we had lost some of our tom-boyishness, and that evening we were decidedly girlish. We flirted clumsily with Rob, and Uncle Jerry feigned jealousy. Later in the evening, Nella and I stood arm in arm, reminiscing over the wonders of that very special January. Talking excitedly about taking photos and reading cards. And about how good it felt to have walked the harbour foreshores, content with each other as two old friends.

When Zelda came and put a hand on my shoulder to tell me it was time to leave, a nervous silence settled on the room. Nella and I kissed our good-byes, holding hands and looking into each other's eyes as we always did. As Zelda ushered me from the room, I looked back to see Nella hugging Sam, and talking into her ear.

In the lift down to the street, Zelda put her arm around me and I didn't cringe. Sam remained silent.

- What was Nella saying to you, Sammy?

- Just that I was to look after you, that we were to look after each other.

Over the next three weeks, Sam and I moaned about school and the fact that so many of the other girls seemed to have acquired breasts and boyfriends during the summer. Every second girl claimed to be 'going around' with someone. Finally, after much hanging out at the shops, and in the car park where the neighbourhood guys rode their skateboards, boys, not just Alex, began to notice us. Admittedly they only said things like, You're in the way there, Give us a chip, or Nice legs, but we were transported. We'd made it.

Almost a month after our surprise party, Nella took a bus from Kings Cross to Bondi Beach on a mid-March afternoon with a chill to it. She sat in the sand, undisturbed by the runners, or the school-kid surfers, or the occasional swimmer. After a while, Nella stood up and delicately removed her shirt and trousers. Wearing a purple bikini of modest proportions, her hair down around her shoulders, she walked into the surf and dived under row after row of breaking waves, just as she'd taught me to do. Having cleared the breakers, she swam further and further out to sea. This is how I imagined it.

THE MOON

The loft has become my vault and I pace its length with my own ghosts pressing in on me. Now it's light, even the seconds have settled in the heat.

I need to shift the weight of this apprehension from my chest. A long hard run over the crusty, excrement-smeared pavements of the East Village will make me remember who I am and what I want. I aim for a square with trees in it, not so I can run among them, but so their calm touches me. I've heard runners say that the pavements of New York City are hard, harder than those in any other city.

While I'm in the shower the phone rings and the machine responds. Somebody from my father's publishing house leaves a reminder that he is, in fact, expecting me today.

'My father'. Since I have known his name, the words have

become taboo. Now I roll them on my tongue to see how they feel. I won't yet be saying 'my father' in public, or in the ominous intimacy of his presence. In the context of my own life, it would seem absurd.

And exactly how long is it that you've been looking for me? he'll ask, perhaps even expecting a simple answer, a number you could count on your hand to signify months or years. But I'll tell him, Ever since I was old enough to perceive your absence. Then I'll sit back and watch him run for cover.

I lay on the floor of my bedroom in one of my long, spangly skirts. Surrounded by the enigmatic cards of the Higher Arcana in all of their baroque detail, I was fixated by the card called The Star; a sylph-like naked girl, kneeling by a pond and pouring water. The Star, shining bright in the inky sky, an emblem of the spirit, the mystical centre and the call of destiny. The waters representing new life and rebirth. The journey represented by the card is not yet over, as the mystic centre has yet to be reached.

Just before ten, the phone rang. I jumped up, sure it was Sam, who sometimes called around then. Zelda was there first. I stood just inside my door, waiting for her to call me to the lounge room. I listened, hearing her only say yes, once, right at the beginning. The ensuing silence unnerved me; it wasn't Zelda's style. After a long silence, she muttered something and hung up. There was no movement from the other room.

- Charlie, she said, shocking me by the silence with which she'd dialled. Yes, I just had a call ... she didn't come back.

The house seemed to shift beneath me, but I realised I was swaying. Zelda never phoned Charlie. She simply had no time for him. The way she frostily met his efforts to engage her in conversation embarrassed me.

At the approach of her footsteps, I dived back onto the rug, giving my right knee carpet burn and tearing my skirt. When Zelda knocked, and opened the door after a few moments, I was lying amid my cards again. She grimaced at the sight. Without asking, she cleared a place on a cushion opposite, and sank slowly into its yielding surface, in the manner of someone who had mysteriously gained weight that she was unaccustomed to bearing.

Her presence there, on my bedroom floor, disconcerted me. Rather than look at her face, I took in the shimmery fabric of her green trousers, the immaculate surface of her khaki pumps, her cream stockinged legs, her billowing ivory silk shirt and her crimson braces. The only part of her that was coming undone was her hair. The finely structured bun that usually sat high on the back of her head was all loose; long, pale strands strayed over her shoulders, one clinging to her neck, twisting around it, looking oddly like a rivulet of blood. For the first time I realised that Zelda's rich auburn hair was fading.

- Sophie, I, I . . . it's about Nella.

Immediately I sat upright, my knees drawn into my chest and my right hand covering The Star.

- She's gone, Sophie. Zelda's voice wavered slightly and she tried to control it.

- Gone where? My voice was hard, defensive.

- She's dead Sophie. Zelda dropped her chin down to her chest.

- No. She's not dead. Nella's not dead. You wish she was, but she's not!

- Sophie, Zelda's voice was full of tears, her eyes dry. Sophie. She's my mother and I love her. I'm telling you that she's dead.

- She can't be, I said, moving back, moving away instinctively. If she's dead, tell me how she died.

- Your grandmother killed herself.

- You're a liar, Zelda, I screamed. Nella would never do that. You're lying and I hate you!

- Nella walked into the surf at Bondi this afternoon, she said, focusing now on the mound of cards, not touching the kohl tears running down her cheeks. They found her clothes on the beach.

The card crumpled in my hand, but I remained silent.

- They haven't found her body yet. They may not.

- No, I howled, turning to face the wall and knocking my forehead against it, feeling nothing. She's just gone for a swim, that's all. She'll be back. Probably come up at Tamarama.

I glanced over my shoulder, terrified, suddenly, that Zelda would approach, but she just sat on the cushion with her head hanging down.

- She'll be back, I whispered. That's a horrible thing to say, that she killed herself. You're such a liar.

- She told me she was going to, said Zelda, almost inaudibly. She found out she had cancer, she'd been ill for a while ... decided the only thing she could bear was to take her own life.

- No, I howled, tearing now at my hair.

- Nella had a rare cancer of the bone marrow. She's been in pain for months. She refused chemotherapy.

- You're lying, I shrieked, knowing that she wasn't, persisting anyway. She would've told me. I would have known.

- That's not necessarily so, said my mother, forcing calm in the face of my hysteria. She's always done everything in her power to protect you ... this was her greatest gesture. She didn't want you to see her suffer.

- You could have stopped her, I said, turning to see my mother holding Nella's cards. Don't touch them. They're mine, she gave them to me.

Rushing forward, I grabbed the cards from Zelda's shaking hand, shoving her as I passed. Clutching the pack I hurled myself through the lounge room and onto the deck, leaving the wind chimes clanging maniacally behind me. Down in the bush I ran, my skirt catching on rocks and branches, my hair bunching in my mouth and my bare feet landing on every jagged edge. Branches dragged across my face and snagged in my hair. I tore the fingers on my left hand as I scaled the rock, my right hand never loosening its grip on the cards.

I lay curled in a ball atop my rock and laughed at the pain in my right foot where a stick had gone in. I sucked my bleeding fingers. The sandstone underneath felt warm; it cradled me. The rock and I were floating on a sea of trees.

- Nella, Nella, I heard myself saying. Nella why? Why? Why didn't you tell me?

Over and over again I asked, and again and again, before I let myself really contemplate her death, her absence, I thought of Zelda. Of how she could have prevented it. Of how she could have saved her mother. Of how, if she had wanted it, Nella would still be there, over in Potts Point, or at Charlie's sitting on the back veranda, listening to the night settle. Listening to him reading to her.

Something in me curled tightly in on itself, became hard and cold. Something that a life's worth of Sydney summers would not thaw. I cursed Zelda. The woman who had so efficiently deprived me of a father and who had now let my grandmother slip away. Easier to be angry than bereaved. Easier to be mad than lost. I stared at the stars, at the sky, until there was nothing more than light and dark. Not a moment of the night of Nella's death escaped me.

By the time the stars faded I was numb both inside and out. The light of day that I believed would never come bled into the sky. Trails of dried blood formed a crazy paving on my legs and my body had grown a shell of dried sweat and grit from the rock. As I climbed down I tumbled, bottom-first, into the dry, scratching branches of a lantana bush.

I sat and contemplated the water, so still in the early morning, velveteen and benevolent. I dropped my clothes onto the dew-damp sand and waded, unthinking, into the cold indigo of the autumn harbour. But when my feet suddenly found only water where there had been sand and my whole body went under, it was shock, not relief that gripped me. I opened my eyes and mouth at once, and both filled with the sting of salt water. I thrashed spasmodically, keeping my head above water, treading frantically to keep afloat, coughing the briny liquid up through mouth and nose.

I was alone. Now there was only me to tend my scrapes, nurse my colds, nourish both body and soul.

I walked back through the bush, treading gingerly now. Feeling the rocks and sticks beneath my lacerated feet, watching for snakes or lizards poking from dark holes in search of the morning sun. I climbed the wooden spiral staircase onto the deck, not knowing what to expect.

The sliding door and fly screen were both open, as I had left them the night before. The house was quiet and ordered, and for a horrible moment, I though that she was still in my room awaiting my return. But my room was empty, hers too, her study awash with manuscript pages. There was no steam in her bathroom, the towels were dry, and in the kitchen, there was no smell of toast and there were no dirty breakfast dishes in the sink. The only sign of Zelda was an empty gin bottle, sitting by the bin for recycling, and an upturned tumbler on the draining board. Her car was gone.

I sat on the deck drinking tea, waiting for something, for some indication that I had dreamt it all. I was waiting for the phone to ring, and for Nella's voice, bright and morning light, to ask me why I wasn't at school. But my foot throbbed, and my head ached, and I knew that this was real, this absence. That this was what we'd always walked towards. This was where Nella's footsteps beside mine in the sand disappeared, and no matter how sorry I felt for myself, no matter how very miserable, I would walk on alone.

In our best gear, Randolphe and I rode in the red Hopper bus from Dartmouth Park, down past the cluster of professional drinkers outside Kentish Town Station and the library and past the charity shops and bric-a-brac emporiums and Guinness-serving pubs into the heart of Camden Town. Striking off in the opposite direction from The Palace, we sauntered past Camden High Street's leather and Doc Marten shops towards the Lock. Below us, on the edge of the canal, some Crusties sat huddled with their dogs, drinking cheap import lager and arguing about the Pogues.

To be going out for dinner with Randolphe caused me both excitement and confusion. Not because he was so very distinguished looking and I was a little infatuated with him, but because it was almost unthinkable to me that a man would take me to dinner and not expect me to show my gratitude by adopting the missionary position almost as soon as coffee and dessert were out of the way.

- So when are you going to tell me what we're celebrating? I asked, lingering over the tart flavour of a Campari soda. Are you going to tell me that it's been nice having me, but it's time I pushed off?

- So grim for one so young, he said, running his right hand along the length of his mercifully narrow tie in a gesture that made me giggle. I know, I know, you're positively ancient for your age thanks to my sister, but today I'm another year older myself ... another year closer to the quieter phase of my life.

- Happy Birthday, I said, jumping up to embrace him, causing him to blush and the man at the next table to lose track of his conversation. You should have told me! I'd have done something.

- But my dear, we are doing something, he said as we were delivered silver platters of fresh artichoke. I can't remember the last time I shared my birthday with a young lady as charming as you.

- You don't have to flatter me, I said, delicately prising leaves from the core and pulling them between my teeth. You already have my undying worship.

- I've seen how quickly your worship can die, he said, raising an eyebrow. I saw my publisher friend the other day. He said that poor sod was quite distraught after his launch ... drank all night alone in his room ... demanded my telephone number in the morning.

- I'm sorry to involve you in that, I said quietly. I'm absolutely reformed now. No more belligerent authors, I promise.

- What do you mean reformed? he asked. Are you in the habit of befriending belligerent authors? It's an odd habit for someone who doesn't read.

- There've been a few, I said, toying with my artichoke leaves and making a great ceremony out of wiping my fingers, of patting the stiff linen napkin against my lips.

Randolphe started to look around the room, as though checking the exits and the whereabouts of the loos as you would in an aeroplane. He cleared his throat a few times and then distractedly tasted the red wine for the insipidly smiling waiter. The silence stretched between us and threatened to break, to come back and slap either one of us in the face.

- You understand that I would never try to tell you what to do, he said with a tight, controlled voice. I'm not a man to make moral judgements ... even about the people close to me. You realise that your mother also had a, well, a predisposition to befriend authors? he said, looking as though he'd just smelt someone's rankest, liquid fart. I know you're not fond of her, but are you sure you're not taking her example a little too literally?

I swallowed hard, the bitter taste of vinegar catching in my throat. Across the table, Randolphe watched me, almost sadly, as I slumped, heavy with self-despair.

- One of those authors out there's my father, I said, hot-faced. I meet a writer of a certain age and I'm drawn in by the sheer possibility ... I'm curious ... have to find out as much as I can about this man ... really want to like him. Just in case, you see?

- Really, he said, his eyes mercifully closed.

- Please don't be disgusted Dolphi ... I couldn't stand it, I said, looking for a waiter to take away the wreck of my artichoke, the wreck of the dinner.

- I'm not disgusted with you Sophia, he said, his voice sharp as a paper cut. It's my sister I'm disgusted with. If she'd only bloody well told us all who the father was there wouldn't be any of this perversity!

` Mm, perversity. He thinks I'm a pervert, I thought. Peas in a pod, Zelda and me.

- If she'd only swallow her damn fool pride and give you a name, you might have some chance of leading a normal life, he muttered. You might start to meet men that you're attracted to, rather than men she'd be attracted to.

- That's not the way Zelda sees things, I said, nearly choking on a surge of defensiveness. She thinks I go out with those men to make her jealous . . . make her feel old . . . just because I can.

He still wasn't looking at me, nor was he eating. Happy Birthday, I thought.

- She won't tell me my father's name because she believes women shouldn't have to know their fathers . . . are better not knowing their fathers.

Randolphe was shaking his head and holding his hand to his brow, oblivious to the traces of vinaigrette that left a shine on his forehead.

- Dear God, he was saying, addressing his plate. Nella would turn in her grave.

- Don't say that. Nella thought it was alright for me to be brought up by women. And it was, Randolphe, wasn't it? Did I turn out that badly?

- You turned out very well indeed, my dear, considering. I just want you to be happy, he said, as though he were wishing me something as inconceivable as the Olympic shot-put medal. I believe you should know your father . . . it's your right.

- I thought I'd find him in London, I said, heartened because he didn't despise me. I mean, it makes sense, doesn't it? Maybe he was even at Dick's launch?

Once again Randolphe rubbed his forehead, and my guess was he was thinking it could have been any of those blokes.

They'd all known her, and it wasn't just the authors she'd slept with.

- I'm going to ring her, he said. I'll force her to tell me.

- Thanks Dolphi, I said, anxious for the loss of his birthday. I don't see how you could succeed where years of attack from Nella and me failed.

- Sophie, don't worry yourself my dear, he was saying. Try to relax and enjoy London.

That night, in my bed in Randolphe's house, I slept curled in a ball, nursing the remains of dinner in my belly and trying to keep my feet warm. I woke at three in the morning, my head filled with a dream of Sam. She was by the water, on the bay where we'd grown up, on a shiny crescent of a beach backed by low sandstone cliffs. A stretch of sand that was only accessible at low tide. It was mid-summer, time of the king tides, and she was stranded with the water still rising. It wasn't a question of just wading over rocks to get out, she'd have to swim for it, but wouldn't. A few hundred metres up the bay was a warning sign; on a lop-sided post was a steel plate threatening a dark, ominous outline. The words Man-Eating Sharks were barely discernible. Although the sign had been there for years, had been used for target practice by local kids with air guns, and was only the token gesture of some local council long defunct, since we first saw it, it had haunted us. I awoke in a cold sweat, convinced that I couldn't help Sam because it was imperative I catch a plane I was already late for.

Nothing prepared me for the neatly boxed finality of Nella's flat. No longer a place where every comfort and detail spoke of the woman who had slipped out for a moment. It had become a place from which Nella had taken her leave. Rugs were rolled and tagged, boxes packed and labelled, the kitchen and bathroom pristine as TV commercials, furniture clustered together to facilitate its removal, to discourage lingering.

Nella had been preparing for her death for months, and I was the only one who hadn't known. Of course I blamed Zelda; the one who placed so little trust in me, the one who spoke to me as adult to slightly backward child. It must have been she who vetoed my involvement in Nella's preparation for death.

With eyes smarting, I stood at the window in the clam-shaped room, looking for what I imagined would be the last time at the trees whose spiky conkers scattered the pavements like soiled confetti. It was late morning and we'd missed the cockatoos' first chorus of the day. By then they would have been feeding across the harbour at the zoo, where the liberally strewn seeds made a welcome change from sandwich crusts and McDonalds' buns. At dusk, they would return, well fed and boasting of the fact, to serenade at Nella's window as the harbour turned purple.

Nella's note said, My darlings, My last day was spent baking you these biscuits. All my love for you both went into them. Please enjoy them, as you enjoy your memories of me, without regret.

- What else does it say? I demanded, once Zelda had stopped reading. There must be more. Some message.

- No, that's it, she said, her voice and her face crumbling in unison.

By the window, I steeled myself against tears and listened, outraged, as Zelda sobbed. Crocodile tears, I kept whispering, and half wondered why she didn't use them more often to get what she wanted.

After a soft knock at the door that neither of us acknowledged, Uncle Jerry slipped into the hallway, stooped with a tea tray. He winced slightly as he slid the tray onto the table beside her biscuits.

- Dear, he said, going immediately to Zelda, embracing her. She loved you so much. She was so proud of you.

- No, said Zelda, sobbing on Jerry's shoulder while her flowing hair tangled in the hand he held at her cheek.

- Yes, she was proud, he repeated, firmly this time. She kept the newspaper reviews from your books. She told me again and again that despite the fact she'd been alone, you'd done so very well . . .

Zelda's keening only intensified, and I wanted to evaporate. Wanted to feel truly invisible so I wasn't asked to participate in this collective grief.

With her hair down over her shoulders, Zelda looked as young and as lost as I felt, but at that time I was determined to appear in control. And so when Uncle Jerry came to stand by me, to place his hand, tentatively, at the base of my skull, I stood up straight and gazed ahead.

- You'll miss her Jerry, I said, using his name on its own for the first time and holding his hand as he squeezed tears from his baggy, old man eyelids.

Behind us, Zelda knelt on the parquet in her immaculate linen suit and poured the tea, just as Nella would have done.

- You drink my cup, I told Uncle Jerry, breezing past Zelda and moving through the hallway to the bedroom.

Cross-legged, I sat on Nella's bed, the bare mattress alarmingly stained in the way of most mattresses, but shocking me all the same. The greyish surface of the harbour was devoid of sails, unlike those summer days when I had lain on that bed having my bandages changed. Zelda had always said Nella had the rooms the wrong way around, that the bedroom, having the best view, should have in fact been the lounge room. But that was the point; the best view had to be the one Nella saw first thing in the morning and last thing at night. In Zelda's world the only place for a view was where her guests could admire it.

When she followed me into the bedroom and offered me her tea, I shook my head, not looking at her. Not wanting to acknowledge her sorrow and loss.

- It's yours, she said, standing by the bed. Nella's left you the flat. This place belongs to you now.

- I want to move in straight away, I said in a monotone, watching a hydrofoil shrink as it flew towards Manly, watching my past fade with the same resolved momentum.

- Don't be so ridiculous, Zelda snapped, then forced her voice to soften. In the will it says we have to let this place out until you're twenty-one. Then you can decide what to do with it . . . the money'll go into a special account, so you have something later.

- What about her things? I asked, trying to muster as much anger as I could, but there on Nella's bed, finding it difficult.

- She wanted most sold or given away, said Zelda, sitting, suddenly deflated, on the bed beside me. Said she didn't want us moping over a bunch of objects.

- Fine, I said, wanting to keep everything, wanting to drag it all to my chest and hold it close.

- I know you'll miss her Sophie, she said, placing a soft, ink-stained hand on my cold fingers. You had the best of her, you know that? More than I ever had of her. She loved you very, very much.

- You never wanted her, I said, pulling my hand away and

drawing my knees to my chest. I want to go home now. I'll take the bus.

- You don't know what you're saying, she said, her voice still disconcertingly gentle. I've arranged a nice treat at the movies for you ... Sam's taking the afternoon off school. It's all organised. She'll be at Hoyts at two.

- You don't have to organise everything for me just because Nella's not here.

- Sophie, I have to go to work this afternoon. I didn't want you to be alone.

- I like being alone. I'm not afraid of being alone like you are.

- Here, she said, businesslike, standing up and picking at the creases in her suit with an irritated expression on her face before pressing two twenties into my hand. Take Sam to the Pizza Hut afterwards. Take a taxi home.

I stood at the doorway in the hall, knowing I couldn't say good-bye to Nella there, under those circumstances, as Zelda was doing. When she finally emerged from the lounge room, Zelda pushed the box of biscuits into my hands, and for a moment, they were Nella's hands, pressing something upon me before I left. Something of herself that I could carry away with me.

With the quilt tucked under my body on three of its four sides, safe in my cocoon, I inhabited only a third of the single bed. The smaller I made myself, all curled inward, the less of me there was to get cold. On the polished wooden floor, my kelim set the room's tone. I'd decorated it with piles of my own clothes; photos I'd carried with me of the bush and harbour adorned the small mantelpiece and the inside edge of the standing mirror. Even with its bachelor air, Randolphe's house felt familiar. For all their differences, Nella, Zelda and Randolphe each had homes that were a mixture of classic simplicity and eastern exoticism. This unexpected similarity, this sense of an echo, must be attributed to my grandfather whose real life lay in the Middle and Far East. His presence in the lives of his family was marked by hand-woven carpets in shades of blood and terracotta, by low-lying, dark wooden furniture and by Arabic parchments and Indian silks that hung on walls in glass cases.

- Betrayal bounty, snorted Zelda when I was clearing the cellar of disintegrating rugs to make a darkroom. Each time he cheated on Nella again, we'd receive notices from the Australian Customs Office announcing the fact!

I heard the floorboards creak in Randolphe's room, but could barely bring myself to stir for fear of moving into one of the bright patches of cold on the bed. From the pillow I could look out the window at the double chimney pots rising like periscopes from the slate of the next-door roof that glinted grey like the harbour in storm. The pigeons were already shitting, bickering, and the pale early morning sky looked almost blue without its uniform of clouds. Inspired by the clarity, and the absence of grey in the sky, I poked a leg out from under the quilt, testing the air, before leaping out and beginning the mad dance of clothing myself before the cold drove me back to bed.

Sock-footed, I thundered downstairs to retrieve my boots from beside the fireplace where I had shed them the night before. By the time Randolphe took the stairs at a more dignified pace, I'd already managed to gulp down half a carton of orange juice and a slice of thickly honeyed rye bread, all in the hope of quietening my morning-sore throat.

I in my boots, leather jacket and Peruvian knitted cap and he in his Barbour and jaunty Harris tweed pork pie were on the heath at 7.30 that brilliant winter Saturday. The great rolling spreads of turf were milky with frost and dark green where dogs had left trails like strung beads. The ponds we passed – the Dog Pond, the Men's Pond, the Fishing Pond, the Duck Pond and the Women's Pond – displayed Dangerous Ice warning signs. I wondered what might become incarcerated as a result of the overnight formation of a solid slab on top of the water. Beneath the ice, it would be as dangerous as the underwharf.

- I'm off to help Stanley sell his t-shirts in Camden, I told Randolphe once we'd been outside long enough to make it decent for me to speak. Just in case you're worried about me turning over a new leaf and invading your mornings ...

- I'm delighted to have company, he said, lingering on the last word as though we both knew that company did not involve idle chit-chat. Sometimes I feel a freak out here. At this time I'm the only one without a dog or a pair of those air shoes.

- Long live freaks!

- You'll be wanting the 24 from Hampstead Heath Station, he said, always ready to dazzle me with his knowledge of the London bus system.

The route to the railway station took us past all but one of the heath's ponds; the one that we spurned was that below Kenwood house, spanned by a Grecian bridge that looked so artificial I assumed it was left over from a performance of one of the summer's operas. At the Mixed Bathing Pond and its twin Fishing Pond, there were already a few optimists with fishing lines cast into the still depths.

- You'll feel at home at Camden Lock, he told me, as he pointed down the hill to the bus stop.

Camden High Street was buzzing with vendors arriving in vans to deposit enormous bundles of wares on the footpaths before driving off to their regular, secret parking spots. Stanley, as promised, arrived in his beat-up Bedford van to find me standing outside a certain pub on a certain corner. I was to mind the green bin-liners full of t-shirts as he screeched off to park, ran around to check on his stall allocation, to argue and negotiate and fill in forms, before coming back to begin the process of moving the stock and setting up.

They all knew Stanley, the bulky-jacketed stall holders. A few of the blokes joked with him, teased him about me. At times I thought I overheard the word 'sheila'. Stanley's spot backed onto the inlet where the touring canal boats docked. On the other side of the inlet was a stall that sold Indian vegetarian food. The smell of the cooking on the massive steel woks would drive me into hunger panics at odd intervals throughout the day, usually when there was a crowd of customers milling around or when Stanley had gone off on one of his jaunts to check out the competition.

He set up the stall in twenty minutes flat, despite numb fingers and my own fumbling attempt to make myself useful. I delighted in the moment of laying out the shirts, having only seen one or two of Stanley's cruder, sloganed efforts. He favoured simple, iconoclastic images in dark, single colours on thick, pale cottons; on white, 'natural' and a grey sweat shade. I yelped at a shirt he displayed with a spectacular flourish. My very own serpent, flattened out on the back of a long-sleeved shirt, and on the front, over the left breast, was a perfect pentagram.

- It's a shame it's not warmer Soph, he said shifting from boot to boot, not looking at me. You could have really showed it off. Hope you don't mind. It just seemed perfect . . .

- I don't think I mind, I said. Guess not. It'll give me an idea of how I'll feel if I ever give you photos for the shirts, I said, awkward in Stanley's domain. I'll have to send Sammy one.

- Hey, he said, stepping gingerly. I'll go and get us some coffee now before the punters crowd us in. We can drink the stuff in the Thermos later.

Abandoned by Stanley, I stared at the woman opposite as she painstakingly laid out strand upon strand of Baltic amber. I refused to miss Jake, but I felt a terrible unease over Sam's near total silence since my arrival in London. Sure, I'd only been gone a few weeks, but I'd already selected a dozen photos I'd taken of people or the Thames or a bare winter tree, and sent them off to her complete with captions. Even if none of the photos were of me, they'd give her some idea of what was going on in my head.

The one bleak little letter Sam sent me voiced all the truths that had been left unsaid in the drunken cacophony of my departure. Who's going to stop Sammy from soliciting at the strip club when she's desperate for money, or tell me that my latest roll of pictures was devoid of inspiration ... that it sucked? Who's going to give a shit, was the bare essence of Sam's only letter, scrawled on the back of four flyers for a new Darlinghurst club.

On an upturned milk-crate behind the table, I could already feel the ache of cold in my knees. The first customers arrived while Stanley was gone; two strawberry-blonde girls cooed over the serpent shirts, declaring them very East Village. I charged them twenty pounds a shot and they bought three between them, one in each colour. They were going to send the third shirt to someone called Rochester, at Yale.

With large Styrofoam cups in each hand and a brown paper bag tucked under his arm, Stanley shimmied between the table and canvas to join me. He handed me a coffee and I handed him sixty pounds.

- What's that for? he asked, looking at the notes as though I might have stolen them.

- Sold three serpent tops, I said, shrugging my shoulders and blowing on my coffee.

- Alright sister, he said, shoving the notes into a pocket. I usually charge twelve for the long sleeved ... ten for the short!

- They didn't think twenty was too much, I countered. Twelve's far too low ... you should charge at least fifteen.

From the brown paper bag Stanley produced a small loaf of banana bread and broke it in half with his dye-stained fingers. I pushed the moist, luscious chunks into my mouth, staring at the people streaming past.

- Soph, you'll put them off, said Stanley, pulling a battered copy of *Death in Venice* from his breast pocket. Get a book from that second-hand stall over by the arch. They'll lend you it for fifty pence for the day if you tell them which stall you're on.

- Nah. I don't read, I said, grumpy that Stanley would prefer to read than talk to me.

- Sorry I mentioned it, he said, examining his mangy hands. Don't feel you have to stay here all the time, I know it gets a bit dull.

Wordlessly, I wandered off, not looking back at Stanley. I walked past stall after stall, and a mandala-like pattern of hand-decorated ceramics, chunky woollen sweaters, art deco clocks, silk ties and battered felt hats blurred before my eyes. Nothing related to me and my denim, black and grey. All the colours now in my life, the purple dress and Sam's knitted Peruvian hat, had been gifts.

I emerged from the chatter of the market grounds onto a

path by the canal, gasping for air as though I'd been trapped underwater. Leaning on a low brick wall I stared at an abandoned office block on the opposite shore, and wondered how undermining the insidious caress of the water was on its very foundations. The water was mud black and fringed with a decorative border of coloured plastic detergent bottles. A long, low canal boat glided by, under the arc of the foot-bridge. A scraggy-haired man, with a beard and black jumper missing an elbow, was at the tiller brushing his teeth, the white gob he spat into the water spreading, not sinking.

The Lock was a series of troughs and heavy wooden sluice gates whose strength and solidity appeared dubious. The water revealed a date, 1915, just above the tide line on the brick wall. One sign informed that the Thames at Limehouse was six miles away, London Zoo three quarters of a mile away, and Little Venice two and a half miles away. Of the three I favoured Limehouse, for the vast possibility the name conjured in my mind. I could not picture a place called Limehouse, but planned to walk along the canal and see it one day.

Away from the markets and towards Kentish Town Road lay a vacant lot contained by the canal, some posh offices and the road itself. A group of homeless kids had set up camp, and demolished the wooden fences in the area to fuel their cheery bonfire. The naked branches of the trees had beer cans impaled on their tips, and in the wan light, as the fire glowed red in the gloom, a late Christmas scene emerged.

I headed back, entering by way of the upstairs gallery of a covered market, less crowded than the markets proper and occupied by shops as well as stalls. Carried along as I was by the tide of people who knew where they were going and what they wanted, I found myself in a smaller antique market. The sort of place that would hold no interest for me if it wasn't for the clairvoyant, reader of cards, sitting in a corner at her table.

As I approached she was just finishing a reading, and a young red-headed woman who could have been my sister got up to leave. The resemblance was lost on her, eyes filling with tears as she walked unseeing, out of the hall. There was a strained, silent moment as the moon-faced woman with the cards composed herself.

- I always feel as though I've been too heavy-handed, too honest, when someone like her walks away distraught, she said, still not offering me the deck to shuffle.

- Some people'll cry at the least sign of understanding, at a hint of warmth, I said, casual, knowing. You just confirmed to her what she already knew.

- You'll find the one you're looking for my dear, she said, smiling at me so her face folded, concertina style around her eyes.

- I haven't asked you anything yet, I said, my skin itching as it flushed.

- We're not going to play games are we? she asked, watching me shuffle the cards with an expert's ease.

- I just want your reading, I said, cutting the cards in front of her and concentrating on emptying my mind.

She laid out the cards in an intricate spread that I was unfamiliar with, then handed me a pack of smaller cards, and indicated that I should shuffle again. I kept trying to ignore her process and keep the question foremost in my mind. It was rare that I asked someone else to read for me, and I knew that my interest in her method could distract her, ultimately render the reading worthless.

- What do you see?

- I see him, your father, she said, all but abandoning the cards. He's got your eyes, but he's much darker than you. You see it in his face, what he's lived.

- What else? I asked, almost without voice, without breath.

- He needs to know you, she said, but sounding unsure. He has people around him, a sort of family, but essentially he's alone.

- Is he close? Will it be soon, our meeting?

- I see him in a forest. I see him by an immense river, she said, looking at some infinitesimal point above my left shoulder. You must travel even further to know him.

- But how? I asked, beseeching, aware that suddenly she seemed tired.

- You must go home to know yourself, she said, looking at the unfamiliar cards, the smaller ones. A crisis will take you home, don't resist its pull.

Then I was aware of the room around us, mahogany and crystal and porcelain. Two young girls were standing shyly to one side, waiting to catch the woman's attention. Immediately I thought of Sammy and me, young and silly and waiting to have our cards read together at Paddington Markets.

- There's nothing, absolutely nothing you can do, she said. Where there's loss there will be gain. When you stop, when you settle, your life will be full and rich.

- What sort of man is my father?

- An immense man, she said, sounding almost awed. There's something in him that burns white hot. But I tell you now, there's nothing he can give you that you haven't already got.

Later, when I moved back through the crowds towards Stanley's stall, I seemed to glide not shuffle. With unfocused eyes I smiled munificently.

- I thought you'd buggered off, he said. I thought you'd walked out of my life like women do.

- But you're my friend Stanley, I said. That's not the way I treat my friends.

- Yes, I'm your friend, he said, voice flat. Your serpents are doing so well nobody's looking at anything else. Means you're lucky for me like I thought you were. Where've you been? You look as though you've just had sex.

- I've got a job that I'll start next weekend, I began, deciding to omit all of the complicated stuff. It's not a job as such, it's a table.

- What? he said, looking at my eyes for signs of drug consumption.

- I'm going to read cards for a couple of months. Near the bookstall, I said, speaking too fast in my sudden excitement.

Stanley just frowned.

- The clairvoyant, from upstairs, had me read her cards and offered me the table!

- I still don't get it, he said. You don't just get asked by some woman in a market to read her tarot cards, Sophie.

- No, you don't, I said, giggling. The woman who does the readings upstairs in the antique market read my cards, we liked each other, she asked me to do a reading for her ...

- Fucking brill, he said, part-sold on the idea now. We can both work all weekend and play all week, just as it should be.

- Yeah ... maybe, I said, already planning other work - anything to distract myself from my mission.

It had seemed so wonderfully ironic that my first lover was one of hers. I was fifteen and dating Alex at the time. Well, Sam and

I were both dating Alex. There was a lot of touching and kissing and stroking and snake stuff, but neither of us had quite got around to 'doing it' with him.

Zelda was seeing some poet whom I guess she actually quite liked, because there was no publishing coup in it for her. Ten years her junior and twenty-five years my senior, he had this glow about him. It was probably because he liked to swim each day off Coogee Beach, but at the time I was in a spiritual phase and liked to attribute it to his enlightened state of mind. He and Zelda made a strange couple, her with her bluster that filled all available space and him with his still, golden presence. His name was Zane; Sam and I used to chant Zane and Zelda, Zane and Zelda, ZZZZ.

He talked about how he'd have to swim an extra mile for each day he breakfasted with me and Zelda. Claiming he needed to sleep much later so he was clear-headed enough to write and blah, blah, blah. I wondered how many times I'd heard men sit at that table and bitch and moan about how difficult it would be for them to write that day. Was this for my mother's benefit, so she'd pay them a better advance? Or just because they had nothing else to discuss with her?

One Saturday morning I heard her car leave around 7.30, and I rolled out of my tangle of purple sheets and pillows to stretch all the way to the kettle. While the water boiled I took a cool shower that wasn't so much about washing as about waking. I wandered back into my room with a pot of jasmine tea, cleared a place on the kelim, and sat down to meditate while it brewed.

I mumbled the mantra of compassion that Nella had taught me and tried not to allow myself to be distracted by the weave of the rug that was imprinting itself on my naked bum. After fifteen minutes of nothingness, I leaned forward to try to ease the stiffness from my back and that's when I saw Zane, standing in the doorway, watching me. It must have been my post-meditation calm or something, because knowing he'd stood there watching me meditate didn't embarrass me. He wore stretchy grey undershorts that stopped half way down his thighs.

- Want some tea? I asked, gesturing towards the tea pot.

- Will you let me share your cup? he asked in his gravelly, English-sounding voice. I'm afraid that if I go away for a moment the spell will be broken.

He padded into the room and sat opposite me. My eyes moved to the whisper of hair between my legs. I knelt to pour the tea, folding my legs beneath me in a protective pose.

- What're you looking at? I asked him in a voice I barely recognised.

- You Sophie, you're very beautiful.

- Yeah? I said, getting up and walking over to a heavy framed mirror. I'm just the same as I was yesterday, 'though the bruises on my knees have faded and I don't have any pimples today. That's rare, I can tell you.

With a feline grace he glided over to stand beside me, sipping tea and then handing the cup to me. He moved behind me and I could feel his cock poking gently, enquiringly into my bottom as he reached around to cup a hand over one of my little white breasts and another over my pubic hair. My body started to tingle, as though suddenly there was too much blood in it, and I wondered if he felt it. He took his hands away suddenly and moved his mouth right up close to my ear.

- You are beautiful, he insisted in a whisper. Would you like me to make you feel beautiful? To show you how your body can sing?

I stood still, feeling all the blood rush down there between my legs, then I put my hands where his had been, fixed my eyes on his in the mirror and nodded yes. He moved swiftly, soundlessly to the door and shut it. Still holding my breast and half protecting, half caressing the hot place between my legs, I watched his reflection in the mirror.

- Have you ever been with a man before? he asked, moving behind me at the mirror again and replacing my hands with his own.

When I shook my head, he pulled me closer and turned me around to press his lips into mine. Before I could decide whether his mouth tasted of strawberry or plum, he had moved it onto one of my breasts and was tickling my nipple with his tongue. Alex had done this once but I'd told him to stop because it seemed he was rubbing me raw.

He swung us both around so I faced myself in the mirror over his shoulder and could watch his honey-coloured back as it tensed and relaxed. He guided my hands to the waistband of his shorts. I rolled the soft fabric down over his buttocks and stared at the dark crack between his legs, reflected in the mirror, as he kicked the shorts away. His tongue made little butterfly movements on my belly as he knelt and moved my legs apart. A faint cry came from some unknown, dark place inside me as his tongue darted between folds of flesh, and found some place that I had only imagined existed. I closed my eyes, and in a flash saw him doing this to my mother.

Mainly it was his fingers and tongue inside me. Teaching me how to sing. His cock was like a roll of pale, warm marble, so different from Alex's purple thing. He was only inside me for a few moments, a few strange panicky moments, when I thought, even with his gentleness, with his reserve, he's going to split me in two. But I remember wanting him to, pulling him to me with impatience and saying his name over and over on my hot breath like they do in movies. He moaned as though he was hurting, too, managing to say my name and not Zelda's.

He withdrew from me so slowly that I thought he was trying to take part of me with him, and then he moved his mouth down there again, mumbling about not wanting to hurt me and that there was only a little, only a little. And when I couldn't sing anymore and begged him to stop, he came to kiss me with full, blood-coloured lips. He guided my hand on his cock until he was all sung out himself.

We lay on the floor of my bedroom just breathing together, he enfolding my back in the damp arc of his body. Gently he slipped away from me, and when he came back to pick me up, to carry me cradled in his arms to the bathroom, the tub was full of suds and the mirror had steamed over. The only person who had ever washed me was Nella, and thinking of her, I felt alright about what we'd done.

Later, over a real breakfast of toast, rhubarb jam and coffee, he asked me my age. I barely noticed his silence, because I was trying to listen to a Blondie song on the radio. Inexplicably he rose and said he had to call a taxi. While he paced the kitchen waiting for it to arrive he told me in a low, shaky voice that I shouldn't tell my mother about the singing lesson. I told him not to worry, I didn't tell my mother anything, but he barely relaxed, and when the taxi honked its horn outside he only just managed to stammer a good-bye over his shoulder. I was glad he'd gone. I wanted to ring Sam and get her to come over straight away. She'd be *so* pissed off I'd done it without her.

THE SUN

In Nella's old Chinese silk robe I clamber past the row of plants onto the fire escape to watch the street come alive. In places, the faded crimson silk is dissolving to nothing.

I sit on the rusted, cast-iron fire escape and clutch a mug of smoky tea. Below, a fire hydrant leaks into the gutter like a rheumy eye, while the rest of the street is dry as bleached bones. Yesterday at ten the first of the hydrants was opened, and at regular intervals throughout the day the police came by to wrench them shut, and to expose themselves to the sneering ridicule of the people of the block. Even as a stranger, I'm with the block, us against them. While the city loses millions of gallons of water a day and there's talk of restrictions, the locals approach the hydrants with monkey wrenches and wicked delight.

All is happening just as it should down there on the street, just as it has happened for the last three days; the traffic is moving, people are going to work and opening their shops and going to the Laundromat and going to buy milk and going to buy the paper. I too, aside from the lack of sleep, have had a normal morning, but within four hours, five at the most, my world will change. Dreams will present themselves for shattering.

I've stared at image after image of that weathered face. Dark straight hair, dark eyes, serious with unknowable intent, and a long, lean jaw. It's the lines on the face that I go back to, predominant in the most recent picture I have of him. A photo so dark the eyes are almost without expression. Eyes, dark as night and twice as seductive.

What leaves so very many lines on a man's face? And where am I in him? Aside from those eyes, almost lost in the wrinkles of his skin, I cannot recognise myself. It's not a disappointing face, I could get lost in that face. It's a face I would choose to photograph. A face I could spend hours shooting and re-shooting in shadow and in light and in laughter and in contemplation.

There had been no sign of Zane since he'd taught my body to sing. From time to time, Sam and I laughed about going over to Coogee to see him – to ask if he'd give us both singing lessons. For weeks, Zelda and I had barely spoken; I could not remember the last time we'd communicated life's small pleasures, one to the other.

She had a new assistant; I knew because it was he who would call me to check when I got home from school. The indignity of it ... I knew he was only a few years older than me.

It was Simon who told me about the party, not Zelda: a Friday night launch at our house for Zelda's bright new star. For the man I'd heard Zelda on the phone to the few nights she'd come home early. She'd be saying No Will, you know you've done a superb job, You know I think you're a genius, You know the critics will adore it ... Hovering in the kitchen, I made gagging sounds, until she hung up in a huff and stormed into her study with much clacking of heels and slamming of doors.

On the night of the party, she came home early, singing. Singing! But she stopped short when she walked past my door and glimpsed me sitting on a cushion, shuffling cards.

- Darling, she said, the word hard on both of us. Simon should have told you to go to Sam's tonight. I'm having a party.

- I know, I said, looking up and smiling sweetly. It's just that Sam's in trouble for swearing. Not that she swore in front of her mother ... it's just that her little sister dobbed ...

- Poor Sam, she said absently, meaning poor Zelda.

- Don't worry, Zelda, I said, easing off on the smile lest she grow suspicious. I'll help. I'll stay in the kitchen all night and do whatever you tell me to ... What's the party for?

- Well, she said, stepping out of her heels. It's for a very special new writer. For someone I've nurtured for nearly a year and who only now is actually ready to enjoy what he's achieved.

Zelda moved into the kitchen where I could hear the plink plink of ice-cubes in a tumbler and the babble of gin being poured.

- He's a highly erudite novelist, she was saying, oblivious to her audience. He's written a beautiful, poignant novel of self-realisation and political disillusionment. He's a very isolated man who needs warmth and support ...

I know what sort of warmth and support you want to give

him, I thought to myself and flushed at an image of Zane guiding my hand on his cock.

I was looking forward to interrogating Zelda's new Boy Wonder. In the kitchen I started sorting the groceries that had been delivered that day. So there I was, up to my elbows in guacamole and singing along to Blondie's *Parallel Lines* album when Zelda pushed Simon into the kitchen. With him came strict instructions: keep the platters of food coming.

- Doesn't want her guests falling off the deck, drunk! I said by way of greeting, perving at him from the corner of my eye. Bet this wasn't in your job description.

Simon was a big, brown boy; six foot two, broad shoulders, bulging forearms, tanned skin, hair bleaching to blond and a nose that looked as though it had lost a few layers to the Pacific sun over the years. In his khaki canvas trousers and his Lacoste t-shirt, there was something decidedly unscholarly about him.

- At least it gets me away from the crones, Simon said before looking at me dubiously. I don't mean your mother ... I mean, all those lecherous old women. The men are even worse, but at least they don't try and touch my bum whenever I walk past!

- Damn! I said, laughter in my voice. I was hoping you wouldn't mind me touching your arse once I lick all this avocado away.

- I don't think that would be such a drag, he said, moving in beside me at the counter and showing a pink tongue. Here, I'll help with that avocado.

We both laughed too loud, as though wanting those outside to hear, and I made a show of kicking him away. Simon took responsibility for the bread and relished working the garlic into the gritty toasted surface as much as I relished sucking his garlic fingers later.

The platters were going out fast enough to save the guests from certain death in the bush below the house and Simon and I were singing badly enough to keep the curious away. Drinking up a storm.

- You're not like her other assistants, I told him as he opened another bottle and took a slug straight from its neck.

- From what I hear, he said with a sober edge to his voice, we all conform in the end.

- In the end, maybe, I said, feeling somehow complicit in Zelda's secretary seduction program. In the beginning though, not many of them look like you.

- I'm relieved to hear it, he said, eyeing the platter before him with contempt. I'm having serious doubts about this publishing thing. Should have just gone surfin'!

- Gone surfing when? I asked. Tonight?

- Nah, only maniacs surf at night, he said, with a tone of voice that distanced him from beach folk and established his solidarity with the waves. This year. Should have just taken the year off. You know, finished university and dropped out for a while.

- Maybe I should read your cards for you. Tell you what you should really be doing with your life, I said, contemplating illicit night surfing.

- That'd be cool ... d'you think we could get some fresh air first?

Rather than going out through the crowd on the deck and into the bush, I led Simon through the front door and around the side of the house. Shameless, I pulled my whole skirt up and slung it over my arm as I would a beach towel, exposing the very top of my thighs and a pale crescent of bum. He didn't try to talk while we walked through the bush, and for that I was grateful.

I lay back on the rock, waiting for him to settle beside me. My head carried with it its own constellation of stars, and the rock seemed to move as though bouyed by the breath of the harbour.

- Is this what it feels like, I asked. Lying on your surfboard under the moon?

- This feels pretty good, he said, stretching like a cat, moving on the sandstone as though trying to dislodge a bit of the day's heat. Surfing's altogether different, though.

- What are you doing working for Zelda?

- What are you doing living with her?

- I asked first, I said, sitting up so I could watch him and catch the reflection of the moon on the water at the same time.

- Wanted to work with books and she was the only one that didn't just write me off as a dumb surfie.

- You like books that much? I asked.

- Used to. Maybe I still do ... the rhythm of the words in a good book and the rhythm of the waves ... there isn't much that means more to me. I guess I don't like all the crap that goes with it. The publishing I mean.

My head filled with an image of Zelda circling her party and I turned, for solace, to Simon's warm body. In much the same way Zane had taught me to sing, Simon taught me to surf.

Stanley was the most tolerant person I'd ever met, but even he couldn't understand my feeling cold all the time. Cold hands, cold feet, cold bottom, and some days, a near total inability to get out of bed because of the cold. My world was divided into clearly defined halves; everything warm and glowing came from Sydney, and all that was cold and mean and blight-stricken represented

London. It wasn't that I didn't like London. It was a city that made me feel free and anonymous, and for that I loved it.

Days, weeks passed and I followed each distraction that led me away from the hunt for my father. I took photos for the *Hampstead and Highgate Gazette*: of elderly men being turfed out of squats, of buses whose routes were to be discontinued and of buildings that'd once housed someone famous. I developed my pictures in a lab that charged by the hour and where no-one acknowledged my arrivals and departures. On weekends, I read tarot cards at the market, shuffling with fingers that found no reassurance in the texture of the cards. I partied with people I'd only just met and would never see again. I rode night buses all over London and watched my breath rise in clouds around me. I tried to forget where I was from.

One morning I stood at my bedroom window, wrapped in a quilt and did a double-take. Alien colour spotted in the landscape! There, between the grey slate rooftops was a tree bravely brandishing a dozen or so blossoms. The mauve of a Sydney sunset, those new blossoms. I had survived the London winter. The standing mirror reflected skin with the pallor of Nella's the last few times I had seen her.

I'd been in London six months. Six months and only one letter from Sam. Nothing from Jake. In the mirror, I looked like someone I no longer knew, someone who might not be recognised by an old friend who passed her on the street.

Randolphe's bathroom was an expanse of pristine white tiles that I called Antarctica. I waited for the tub to fill, the chill of the small hexagons on the floor creeping slowly up through the soles of my feet. My nipples were hard and puckered like lips pursed in bitter disapproval. I hadn't been with a man since Dick, and that was a long time for me. Perhaps if I went on surrounding myself with men I didn't want to sleep with I'd eventually find some sort of peace ...

With only my head and toes breaking the water, I tried to remember whether Zelda had ever gone six months without bringing a lover home. I doubted it. For a moment, I wondered whether she missed me. She'd had Jonathan send me a cheque for Christmas in a company Christmas card saying Zelda sends her love. PS. I had fun driving you to the airport – Jonathan.

Because of my decision to phone Sam, I wallowed in the bath long enough to need hot water added twice. I ran my hands over my thighs and buttocks and thought how aphysical I'd become, and how thoughtlessly I slipped into my army disposal leggings and jeans every day. How in London I'd curled in on myself, and only became an exhibitionist once or twice a week on a chemical-induced high at a club. I ran my hands over my shin bones, knee-caps, the long bones of my thighs, hip-bones where my fingers could actually get some sort of grip, as though the bone was designed with special finger-holds. With a sudden heave that caused water to slosh over the back of the bath and collect on the floor like so many pools in holes in the ice, I forced myself to face the day.

In an attempt to delay the inevitable further yet, I made real coffee and scrambled some eggs with fresh parsley. I even phoned Stanley to make sure he was home so I could visit later. He told me he'd 'met someone' and was going out with her in the evening, but to come over in the afternoon. Fine, good, see you later. I wasn't really in Stanley mode, and hoped I hadn't offended him by my lack of interest. Stanley was my best friend in London, but there was a distance between us that Sam and I had never known. Maybe it was the strain of unfulfilled lust.

As I lingered over the eggs and toast I tried to put myself

into Marlborough Street mood. Sam's place. Tried to imagine them sitting out the back in the big breezy kitchen, drinking Coopers and throwing shoes at cockroaches on manoeuvre. I tried to see the girls parading around in different outfits in order to decide what to wear to the evening's dance party or club opening or café crawl. I thought about the next-door neighbours, hanging over the paling fence to ask if anyone had any good mull. Someone would be cooking pasta, and someone else would be going through *On The Street* to find out when the next Big Pig gig was, or whether the band playing at Selina's Coogee Bay Hotel warranted a trip to the beach.

What I didn't expect was an answering machine with Lila's voice saying We're probably all tied up right now, snicker, snicker. But do leave a message. Jake can be contacted at his studio on ... And before the message had even ended I was dialling the other number, knowing that Sam couldn't let a phone ring and not answer it. If she was there she would have picked it up. The phone at Jake's studio rang for a long time and I thrilled at the different, hollow, very distinctly Australian-sounding ring of the telephone that made me think of space, emptiness. I dreaded another answering machine.

- Yep, he said, in a tone of voice that said This better be good.

- Jake, it's me, I said, unprepared for how his voice would make me feel.

- Soph? he asked, almost cautiously.

- Yeah. Who were you expecting? I asked, surprised at how catty it sounded. What's this bullshit about a studio? You doing well or what?

- Doing OK, he said. Doing fine. Some gallery's got me working on an exhibition so they've given me this space in Ultimo. View of the city and all, from behind of course. Its best side.

I wanted to be there in Ultimo, looking at the city's arse.

- Hey, the photos you've been sending are great. London looks like a dump, he said.

- It's not so bad. I don't compare it to where Sammy and I grew up ...

- Mm, he said, faltering. I was going to write to you about Sammy, but I couldn't work out what to say.

- Why? What's wrong with her? I said, too loudly. Tell me.

- I haven't seen her for a while Soph, he said cautiously. I mean, she hasn't been home for about three weeks, and before, before ...

- Before what?

- Before she was just strung out all the time. Speeding, dropping acid. Either not sleeping at all or sleeping all the bloody time. And the men she brought home. Jesus, he said, on a roll. One night the girls had to throw one of the bastards out. Reckoned he was slapping her around and she was too out of it to know.

- You think she's alright don't you? I said, pressing the fleshy part of my thumb against the greasy tines of the fork. You don't think anything's happened to her?

- I dunno. Nah, I think she's OK, he said, trying to sound casual. Jessie saw her last. She'd met some Sanyassin who she was getting drugs from, reckons they fell in love and were planning some odyssey to the spiritual centre of the world.

- What do you think that means? I asked, envisioning sacrifice rituals.

- A trip to Uluru, he said blandly. I reckon they've gone bush.

- D'you think I should come home? I asked, giving him the responsibility of making it better.

- Do you want to come home?

- I don't know. I miss Sydney, but I don't know, I said.

- Don't come back unless you've done whatever it was that you wanted to do.

- Oh Jake, I said. But what about Sam? Shouldn't I be there for her?

- Soph, I reckon Sam's been heading for trouble for a while now.

I sat and drew my knees into my chest, hoping there was no more.

- If anything, your sense of purpose beside her floundering for direction made her feel worse, he said gently. Anyone who's mentioned drugs or her lifestyle has been completely frozen out. She's got to deal with it herself. She's got to decide what sort of life she wants.

- Do one thing for me Jake, I said. Call me the minute you think I can do something. Will you promise?

- I promise, he said, sounding much further than a twenty-eight-hour flight away.

- Jake?

- Yes?

- Do you miss me? Do you ever think about me?

- I don't know how to answer that Soph, he said quietly. My life's different now. I work harder than I used to. I don't have time to sit around. I eat, sleep, swim some mornings, work at Clyde's in the day and work here most of the night. On the seventh day, if there ever is one, I sleep.

- So long as you're happy, I said weakly.

- Who's happy? he asked, and all of a sudden I could hear the roar of the ocean coming down the line, and remembered it was a long-distance call.

- Gotta go Jake. Take care.

- Search hard Soph, he said, fading.

Walking to the tube I became aware that part of the sky was obscured by bright foam wads like the synthetic filling of pillows. In deference to the arrival of spring I'd changed into my tunic dress and leggings, and was already regretting it. With the cold air on my legs and rushing up my skirt like stars into a black hole I felt naked. Like I felt when I spoke to Jake on the phone.

I entered the grubby, piss-stinking innards of the Underground in a trance, and navigated the change of trains at Euston without breaking it. Barely noticing the ten-year-old street kid feeding pennies into the chocolate machine and then squatting against the wall to share the treasure with his dog. I was trying to see Sam in the desert with a Sanyassin, but instead, my mind's eye kept filling with images of Jake in a blue shearer's singlet and old jeans. Working in his bare studio with windows thrown open to an impossible image of Sydney's rear.

Finishing school is one of the best things that ever happened to me. Despite its air of hedonism, the last day epitomised the things I hated most about the place. The day kicked off with a champagne breakfast that we were all expected to wear our pyjamas to. I couldn't believe that kids my age actually wore pyjamas! Zelda dropped me off at the park by the water on her way to work, Nella's silk robe flapping around me as I got out of the car. The tar underfoot was already hoarding the day's heat.

In the park, some of the tough girls were sitting around in groups on the grass with their boyfriends from what was referred to as our brother school. Crumpled clothes, empty chip bags and the chaos of empty bottles suggested many of them had been there all night. Group sex, 1 thought with a shudder.

The camera had become a means of distancing myself from the group in a way that the cards never had. Even in the photography class 1 attended during my last year of school, the camera isolated me. If 1 wandered around with a camera in my hands, 1 wasn't expected to say anything, and conversations didn't struggle, politely, to include me. 1 moved from group to group, always hovering somewhere on the periphery.

1 knelt with my camera in front of me, a little closer to one group, the ones 1 hung out with, if 1 hung out with anyone. They were talking about the planned week-long party, after the last exam, in one of the small Central Coast resort towns. These trips had become a school institution, not just with our school, but with the other private schools in that part of Sydney. The idea was that a group of kids pitch in and rent rooms in a motel or a house for the week, convince the landlord that they were well-behaved and very middle class, then turn up with thirty friends and trash the place. A foray into the world of piss and vomit.

- Oh, Soph, sorry but we can only have ten people in the house and we've already got fifteen, said Katie, hiccoughing mid-sentence. Have you organised anywhere to stay?

- Why should 1 have? 1 asked, pointing my camera at two girls embracing.

- What do you mean, Why should you? asked Mary, laughing nervously as she fiddled with her night-dress, which was revealing too much of her pale, freckled thighs. Everyone goes. Everyone's always gone.

- You might meet someone if you go Soph, someone to go to the Formal with, said Sarah, struggling with a cork. Don't you like boys?

- Sure I do, I said, focusing again on the two girls crying in each other's arms. I just prefer them a little older than those around here.

- So are you going to the Formal? asked Sarah again, probably so I'd ask her who she was taking once she'd asked me. Who are you going with? You haven't told anyone.

- None of you know him, I said, photographing a tangle of dirty feet in the middle of a circle of bodies. He's just a guy I know. Don't know if we'll stay long or anything. There's another party on that night.

- What school does he go to?

- He doesn't go to school, I said, getting bored with the conversation, with the visual potential of the group. He's an actor, alright?

- Is he a film star? asked Sarah, slurring her words. Do we know him? Will he give us an autograph?

- Oh, please, I said, standing up, snapping both sides of my robe together where it was gaping at the neck. He's just a guy.

I wandered through the maze of sprawled, drunken bodies, almost too bored to raise my camera. At the edge of the park I climbed onto a rock that formed part of the harbour wall, and sat with my feet dangling in the cool green water. The night before, Sam and I had split a bottle of vodka, drinking a few shots but pouring most of it into two silver hip-flasks.

One of the smarter boys, called something biblical, came over and sat down beside me with a plastic bottle full of scotch and coke. When he offered me a slug, I raised my own flask to my lips and tossed my head back. I turned and photographed him as he stared down the top of my robe.

- What are you looking at, buddy? I asked him, still holding the camera to my eye.

I had this theory that someone wouldn't lie to you if they thought you were going to photograph them doing so.

- Is it true that you've got a tattoo? he asked, looking at his feet refracted through a few inches of water so he wouldn't be tempted to go on staring into my cleavage.

When Sam and I got our hips tattooed a year earlier, we'd decided on a part of the body that was rarely viewed but that wasn't too sensitive. It only took three class swims down at the Olympic Pool for our little secret to become public currency.

- I guess I must if that's what you've been told.

- Will you show me? he stammered.

- What will you give me if I let you see it? It's sort of in an intimate position.

- What do you want? he asked, animated, imagining something simple like a gin and tonic in a bar one night.

- We go over into the bush down there, I said, gesturing to where the park ended at the water. I open my robe so you can get a good look, and you let me photograph you masturbating.

His only reaction was a rapid intake of breath, and a quick slug of that dark sticky liquid.

- You'd like that, wouldn't you? I asked, putting a hand inside my robe to touch a nipple. You want to get out your cock and look at my body, don't you?

I followed his hurried tread into the bushes as he surreptitiously turned to make sure no-one was watching. I made him go all the way through the scrub, right to the water's edge, to have the whole harbour in view. He sat on a rock, waiting for me to put down my bag and focus my camera, not daring to make a move. Frightened I'd trick him into getting a cheap shot of him with his pants down.

- Come on, I said, easing my robe off one shoulder. Take those shorts off.

He just sat and gaped for a moment or two after my robe had dropped to the grass with a sigh, but then he was clawing at his fly and pulling frantically at his cock. I started snapping and moved to unbutton his shirt.

- Let me fuck you, he said, reaching out and grabbing one of my breasts.

I pushed his hand away and stepped back, trying to catch the contortions of his mouth on film. Trying to get the arch of his back and the tension in his thigh muscles.

- Maybe this'll help, I said, reaching down and touching my -self.

- God, God, he said, gasping as hot sperm dropped onto his feet and the bundle of his shorts. God.

I took two more shots of him, head slumped on his chest, one hand covering his genitals, before I put my camera away and covered myself.

- Hey, he said, his voice low, hoarse. Don't you want me to give you an orgasm?

- Thanks, I said, surprised at his use of the word. Really, I can do it myself.

- I just thought, he said, confused rather than crestfallen. Um, do you want to go to my Formal with me?

- No, I said, zipping up my bag. You've invited one of the Kates, remember?

- Oh yeah, he said, fumbling with his shorts and starting to colour. What're you going to do with those photos anyway? Bet you're going to show Kate. Bitch!

- Why'd I show her? I asked, all genuine innocence. She must have seen it all before.

- Because you're weird, he said, growing increasingly alarmed at the damage I could do him.

He was going off to study law; he'd be a famous barrister one day. A famous, corrupt barrister.

- If you show anyone I'll tell them you're a slut and a nympho, he said, sounding pathetic, and making me stop liking him. I'll tell them you dragged me into the bushes and then prick-teased me. Which is the truth.

- I don't care what you tell them, I said, walking away fast so he didn't get any ideas about grabbing my camera.

Later that day in our last school mass, one of the Kates vomited all over the back of the Mary who was sitting on the floor in front of her. It was hot and airless in the tiny chapel, and you could smell the alcohol rising in waves from the sixth form. I was close enough to know what had happened, but not close enough to be badly affected by the stench. None of the teachers knew what was going on; in the middle of our farewell sermon there had been a deep, burping sound and a bit of localised commotion, but all in all it was a fine cover-up. The hymn sheets were piled on top of that puddle of spew faster than the priest was able to change the subject of his sermon to the issue of seemly conduct for young ladies or some such shit. I felt sorry for the Kate, and the Mary, who both had to sit there with vomit down their front and back respectively, but really, it was just too perfect.

I walked out of the school gates and up to the station, drinking the rest of the vodka in the flask, making no attempt at concealment. Most of them were off to some party at someone's waterfront house where everybody would end up throwing themselves in the harbour in their school uniforms. Some would have their legs so badly gouged by barnacles that they'd spend half of the next day at the Royal North Shore Hospital having the tiny particles of shell surgically removed. The others would find hard, festering lumps of shell under their skin a few weeks later, a souvenir for the empty expanse ahead. Funny how alcohol makes people look dried up and spat out, not like school leavers with their whole lives before them.

Some of the others, in their crumpled school uniforms, caught the train and got off with me at the Cross. I wondered if they were going to buy drugs, or were off to a dark bar, or were even heading for a strip joint. I walked straight out onto the expressway that barrelled underneath the Cross itself towards the more leafy, genteel environs of Sydney's eastern suburbs. Heading back towards the city, only three blocks from the station, was Bud's, complete with Harley Davidson in the front of the shop and the sign in the window that year-round asked for girl models.

Sam and I had been to Bud's a year earlier, out of uniform and speeding like maniacs. They gave us our tattoos for free because they believed that we were, in fact, girl models. They even put a photo of us both on the wall with our heads chopped off, pointing our freshly decorated hips at the camera, once the scabs had healed. The Sun and Star duet.

Bud did a double take when he saw me come in wearing my uniform, but was bored enough to listen to my request. When I described the serpent that was to wrap itself around my calf, his eyes lit up.

- Sweetheart, he said, part patronising, part sleazy. We're not talking about a few pin pricks. We're talking two four-hour sessions. We're talking intense.

- So what, I said, with false joviality, and shook the half of vodka that I'd just bought, thinking vaguely of penance for behaving like such a prat at the park by the water.

- And I suppose you're going to tell me that you're a model?

he said, rolling his eyes and trying to look pissed off.

I knew I'd won already, but was determined to give him no grounds for talking himself out of it.

- I'll do the pictures afterwards, I said, flashing him my hip so he knew just how good a deal he was in for.

- Oh yeah, he said. Sun and Star, almost forgot. Where's The Sun today?

- Man, I don't know, I said, offering him a taste of vodka. Probably getting stoned or something, y'know?

Rain-yellowed sheets of newspaper blew down Stanley's street and clung to my ankles, needy. Two toddlers played barefoot in the gutter and I shivered as I walked past their council house. Stanley was not home. His flatmate, Marina, opened the door, tongue-tied with embarrassment over Stanley's absence. It occurred to me dully that she thought Stanley and I were an item and he was seeing someone else behind my back.

- Come on in, I was just about to open a beer, she said, rolling her ankles so she stood on the edge of her black lace-up shoes.

Marina and I had barely spoken to each other, not so much out of choice as circumstance. She'd once cornered me in the kitchen to ask whether Stanley had known about Dick. Working in one of the big book shops on Charing Cross Road, she was up with the literary gossip. She'd even read his book, and while she told me he was a brilliant writer, she assured me I was well-off out of there. I was so disarmed by her presumption at commenting on my private life that I actually thanked her for her concern.

In the darkened kitchen, we sat marooned in oversized garden furniture and drank our beers in a companionable silence.

- I'm going to help at a reading in the shop tonight, she said. Free booze. Want to come?

- I dunno, I said, feeling something hard and ugly stir in me. Who's reading? Who published the book?

She mentioned the name of a Scottish writer that meant nothing to me, and then the name of a publisher that I knew well. I thought of rivers and forests somewhere further yet; Scotland!

- Oh, sure, might as well come along. Bit of culture can't hurt.

As casually as she'd questioned me about Dick, Marina started telling me about a man she'd picked up at the Fridge a few nights ago. A Nigerian guy who liked to dance with his body up close to hers so sometimes their pelvises would move together. They'd exchanged phone numbers and saliva at the end of the evening, and she'd called him the following night to arrange a date. She said his voice was smooth as clotted cream, and she knew that after their dinner in Covent Garden the next night they'd go home to one of their beds together.

- Whatever happened to romance? she asked, bored already with the prospect of a date and a fuck. Have you ever been in love, Sophie?

- I've never even been close, I said, almost feeling bereft of romance. You?

- When I was sixteen, I fell in love with my best friend's older brother, she said, wistful. The town I come from in Donegal was small enough for me to know that if Eamon and I ever did *it*, everybody would know and my parents'd either kick me out or lock me in and throw away the key.

- So what happened?

- Oh, he was very sweet . . . very understanding . . . but also disapproving of my compliance, she said. He moved to London and got an apprenticeship ... I followed him two years later.

She got up to go to the fridge and I thought, end of story. Nobody tells you anything in this city!

- By the time I arrived he was living with a blonde-haired English woman who wore floral skirts by day and fucked him till his dick was blue at night, she continued after an angry pull at her beer. He treated me like the snotty-nosed friend of his sister that I was.

- So by not sleeping with this guy, you were able to fall in love with him. Not that it mattered, because by then you'd lost him!

We both laughed too loud and took great slugs of Heineken, but the laughter was to conceal the fact that for acquaintances we'd gone too far.

On the tube into the West End, Marina and I swapped tales of the coastlines that dominated our childhoods. Both aching for ocean and for the dreamscape that is the water's edge. By the time we reached the Charing Cross Road she'd invited me home to Donegal with her, on the understanding that it would take her a while to get the money for the train and the crossing and all.

In his mid-fifties, the Scottish author's brilliant blue eyes immediately ruled him out. A strawberry blond with a sprinkling of treacle-coloured freckles on his face and the backs of his hands, he had the air of a Highlander gone soft in the pubs of Glasgow. Lean as he was, I could tell he was a drinker. His granite grey sweater that looked as though it should smell of heather reeked of tobacco on closer inspection. This wasn't the outdoorsman the clairvoyant had described and whose enigmatic image had become that of my father.

Clutching a bottle of poncey Mexican beer, I sat in the front row and watched rather than listened. Trying to imagine how I'd feel or what I'd have done if I had indeed encountered a stranger who I believed was my father.

In a lyrical half song he read of the sea, of a man working on a fishing boat, who watches his best friend swept away. Although the ocean was the culprit, the agent of death, the sea's rhythm was the only thing that could soothe the bereft sailor. The lull of the undertow was as powerful in his life as in my own.

I accepted Marina's invitation to the pub, and as a simple matter of course, engaged the Glaswegian in a conversation about his work that I could carry out in my sleep. McKee, as they all called him, was delighted to have a young woman take such an interest in what he kept calling men's writing. Scottish male writing.

Marina didn't flinch when I told her I was going back to the hotel with McKee, and then I knew that she and I would indeed be friends. Awkward in the glitzy opulence of the Bloomsbury hotel's bar, McKee described a croft house by the water where he wrote, looking across to the Island of Skye, and I told him about the rock I dreamt on as a child. We were drinking whisky, and he had become peacefully mellow rather than laddish. When he talked about how good the booksellers had been to him, and how sensitive his editor was, and how afraid he was of the interviews I nearly cried at my own cynicism. This McKee was an ordinary bloke. Just a guy who got tears in his eyes when he spoke about the Western Isles and the small communities that had been starved to oblivion.

- McKee, I said, taking his hand in mine and moving close. I've really enjoyed talking to you, but I should go home now.

- Och. He squeezed my hand and gave me a warm whisky kiss on the cheek. You must come and visit me. The further north you go, the better the people. My wife Maggie's a painter. You two gels'd get on just fine. Bring yer man if you like.

Two days later, Randolphe cleared his throat and presented me with a copy of the *Evening Standard*, open at the *Londoner's Diary*. Beside a photo of Zelda looking only slightly older than me, a caustic paragraph wrote of the Australian publisher's daughter who was in the business of seducing authors.

I spent the morning of the last day of the year by the El Alamein Fountain on a slab of concrete in Kings Cross that some referred to as a park. By night it was a no-man's land, peopled by drunks, drug dealers and tired hookers, who congregated by clusters of anaemic-looking palm trees. The park's name, its palms and its fountain were all supposed to evoke the atmosphere of a desert oasis.

I'd set up the little card table, borrowed from Uncle Jerry, covered it with a crimson silk scarf that once belonged to Nella, and hung an arty cardboard sign from the front of the table saying 'Know Your New Year. Only $12 for the Next Twelve Months.' It went down a storm. At times there was even a queue. I read cards for the entire staff of the St George Building Society in their dinky red and white uniforms, each scurrying across the road in her break, standing eagerly in line and chewing on a sandwich while worrying that her reading wouldn't be as fab as her colleagues'.

The combination of the morning's brilliant light, dry heat, and a sense of vague optimism for the New Year was good for business. I didn't have to grope for positive interpretations of cards promising doom. The proliferation of cards like The World, The Sun and The Lovers sent a series of punters reeling from my table in joyous disbelief.

Towards the end of the session a young guy, not much older than me, approached the table, approached me, as though he was sitting down with an old friend. Though I could swear I'd never met him before, I half expected him to say, Hi Soph, How's it going? There was nothing so exceptional about this guy, sure his t-shirt was hot white, but then it was a time of whiter than white Haines Ts, threadbare Levis and coloured Converse basketball boots.

His cards were the best I'd turned in a morning of extraordinary readings. As I flipped The Sun, The Pope and finally The Lovers, he sat there, holding his head in his pale hands, arms all sinewy. In his aquamarine eyes I read such a look of languid pleasure that I felt myself blush. It was as though, rather than just sitting there reading cards for him, I had one hand under the table stroking the top of his thigh.

The Sun on its own, promising satisfaction, earthly happiness, joy, achievement in the arts, and finally love, is such a powerful card that it can completely overwhelm the influence of more negative cards around it. Combined with The Pope, a card denoting goodness and inspiration, and with The Lovers, The Sun is such a dominant force that its presence in the reading heralds an exceptional period of one's life. As I turned over each card, I became increasingly sure that in the near future this stranger's life would touch my own. Not that I would tell him ... how could I?

- So, it looks like it's gonna to be an alright year, he said, his tone laconic, running his hand through his sweep of dirty-blond hair.

- What's your name? I asked.

- Do you need that for the reading? he asked, dirty grin, settling on the upturned milk-crate like someone with no place to go.

- Course not, I said, laughing to cover my embarrassment, fingering the cards. It's just that the cards say you're gonna be famous one day. I want to recognise your name when I hear it dropped at dinner parties around chic inner-city tables.

- Jake, he said. And yours?

- Sophia, I said with mock hauteur. But you can call me Sophie like the rest of the world.

- I like Sophia, he said, pulling a pen knife from his hip pocket. Do you ever go to Clyde's?

- Sure.

Clyde's was one of the Cross's crustiest all night cafés, tucked away in a tree-lined street of balconied Victorian terraces, boasting an old-fashioned juke box with Formica panels and a Dalmatian that farted at familiar customers.

- I work there sometimes, he said, poking the tip of his knife at the hard skin of his thumb. I was thinking that Clyde might be into the idea of you reading cards there on a Monday night, when it's a bit on the slow side. You want me to ask him?

- Why not? I replied, trying to be off-hand but unable to quiet the way my knee was knocking against the flimsy leg of the table. You're not a waiter . . . the cards say you're some sort of artist . . .

- I'm only masquerading as a waiter, he said. In real life I'm a sculptor.

- The cards don't lie, I said, beginning to tap the pack up and down on the table, nodding at a woman waiting her turn and glancing anxiously at her Swatch. So I'll drop in some time and see you, or speak to the Clyde guy. Right now I've got another reading to do.

- Oh yeah, sorry, he said, now scraping the pen knife along the soft denim at his thigh. Mind if I watch?

- Yes, I said, my voice linen crisp. See ya, Jake.

- See ya, Sophia, he said, shuffling away then looking back. You made my day, you know?

A little over an hour later, business slowed. Weary but satisfied, I whisked away my sign, uncovered the table and tucked its spindly legs inwards before heading off down Macleay Street. At the Croissant D'Or I stopped to buy an apricot pastry for Uncle Jerry. The rich, butter smell of croissants lingered in my hair.

Back on the street, my hip pocket bulged with the morning's takings and my cards rattled inside my Globite suitcase covered in JJJ Radio stickers. The heat had become so intense that as I walked along the few exposed sections of Victoria Street, the rubber soles of my boots seemed to melt and stick to the pavement. Acid-proof or not, the boots were only just holding up to a Sydney summer afternoon. There was already a ripple of energy in the air that heralded the coming of an event. Women were hanging out on the latticed balconies of the backpackers' hostels, drying their bleached hair and offering their newly shaved legs to the sun. The bottle shop of the Piccadilly Hotel was doing a brisk trade as city dwellers came with bulging wallets and left weighed down by the dozen stubbies on their right shoulder that counterbalanced the brown paper bag in the left hand, straining with its two bottles of J.D.

I crossed William Street at the raw gash where it ducked through a tunnel and fled beachwards. The Coca-Cola sign on the Hyatt screamed Coke Adds Life – my very own, Sydney symbol. It was at this ugly intersection that cars from the suburbs were already negotiating their way into the narrow streets of the Cross. The object was to arrive early enough to get a park and to put in a few good solid drinking hours at The Rex before going back to the car for the esky, its foam hull packed with melting ice and sweating bottles. Then began the trek to some vantage point – Mrs Macquarie's Chair or the top of the navy car park – to stake out a claim for firework viewing.

A carload of straw-headed blokes from the beaches, the zinc barely scrubbed off their noses, invited me into their Holden station wagon for a quickie before they got too shit-faced.

– Sorry fellas, you're a bit young for me, I said, throwing my head back as I pulled dark glasses down over my eyes, aware that later in the evening a comment like that could get my head kicked in.

I left the Cross for the more serious groove of Darlinghurst, feeling the sun hot on my bare shoulders. Imagining the freckles darkening in the early afternoon's sunshine and turning cancerous. I walked past the Hospice where it seemed like half the city's beautiful young men lay dying, before turning into Oxford Street and its haze of idling traffic, heading out to Bondi Beach. I walked past the sandstone monolith of the law courts and the patch of scorched grass that divided the traffic and was named Gilligan's Island in deference to its crew of castaway drunks.

The pub that Sam and I were to meet in was still ungentrified, and attracted a clientele of returned servicemen, shabbily dressed civil servants and old-age pensioners with potato-sack figures.

The common denominator was a love of good draft beer and a mutual disdain for the loud music that throbbed from the gloom of most of the other Oxford Street pubs. The walls were tiled with textured slabs, a piss-stained, caramelised look to them.

The carpet sported jaunty brown and red swirls and was sticky with years of spilt beer and cigarette ash. Around the base of the bar was a stainless steel trough for cigarette butts and gobs of phlegm and the occasional stream of piss. The top of the bar was decorated with cigarette burns in keeping with the tops on the high, round tables that sprouted like toadstools from the fertile turf of the carpet. The bartenders wore grey flannel shorts, long white socks and beige t-shirts, stretched down over their guts, with strands of greased hair breaking free from the elegant sweep that covered the bare crowns of their heads. This was Australia.

My stomach convulsed as Sam's voice rose from a group of serious party types clustered around one of the fungoid tables. I was taken aback by the lycra and denim-clad bodies that jarred so strongly against the pub's muted background and its less stylised clientele. I would suffer a similar reaction when seeing Sam with her two sisters – our bond was weakened by the presence of others. It was all about belonging. I belonged with Sam in the same way I had belonged with Nella. I didn't belong with this group of air-brushed, glamorous hairdressers. They'd all stumbled across the road together, high on shots of vodka after a frenzied morning of creating New Year's Eve 'looks'. In her first week out of school Sam had talked them into letting her sweep the salon floor and wash the occasional head of hair in exchange for free attention to her own hair and some meagre pocket money.

I went straight to the bar to order two double voddies without even greeting Sam. I'd swallowed one of them before the second had been deposited before me, and the bartender did a double take, narrowing his eyes when I peeled a ten dollar note from my wad. The poor bugger would really have cause to scowl in a couple of years time, I thought, when they renovated the place and he lost his job to a glamorous young boy. To someone who spent most of his week's wages on a pair of black and white jeans that defined the curve of his arse so sweetly.

As I nudged into the little clique beside Sam, she turned and hurled herself at me, planting a purple lipstick flower on my clammy cheek and executing a tight little turn on one heel to display 'her new haircut' from all angles. And all angles it was. Most of it had been clipped away with a number one shear, but what was left was tapered from her crown to a point halfway down her skull. Dyed luminous purple, the two inches of hair on the top of Sam's head had been gelled to a breathtakingly upright stance. Shazam slashes of eyeshadow in the same shade of purple went from the corners of her eyes to her hairline. On her cheekbones, pink glitter caught the light like the trace of frozen tears.

- What do you think Soph? What do you think? she asked, voice kettle shrill. Jazzie did it.

Sam pointed at another similarly decorated woman whose blueblack hair was so firmly gelled it looked dangerous. As Sam introduced the team, I felt like I'd walked onto the set for a science fiction film and patted my lank locks self-consciously. The guy beside me joined in, patting my hair in that appraising manner particular to hairdressers.

- Feels good, he purred, running his tongue over his rouged lips. Long hair is a bit passé for women though, don't you think? I'd love to give you something a little more chic.

The conversation turned quickly to drugs, and which trips were available for the evening's amusement. It was only Sam and her four new friends, but from my outsider's point of view, they were an impenetrable mass. Their names sounded like a cocktail menu when strung together: Jazzie, Red Sally, Billy and Bee Bee.

- Who wants a drink? asked Sam, standing precariously on the metal foot-rest of her bar-stool while she took the complicated order for mixers and chasers.

I followed her to the bar, ostensibly to help carry, but really to be there in case she didn't have the money. She had the cash – more than I'd ever seen on her. The sort of money you didn't make as someone who swept the floor at the hairdresser's across the road.

- Did you break into your piggy-bank Sammy?

- Nah, borrowed some money from the old man, she said.

- That was pretty generous of him, wasn't it? I asked, feeling like a slime bag but unable to restrain myself.

- What's that supposed to mean? she said, turning to smile, not at me but at Billy. What do you think of him?

- Who? What? I asked, wondering whether, after all these years, she wanted my opinion on her father. Oh, Billy? He's kind of cute. Does he work at the salon?

He was alright looking; at the very least he knew how to fill his black leather jeans. Though black leather jeans on a steamy summer night in Sydney town were a foolish if brave gesture. I hoped they were lined and frequently dry-cleaned. His head was shaved, displaying a gold stud high in his right ear. His white t-shirt stretched taut across his chest and defined two turgid pectorals. A walking sexual ambiguity.

- Billy? Cut hair? she spat a mouthful of vodka and coke at the surface of the bar. Does he look like a hairdresser? He's a dealer, Soph.

- Great, I said, injecting more enthusiasm than I felt.

- He's really, really cool . . . lives in a warehouse on Wentworth

Avenue, her voice rising, annoying me. He lives on his own . . . imagine. He's going to take me there later.

As the round of drinks was necked in the time it took Sam to reapply her purple lipstick and the little troup dismounted from its stools, I felt a hot pang of regret for not bringing my camera. The two bartenders jeered as we walked out, and one of the drunken rissoles speculated loudly on the gender of each one of us. Oblivious to the returned serviceman's comments, the others faced the onslaught of afternoon heat and fumes while I hovered on the threshold, smiling my thanks and apologies to the unseeing regulars. Billy led us around the corner and into the alley at the back of the pub where the kegs were rolled into the cellar.

Three joints and a few slugs of vodka later, we stumbled up onto Oxford Street again. Billy and Sam encircled each other with their arms, and I watched from behind as he stuck his succulent red tongue into her studded ear. I struck up a conversation about reading cards with Red Sally, who divulged her *big* secret – she always wore red underwear.

Next en route to oblivion was one of the early openers that overlooked Gilligan's Island. Surging up the stairs from the din of the street, as one can only do when part of a large drunken mass, we took that quiet, palm-filled room like a bunch of desperate shoppers at the January sales. Full of dope and vodka I decided I didn't mind when Bee Bee stroked my hair again. It occurred to me that hairdressers actually got off on having their hands in people's hair, and at that moment it seemed like quite an acceptable pastime.

We slumped in beige vinyl couches whose sheer ugliness was only partially redeemed by the palms. Billy, the leather-crotched stud, started to pontificate about how dull sex had become.

What was the point of having intercourse again and again and again? Even if you did switch partners every few weeks, it was still an essentially repetitive activity. I hate people who ask questions to which there is no answer.

Sam puffed up her chest and ran her be-ringed fingers up and down her thighs. I knew she was thinking that she'd show him. That he was probably just throwing down some public challenge, barely concealing the fact that he was desperate for a good root.

- You know, Billy said. Most people have such a conservative attitude towards sex ... in my opinion, the more holes in the ear ... the more tattoos only amount to an apology for the fact that they just want to be petted and held. That they're crap in the sack.

At that, I plonked my tattooed leg onto the table. Red Sally knelt down to caress the serpent's head, crooning at it all the while, putting her tiny pink tongue out to meet its black pointed one in a gesture that made the hair at the back of my neck stand on end.

- You just haven't been to bed with the right sort of girl yet Billy, said Sam, in a voice that made me want to drag her from the pub, take her off somewhere quiet, and feed her chocolate cake and hot milk.

I was fiercely, foolishly protective when I was around her. Compensating for the fact that one day, without doubt, I would leave her all alone.

We moved from the barely fading late afternoon into the midnight blue cavern of a club above one of the Lebanese food joints. Jimmy Somerville's 'Baby Don't Leave Me This Way' was blasting so hard and so loud that the only thing to do was dance. We scattered the pairs of boys getting sexy, pelvis to pelvis, in the pulsating womb of the dance floor. It was a time of dancing with arms raised above the head and much stomping of heavily booted feet.

It was Billy and Bee Bee who had the performance down to a fine art. They stomped around the floor, swaying their hips towards each other and exchanging simpering, burning stares. When Jimmy sang 'My heart is full of love and desire for you', Billy moved in behind Bee Bee and thrust his crotch at the other's denim arse. There was a familiarity about the way they treated each other's bodies that made me certain they'd been lovers.

As Prince bayed out the words to 'Raspberry Beret', Billy drew Sam to him and stuck his tongue down her throat, with one hand still on Bee Bee's crotch. Through my state of dance floor euphoria I wondered what was real and what was show, and whether it was moralistic of me to assume that both gestures couldn't be true. But then Red Sally pulled me to her to dance close and I started to think that really it didn't matter whose flesh came into contact with yours on a dance floor, so long as you weren't left rubbing your hands over your own body.

The plan was to pub-crawl along Oxford Street, all three miles of it, to the Hotel Bondi. The route was to be punctuated by back alley sessions with grass. Somewhere along the way Jazzie pointed out that we'd never make it all the way to Bondi and get back to the party in the Cross if we carried on in our meandering, indulgent fashion. Red Sally managed to find us a taxi driver who turned a blind eye as we all piled into the back seat in an attempt at the Guinness Book of Records. Halfway to Bondi it was decided that in order to commemorate our evening of spiritual bonding we would all have one ear pierced in exactly the same place. Billy knew someone who worked near the Hotel Bondi who probably wouldn't charge.

At Irene's chintzy salon, the hairdressers were finishing off their last customers for the year, arguing about who should go out to buy the champagne. It was quickly agreed that they'd stick around to do our ears if one of us agreed to buy the booze. Jazzie volunteered to go; she was the one who said she needed to be even drunker before she could deal with the pain of upper ear piercing.

The smell of peroxide gave me something akin to an amyl rush as an emaciated woman wearing a pink boob-tube sank a stud into the cartilaged rim of my ear. As I opened my mouth to wail, Sammy shoved the open neck of a bottle of Great Western in my gaping gob and turned head and bottle back in unison. I fought to breathe through bubbles, oblivious to the random bursts of pain that were coursing from my right ear into my brain. Around me the hairdressers fiddled with combs and sprays, staring into mirrors that were still adorned with silver and green Christmas tinsel. I sat clutching my Globite, painfully sober. It wasn't that I didn't want to be there, or that there was some place I thought I'd rather be; I was restless, with the overwhelming sensation of having outgrown every stitch of clothing on my body.

Armed with bottles, and kebabs from a beach-front milk bar, we wove our way to the water's edge, skirting the groups of half-naked men and women clustered around massive ghetto-blasters, dwarfed only by the girth of orange and yellow eskies.

Down at the tide line we fumbled with the laces of our boots so we could stick our feet in the water and moved off down the beach southwards for the viewing of the last sunset of the year. On an empty expanse, we planted our bottoms in sand still warm from the long summer afternoon. An awed hush fell over us as a softer light inhabited the lurid beach-front, alive with the colour of so many different beer cans and the curves of brown and green glass.

On that beach, at that time of day, looking out into the Pacific, images of Nella washed over me; Nella in the surf, Nella swimming towards the horizon, Nella's white hair floating on the water before it became heavy with the sea, dragged her down. When I finally blinked and swallowed hard on the past, a major shift in the group's composition had taken place and the fool's sense of belonging I'd been nurturing fell away with a graceless thud. Sam and Billy had moved further down the beach and were lying in the sand kissing, Billy kneeling over Sam's body, as though pinning her to the ground ... but my Sammy wasn't offering even a whisper of resistance. A few feet behind me, Jazzie and Red Sally huddled, kissing and grabbing at each other's tits. Sally pulled Jazzie's stretch top up to reveal an erect, purple nipple and moved to put her tongue to it.

Beside me, Bee Bee watched Billy and Sam, a mournful expression on his face. Abruptly rearranging his features he turned to me, and with his hand at the back of my head pulled me to him.

- I've got to go to the toilet, I mumbled, as he tried to press his cold lips to mine. Sorry Bee Bee, I won't be long. Keep my place warm.

With barely a look in Sam's direction, I strode up the beach, feeling the sand between my foot and sock, clutching the Globite case to my chest. Bee Bee wore his obsession for Billy all over his face like a loud, cheap after-shave. I doubted it would be much fun standing in for a boy ... standing in for anyone.

I sat in a taxi on the approach to the Cross, where the traffic ran as slowly as Golden Syrup when it's been put in the fridge by mistake. Rather than the predictable anger and cursing and futile blowing of horns, people were beginning the party inside their cars. Radios blasted on a dozen different stations, and women passed iced cans of beer from the back seat to their blokes in the front like a scene from a vintage Four X advertisement. At that rate, it was likely I'd see in the New Year with an incensed and lecherous cabbie in a car that reeked of day-old puke.

I dropped a five dollar note over the back of the seat and slipped out the passenger door into the stasis. It was good to walk, I told myself, trudging up the hill from Rushcutter's Bay into the Cross. I stood on the pavement outside the fire station, waiting for my head to clear, waiting to regain my land legs. If there were to be a fire in the area that night, the engines would be trapped in their garages by the fleet of cars from the suburbs. I crossed roads, weaving between stationary cars, and headed into the heart of the Cross.

A warm, orange glow emanated from Clyde's, and there was an aloofness about the café's clientele that suggested they thought New Year's Eve parties uncouth. I squeezed into a corner table under a plastic palm tree, where I could watch the workings of the jukebox as it spun its selection of records before stopping, seemingly at random, to settle a piece of thick black vinyl on the turntable. As the jukebox began to play a song from another era that I happened to know and love, I ordered iced chocolate from a skinny waitress with a helmet head of straight black hair. I opened the case in my lap and turned up cards at random, dissatisfied with each.

Behind the counter that nestled half way down the room's side wall, Jake sank a stainless steel blade into the moist depths of a chocolate cake, and sang along with the box.

Sitting in Clyde's, on my own but watching Jake sing, I began to feel much, much better. Not great, but I didn't feel as though I was being dragged down a steep hill by my feet, either. I didn't feel as though someone was suddenly going to put their tongue in my ear and that I'd have to pretend I liked it.

For the second time that day the Jimmy Somerville song played, and I thought about how life was like that, the same song playing over and over, until some imperceptible flaw in the vinyl sent the needle off into another groove. This time I didn't jump around with my hands in the air. I was content to watch Jake dance with the skinny waitress as they mouthed the words to each other. Those waiting for coffee and cake seemed pleased to have a reason to put down their books, to be touched by just a little festivity.

A few minutes before eleven, Jake and the waitress consulted their watches and flipped a coin. Punching a victorious fist in the air, Jake eased from behind the counter and breezed past my table, saying, Come on psychic lady, let's go look at the sky.

Three storeys above the world, Clyde's rooftop felt like a pontoon fixed precariously in a storm-torn harbour. The music of a hundred stereos, car radios and ghetto-blasters combined to produce the city's own unearthly scratch mix. On the rooftop I felt a sense of stillness, of distance from the swell of the crowd. To the west, some, but not all, of the city's tall buildings emerged from the roofs of the Cross's bigger blocks of flats. Jake sat on a low brick wall that marked the edge of Clyde's roof, and dangled his feet into nothingness – the corrugated iron of the neighbour's roof was eight feet down. He chewed loudly on a Granny Smith and looked impossibly fresh.

I felt tarnished by the afternoon's revelry, a victim of it rather than a survivor. My boots felt heavy on my feet and my toes kept struggling to push the sand out from under them. My mouth, too, felt coated in a fine layer of Bondi sand.

- Well, psychic lady, said Jake, not moving from his perch or turning to me. What happened to you this afternoon?

- A few drinks with a friend, I said, lifting my voice on the last word as though challenging him to disagree.

- And what are you doing here, on a rooftop with some stranger? You should be careful. Anyone could take advantage of you when you're so wasted.

- Wasted! You ain't seen nothing, I said, feigning brashness.

- Downstairs your skin was the colour of pistachio ice-cream and your pupils were as big as the bowls we serve it in.

- Oh, I said, my head in my hands, my mood so at odds with the music from the street and the spray of excited voices from the block of flats across the way.

- Hey. Come and sit beside me. I promise I won't say anything nasty to you. The fireworks are about to begin.

Leaving my little suitcase standing forlorn, threatening to lose its balance on the sloping roof, I went and sat close to Jake, inhaling the scent of him. With my back slightly towards him and feet dangling without certainty on either side of the wall, I wondered whether anyone really still used Sunlight soap. He put his arm around my waist and pulled me closer. I held my breath, trying to still my sobs, afraid that the shudders that had been wracking my body would topple us both from our perch. That our fall would stop the old year in its departing tracks.

As the first of the fireworks filled the sky above Sydney with the vermilion trails of angel dust, a strong, almost conclusive calm came over me and I relaxed into Jake's body. As golden, green, red and blue fountains of liquid passion coursed down over the city, warm, healing tears ran down my cheeks. It was loss that I was overcome by; the loss of a friend, the loss of a sanctuary, the loss as always of my grandmother, and finally the loss of an excuse to stay in Sydney. Sam and I were no longer in it together.

- Jake, I said, a few moments after the last of the colour had slipped from the sky and into the unseen harbour, into Woolloomooloo Bay. Can I go home with you tonight?

- Psychic lady, he said, chuckling quietly. Why ask when you know the answer?

- Can we go now? I said, leaning forward to rest my forehead on the cold brick of the wall. I don't feel very well.

- Take my keys. I've got to work 'til one, he said, helping me from the wall. You don't have to wait up.

Jake put me in another taxi with keys and directions and stood on a corner near Clyde's with his arms across his chest, laughing from deep down inside himself. A warm, wondering laugh. Meanwhile, I was on my way to Marlborough Street, centre of inner-city Sydney's mega-grunge. When I got out of the cab and staggered down a narrow lane-way to vomit, I was already part of a fine Marlborough Street tradition.

After wrestling with the unfamiliar locks, I stepped into the dark, silent house and felt the hall sigh around me. In an upstairs bathroom I left my clothes in a heap on the floor and stood under a hot stream of water until the room had disappeared in steam. In the downstairs front room that Jake had told me was his, I found a Velvet Underground t-shirt to cover my damp body, and crawled into a bed that smelt of sandalwood.

THE HANGED MAN

I could just turn up, stick to my story, take my photos, rolls and rolls and rolls of them, and then go home. And it would be a job well done, nothing disturbed. No-one's life tampered with. His ordered, tranquil world wouldn't implode. There'd be no new and burdensome mantle of guilt cast onto his shoulders. No sorrow at a loss that was never felt.

There'd be no joy, either. The promise, the possibility of a whole new shared world would simply cease to exist. I would leave, having denied myself the comfort of kinship. And he would be left to believe that what will outlive him are his books alone.

When I finally draw myself away from the fire escape and the streets where I'm no-one, my skin is already damp with perspiration that I pretend is dew. Still no breeze to disturb the

*light gauze curtains at the back of the loft, as I pat myself dry
with a towel. The Levis and the fat-soled boots are inevitable,
but not the fine cotton vest with the green, crushed silk blouse
tied loosely at the waist. I'd like to wear Nella's jade, but no
professional photographer would attempt to work with a heavy
string of beads around her neck, getting tangled in the straps
of the camera and the bags, and swinging each time she bent
to retrieve something from her case.*

*In the wall of mirrors in the bathroom I'm relieved to see
that I look like myself, at the same time as looking like someone
who could pass for a working photographer. My hair's sort of
behaving today; curly, only bordering on frizzy. The dark circles
only make my eyes look bigger. My pale skin will look like a
baby's beside his. I have not chosen to wear shorts or a skirt;
exposing my tattoo straight off would be the sort of thing that
the old Sophie would do.*

*I gather my gear, hasty, having lingered too long on the fire
escape. The cat is already lying in the kitchen by the open
window, waiting to catch the breeze. With its legs splayed and
its big tummy falling to one side, lying on its back, it is a
picture of trust, safe and content in its small, known world. Of
course, we all believe to a certain extent that our worlds are
impenetrable. Inviolable. My father cannot be alone in this.*

With the consistency of the finest amber-coloured honey, Sydney's
weather weighed heavily on us for the first ten days of the year.
The insurmountable task of kick-starting the party-spent beast
into action had never seemed more odious. Nothing really
happens, much to Zelda's intense frustration, in those two weeks
before and after New Year. Come mid-January, though, the world

returns from its collective Gold Coast holiday, university acceptances appear, terrifying and public in the *Sydney Morning Herald*, and the month of revelry calls in its dues.

Two days into the New Year and Sam and I were sitting on the deck, content in the knowledge that Zelda wouldn't come bustling in on her unsteady heels. No sooner had she supervised the cleaning away of her New Year's party than she was gone. Off for a week at a Central Coast health farm where she could read to her heart's content and detox with relative dignity. When I got back from Marlborough Street on New Year's Day she'd already disappeared, no doubt relieved that the first day of the year wasn't marred by my presence. She never knew about the first tattoo – but my serpent was cause for comment. It was easier for her to focus her wrath on the way I'd looked, than on what I'd done with Simon and what she must have suspected I'd done with Zane.

The New Year saw a similar shift in Sam's relationship with her own parents. Her 'borrowing' of two hundred dollars from her father was one thing, but it was quite another thing to come home still tripping on New Year's Day and insist that her youngest sister hear every detail of the evening's adventure. It wasn't that we'd pub-crawled, stoned all the way, down Oxford Street, or that we'd had our ears pierced. It was the details of what Billy had done to Sam in his warehouse in the early hours of the year. Indeed, which mother and which sister, in their gum-shrouded suburban red brick, can endure a tale of bondage and exhibitionism? Sam, her tongue loosened and judgement absent, had burbled out the story of Billy's penchant for tying girls up, and fucking them doggy style while his boy lover looked on.

Having taken nearly twenty-four hours to return to the

point where she didn't merely crawl back and forth between the bedroom and the bathroom, Sam was finally ready for the New Year's Eve post-mortem. For the show and tell session. She was ready to call the gang and invite them around for something she promised me would only be the mildest of recovery parties.

- Soph, why won't you tell me what you did? asked Sam, wounded, scowling at the turquoise glimmer of water through the trees. We always tell ... I've told you about me and Billy.

- Sam, I said, unable to look at her, fixing my attention on the blue and gold flowers of the teapot. We didn't do anything. We slept in the same bed, I woke up all tangled in his legs, and then we talked ... he brought me breakfast, and while I lay in bed and ate, he showed me his sculptures.

- But in the night, when you went to bed? she asked, frightened lest we might have somehow wound up on different paths, alone.

- I told you, I said again, annoyed. I was sound asleep, had been for hours by the time he got into bed. I wasn't out of my head Sammy, I would have noticed if he'd as much as touched me let alone tied me up.

I hadn't meant to say anything about that. I really hadn't intended to even mention it until I'd had a chance to think about it, to rationalise it. I wanted to see this Billy guy again when I wasn't drunk or stoned, to make sure I wasn't judging Sam too harshly.

- I see, she said, voice choked with bile. You've undergone a sexual reform. A celibacy vow for your New Year's resolution, and I'm the slut, just like my mother says.

She jumped out of the deck chair to turn on me, hands on her hips, legs spread wide. With the sun beating down hard behind her, all I could make out was her warrior woman's silhouette.

- It's all very well for you to fuck your mother's lovers in her house, but when I do a little S & M I'm the weird one? she said, her chin sticking out beyond her face's profile. Is that how it is Soph? Go on. Tell me.

Sam was shrieking, and greasy tears fell on her cheeks. I knew that despite all the sleep, and the tea and mineral water she'd been guzzling, she was still coming down. Not that I dismissed her comments on those grounds, despite my rationalisations. Her words stung like the tang of deodorant on newly shaved skin.

- I'm not judging you Sammy, I said, standing and gingerly putting an arm around her shoulders.

We started to laugh out our angst and tears, but it was no hearty soul laugh. Over the last few days, we'd crossed some line that measured self-preservation and self-respect. What was left unsaid was that since we'd finished school six weeks before, Sammy had been careening out of control, and I, rather than taking the accomplice's role, had somehow become the witness. I'd been developing film and reading up on the photography course I wanted to enrol in, and she despaired at my abandonment of hedonism.

The afternoon, which promised hours of talk, was lost to us before it had even begun. Before we'd had a chance to get anywhere near what was really dividing us, the doorbell rang and the house filled with the New Year's Eve gang, reeling with the adventure of having fled the baking, fermenting streets of the inner-city.

- But darling, crooned Bee Bee, close to my throbbing, newly pierced ear. Where's the swimming pool?

- Down there, I said, pointing through the trees at the crystalline promise of the bay.

- Oh, but that's miles away, he said, deflated. I couldn't possibly walk all that way in my condition. I'll just have to settle for this charming deck.

I told Sam across the room that I was going off to read for a while, gesturing in the direction of the bush, the harbour and my rock. She barely took her eyes from Billy, who was kneading her buttocks with big, veined hands and drawing her hips to his in some semblance of dance.

Away from the house, the music faded in the cicada din. I stood for a few moments at the deepest of the creek's pools, waiting for one of the creatures I knew to be hidden in the dark chasms. When nothing stirred, I moved on, humbled. Feeling that my relationship with the place was already tainted by the stench of party smoke that still seemed to cling to my skin and my hair. There was too much of the outside world smeared over my body for me to be able to melt and blend as I'd once done.

In the late afternoon heat haze, rivulets of perspiration traced my calves like varicose veins. I mused over the vodka content in my sweat. The mysterious synthetic of my bra top stuck to my skin. The rock was a still, private place for me, more a room of my own than the room I slept in at Zelda's. Over the last two years, I'd watched as trees had grown to obscure the rock completely from the watchful windows of the house on the cliff.

I stared into the blue of the distance and the dull eucalyptus green of the other shore, distracted, suddenly, by the gull-like surge of a sailing dinghy as it tacked back and forth up the bay.

The near noiseless approach of the person who stopped at

the foot of my fortress rock made me recoil. I sat and waited. Stealthily, Jake looked over the rock's edge, but smiled when he saw me, watching his ascent.

- I was going to sit here and wait till you woke up. From further up that way it looked as though you'd passed out in the sun.

I nodded my head gravely, waiting for an apology for the intrusion, though part of me didn't want to spoil his getting acquainted with the bay.

- What are you doing here?

- Didn't your friend tell you I phoned? he asked, puzzled, unselfconscious. She invited me over. Told me to bring friends and booze and gave me some woman's account number for a taxi.

- I see, I said, more irritated with him than with the true culprit, Sam.

- I brought two of the girls I live with. Jessie and Lila. Lila knows one of those women up at the house from where she gets her hair cut ... they're all getting on down.

- I felt hot, pissed off, and resumed the all-encompassing task of observing the buffing, scudding trail of the wind on the water.

- You do a pretty good imitation of the angry young woman, he said softly, turning my face towards him with work-toughened fingers.

With the leathery thumb and forefinger of his right hand, he brushed away the grains of sand that coated my tear-wet cheek. The gesture brought on fresh vodka tears. I pushed away his hand and shaded my eyes, as if against the glare.

- Why are you so sad, Sophia? he asked, watching the water so I didn't have to feel so exposed by his ocean eyes.

- My grandmother died.

- I'm sorry. I didn't know, he said, sounding as though he was suppressing a sob himself. When?

- Five years ago.

- Oh, he said. That recently?

- Yes, I said, my voice all jagged and catching in my throat. And I'm going away and leaving Sammy all on her own. Well, I've got to save some money first.

I glanced at him, cool and distant in his threadbare jeans and white t-shirt. Even though he didn't look as though he was melting under there, I knew he must have been if my temperature, scarcely clad, was anything to go by.

- Swim? I asked, suspicious of his concern, his interest.

- That'd be great.

He followed me, cat-like, down the right side of the rock and through the gums and vines on a vanishing path to the water that came out behind someone's derelict boat-shed. I led him out towards the point over algae-covered rocks and sandstone slabs punctuated by shallow, warm-water rock pools. Leaving my shoes on, I waded knee-deep across an inlet, and scaled the rocks that concealed a small sandy beach from the rest of the bay. I dropped my top and shorts on the sand and darted into the cool shallows.

I squatted, half standing and half floating on the edge of a sandy ledge that fell away abruptly, so the water covered my shoulders. With my feet still touching the ground I felt safe, caressed by the cool salt water. I knew if I moved out further though, where I couldn't touch the bottom or see what might lie beneath me, I'd feel the chill of vulnerability. I'd imagine that each downward tread would be my last. The vice-like grip of a shark's jaws. Of course, in the shallows I was no safer, and knew it, having grown up on stories of waders being taken in knee-deep water.

From the top of the rock I'd just climbed over, Jake threw first one then the second of his cracked brown work boots, and followed them himself. I watched him pull his t-shirt over his head and smile as he felt the sun on his chest, then hesitate before he turned around to slide his jeans over his slim hips. I laughed when I saw he didn't wear underwear either, but modestly gazed out into the open harbour as he turned to hurl himself into the water in the way that guys do. I almost reached out to draw him back as he glided past me underwater, pale shadow, and out into the depths.

- This feels good, he said, as his head broke the water twenty feet from shore. Why does skinny-dipping feel so much better?

- It's more sensual, I said, not really thinking. I'd feel better if you came in a bit closer; a dog was taken near here last summer.

I lay on my back and floated, feeling the sun through the water on my breasts and belly. Jake made no move to come in.

- When I die, I want it to be somewhere every bit as beautiful as this, he said, and though I was looking up at the sky, I could tell from the direction of his voice that he was looking at me not the harbour.

Jake swore at two young boys in a dinghy, who'd come in for a perv, and told them to get the hell away. I walked out of the water and lay on my stomach on a flat rock on the edge of the beach, almost purring at the sensation of the sun on my back and legs. With eyes shut and fingers splayed on the warm, textured rock-face, I listened to Jake splash around in the water, and then come and lie face down beside me. He put his palm on the rock next to mine and our little fingers touched. With my eyes shut I could feel the heat of his stare, and the light against my eyelids looked like fireworks.

- Jake, I said, making a panicky, split-second decision. I just wanted you to know that I think you're really attractive.

- Uh, thanks Sophia, he said, and laughed, embarrassed.

- But, I said, opening my eyes to look across the toffee-coloured rock at him. I don't sleep with men my own age.

I watched his face to see if he was hurt or relieved or flattered or pissed off, but found his bemused expression inscrutable.

- Hey, no sweat, he shrugged. I'm pretty much celibate these days. I need my energy for work.

- You don't expect me to believe that do you? I asked, trying to sound street smart, not incredulous.

- It sounds as likely as you not sleeping with guys your own age, he said. If you want me to believe you, you'll have to believe me.

- But celibacy's intense, I said, propping myself up on my elbows to be able to watch him better, conscious of my sand-covered breasts, maybe wanting him to brush the sand from them as he'd done so carefully with my cheek.

- So is sleeping with older men, he said, an eyebrow raised in challenge, inviting denial.

- Don't you like sex, Jake? I asked, turning quickly to sit in a ball, my knees pressed up to my chest.

A southerly breeze rose almost on cue. The perving boys in their dinghy leaned out over the water to counterbalance the weight of the gust that filled their sail.

- Well, sex, for me, goes with involvement, he said. I ended up hurting the last woman I went out with ... she always thought I was hiding something from her.

- Were you? I asked.

- In a way, he said, distant. I was working on a piece I was really excited by, but was too shy to discuss it with her in case she called it stupid ... sort of withdrew all my emotional energy from her. Not very nice, eh?

- I don't know, I said. You can only give what you can give.

Dry but chilled, I got up to put my clothes on. I felt more uncomfortable with Jake's naked flesh than my own.

- Tell me about the cards, he said.

- What do you want to know?

- Everything, tell me everything, he said, finally getting up to put his jeans on.

As the harbour turned shades of lavender and grey in the dusk, I began the gradual process of telling Jake everything.

I wandered the corridors of Covent Garden and gazed, uncomprehending, into shop windows. At the tap, tap, tap and stumble of stiletto heels on cobble-stones, I turned and looked hopefully at the passing faces, like a lost dog waiting for a passer-by to pat her head and send her off on the right path home. I walked in concentric circles, cutting gaping holes in the dense cold, mapping out my own urban songlines. Searching in vain for the scent of a bloodline.

My destination had remained for years a scene I witnessed with the clarity of both spatial and temporal distance. In it, I'd be engaged in conversation with a tall, sensitive man. Our talk would meander luxuriously through worlds that charmed us both. And when he finally looks at me, wonderingly, as if to say, how can this be, this great and terrifying rapport? I would tell him my name, announce simply that I was Zelda's daughter ... that together the three of us formed the corners of a crazy, ungainly triangle ... together we formed some dysfunctional whole.

I drifted through Soho's innards, drawn to the grit and sleaze, perversely comforted by the posses of drunken men. Reassured by the barrel-chested, broken-toothed bouncers who fancied themselves as debonair front-men, I found myself in a world more familiar to me than the leafy north London streets or the shifting kaleidoscope of chaos that was Brixton Market. Walking past rooms that offered glimpses of girls in synthetic leopard-skin frocks, Sam's absence, or her memory, weighed on my already slumped shoulders.

- Oi, sweetheart, said a man in a brown leather jacket walking in step with me. You want to sit on my face?

Ignoring him, I increased my pace and thrust my chin out in tough-girl fashion. Behind me I heard his mates snickering and saying She likes you Duggie, that's obvious.

- Come on darling, he said, drunk enough to remain undeterred. Let's party together. I want to see if you're a natural redhead or not.

At that, I stopped, aware that his friends had halted in unison a few feet behind as if on parade. I looked down at my toes, feigning embarrassment, and smiling, threw my head back to launch a spit ball at his chin with all the force I could muster. Not waiting to take in the reaction, I ran for the bright lights and more sanitised atmosphere of Old Compton Street, cursing men, cursing drunks, cursing myself for the naiveté of being surprised by such an encounter.

On Charing Cross Road I peered in windows at books and wondered. Any of the dozens of new titles could be his, and any of those names could have been mine. How would I know? I could walk past him in the street and not know. Could be introduced to him in a bar and not know. Could sleep with him and still not know.

Buses wheezed by that could have sped me to Randolphe's, but the prospect of finding myself there alone made me nervous. How would I restrain myself from doing something stupid, like booking a flight home, or drinking a whole bottle of Randolphe's vodka and calling my mother to scream at her. To howl, to shriek at her so she would realise that I was lost in the world.

By the middle of that torpid January, Sam was living in Jake's house on Marlborough Street. In the wake of New Year's Eve there'd been screaming matches at home about the 'borrowed money', about 'the future', and finally, most brutally, about what she and her new 'boyfriend' got up to. Tears were shed, feet were stamped, doors were slammed and records were thrown against the wall, though it was only the last of these that my Sammy regretted. It was not a time to feel remorse.

A friend of a friend lent us a beat-up combi van spray-painted a faded aubergine purple. While her parents were both at work, we gathered together a short lifetime's worth of ephemera: cheap cosmetics, strings of shiny beads, the sort of perfume that adults give children, a skateboard that was never tamed, a drooled-on blue teddy-bear, bundles of letters and birthday cards, paperback romances, tired looking sandals and clothes. Half of these things would remain in the van when we unloaded at Marlborough Street, and later end up at The Smith Family. Sam's older sister cried behind her locked bedroom door and refused to say good-bye when we left.

As last one in, Sam got the smallest room. A room completely overwhelmed by a double futon that touched the walls on three sides, and decorated with a clothes rail that hung somewhere up near the ceiling. The window above the bed overlooked the back-yard; the swollen frame made it almost impossible to close, so most of the year the room was filled with the sounds of back-yard barbies and the neighbours' late night sex.

Before Sam moved in, we shove-dragged the futon out into the hall where it was stumbled over for two days while we painted. From a depressing shade of off-white, more off than white, the walls turned a lilac blue, and the ceiling a velvet, midnight hue. Later, Sam nearly killed herself by balancing crazily on a ladder and drawing stars on the ceiling with a gold-inked felt-tipped pen. As she acclimatised to the sudden shrinkage of her living space, she also learnt tolerance for the cockroaches that crawled over the top of the futon at night. Knowing I would never be able to restrain myself from sleeping in something akin to a body-bag to keep the nasties away from my skin, I was only marginally envious of that room of Sam's own. Jake's room, perversely, was a roach-free zone, a miracle he ascribed to the chemicals he used to treat his metal forms.

The decline of the private school girl began. Offered a place at a technical college to study child-care, Sam just laughed and dropped a trip, not even bothering to respond. Offered a job as a receptionist at the firm of one of her father's colleagues, Sam spat a mouthful of good vodka out the door and swore that the bastard had always had his eye on her arse. I admired Sam's lofty ideals, but feared for her ability to pay the rent, buy clothes, buy drugs, go to night clubs and feed herself as well.

On the day Sam moved in, we got in the purple combi and drove cross-country to the fish markets, where we both walked around shrieking at the live crabs and getting high on the briny smell of all of those sea creatures. Bare-footed we leapt over puddles, jumping up and down on the cold, wet tiles of the market halls to try to keep the fish swill from permanently scenting our feet. We bought five kilos of king prawns.

At the hour of Sam's first Marlborough Street dusk, we covered the round green table in the kitchen with massive bowls of prawns, satellite dishes of mayonnaise and lemon, lengths of a sweet smelling crusty French bread, and a mozzarella and spinach salad that we were both proud of. Jessie and Lila were disturbed from their dressing-up games, and Jake was dragged from his metal-bashing to come and partake of the moving-in feast. The sight of the candle-lit table covered with a monstrosity of food made Lila squeal with delight, and Jessie change her mind about wearing a clinging frock out later.

- Will you be feeding us like this every night? asked Lila, flipping the lid off a bottle of beer and filling the tumblers we waved at her.

- Actually, it's Soph who's feeding you tonight, she said, giving me a prawn-scented hug. She's supposed to be saving the money she makes telling people lies about their lives for a trip to London.

- She didn't tell lies to me, said Jake.

- What did she tell you that's come true? asked Jessie, peeling the first prawn.

- She told me that we'd become close friends, he said, grinning like a maniac.

- I didn't tell you that in the reading! I said, vulnerable on the cards' behalf. I told you the morning after when we'd already spent most of New Year's Eve together.

- What else did they say? asked Jessie.

- They said he's going to be a star one day ... that he's got a big year ahead of him.

- Yay, cheered Lila, raising her glass. Jake's gonna be famous, Jake'll be a star. We'll eat prawns every night.

Even amid the tar and concrete of Surry Hills, crickets sang at the end of the hot day. Left-over shiny, black-green Christmas beetles flew into the lights with hollow plonking sounds when they hit the shades. In one of the Marlborough Street back-yards, a dog howled each time our talk or laughter rose above a certain level.

- So what do you think of that for a money-making venture? Sam asked, throwing a chunk of bread at me across the table.

- Sorry, I missed it, I said, Jake's gaze on my face even as he peeled another prawn.

- Stripping, said Jake, still watching.

- You're joking.

- Oh, come on Soph. Why not? asked Sam in a voice that told me she'd already made up her mind.

- You'd make much more money in a night, even at a peep show, than you would in a whole day reading those cards, said Lila, goading me. Have you got something under there that the rest of us haven't?

- Only a star on her hip-bone and a serpent around her calf, said Sam, my loyal friend.

- It's a pentagram, not a star, said Jake. It's a sacred, secret thing that should be protected.

- Why the fuck not? I laughed. What do we have to do?

- We just do what we'd be doing in our bedroom anyway, said Jessie, licking her fingers with a feline expression on her face. Men love watching women touch each other.

- Is that so Jake? I asked, returning his stare. Do you like watching girls together?

- Jake just can't bear to be left out, said Lila, stroking his thigh and cat-licking his ear. He's such a hands-on sort of guy. You know what I mean?

- I'm not sure that I do, I said, watching Jake squirm more at Lila's words than her touch. Will one of you tell me more about this wonderful career, and I'll eat prawns while I still can. While strange men won't ogle the bulges around my waist.

When the kitchen table had turned into a mess of prawn skins and dead beer bottles, I felt obscenely heavy, as though I'd eaten two kilos of the orange beasties myself. Jake had dripped mayonnaise and lemon down the front of his shirt, and when Lila pointed this out to him, he wiped his hands on the white cotton, dragged it over his head and slung it into the corner. His own striptease ended there, but still provoked a chorus of drunken approval.

Jessie tweaked a nipple the colour of burnt toffee and told Jake that he was now dressed for the washing up. The girls were going out to drink in a new bar overlooking Gilligan's Island and to shoot some pool. Sam barely registered my decision to stay in and let the beer and prawns ferment quietly. I hadn't been 'out' since New Year's Eve and still didn't feel up to it.

I remained slumped in a chair, a mass of warm prawn flesh, as I watched Jake's back while he washed the dishes. In the bare bulb light of the kitchen his skin glowed moonlike and his jeans sat pertly on his hips just below his tapered waist. Poor artist be damned. Jake could have been the new Levis boy! I wanted to know what he was wearing under there, but my tongue didn't remember how to form the words. The commotion of the girls' departure had left a relieved silence in the house that overwhelmed me.

After a while, we moved to the back steps with the bowl of prawn heads at our feet, calling in the neighbourhood cats. The concrete of the step was still warm from the sun, though it had been dark for nearly two hours. A sickle moon gave the yard a silver sheen.

An obese tortoiseshell tom appeared from next door, and purring, stuck his nose into the prawn bowl. The purr grew louder and deeper the more he ate, and I marvelled that so many prawn heads didn't drown out the rumble.

- Not too many Gough, said Jake, nudging the beast in its tummy but not stopping it.

- Gough?

- Yeah, Gough, he said, pushing him away from the bowl. They called their new cat Malcolm because he's tall and lean and hates Gough.

- Do you get on with your mother? I asked, suddenly.

- Yeah. I love my mother, he said. Why?

- You don't sound all that certain.

- Uh. It's just that I don't see much of her ... Dad's a drunk and she sticks around to watch. That hurts.

In the space between words, I heard the mournful clatter of a country train pulling into Central.

- How'd you meet Jessie and Lila?

- What is this? Twenty questions? Why do you ask?

- Oh, just because they're such a wild pair. Such characters, I said, not caring how my question sounded.

- They saw me in a bar one night, pissed as a fart, liked the look of me and brought me home to play with. I just never left.

- Hah, that's a good one.

- It's the truth, he said. It's them that likes an audience, not me that likes to get off on other people's thrills.

- So why did you stay then, if they were just other people's thrills?

- I liked the girls ... I liked the vibe in this house, he said. And I needed to get out of the place I was living.

- Why?

- I was living with my best friend from school, he mused. The two of us hurtling in opposite directions.

The lean cat, Malcolm, came to sit at the far end of the yard, but declined our leftovers.

- He got a flash job and started wearing fancy suits, he continued. I spent more time alone. He was on an upward spiral and I was on an inward spiral. That's it.

- I wonder which way Sam and I are spiralling?

- You're moving inwards and she's moving downwards.

- She is not, I snapped. You barely know her, how can you say that?

- You're right. I barely know her, but because you know her so well you can't see it.

- Thanks for the vote of confidence.

- Hey, why so touchy? he asked, throwing his arm around me and pulling me into his chest.

- Dunno, I said, inhaling the sandalwood odour of his skin and feeling the warmth from his chest moving right through my shirt, moving me. Guess I feel funny about Sam moving ... change ... even though I'm always desperate for it, I'm not used to it.

- What's this sorrow you carry around?

- It's the invisible, intangible sorrow that only you ever seem to see, I said, glibly. Maybe I'm only sorrowful around you?

- Now why would that be? he asked, releasing me and walking inside.

At the Camden Markets I read in a daze. I became an oracular voice and a pair of unfocused eyes making hollow pronouncements that frightened people. Stanley came and sat opposite me, his dye-stained hands shuffling cards, and asked if I'd changed my mind about reading for friends. No, I told him, no. Unfazed and sweet-voiced, he reminded me about the dinner at his house that night. In my mind's eye, I had a vision of Stanley in twenty years' time, trying to enact some Peter Pan fantasy of endless clubbing while anchored to another world by kids and a wife.

During a brief lull in the flow of customers, the sun, for the first time in months, touched my face with a warmth I could feel. I closed my eyes, tilted my head back, and for a moment, my head was clear of all the voices. Perhaps I even smiled. London life was fine: I had my readings; I was taking photos; I had Randolphe and Stanley and Marina ... but I wasn't doing what I said I'd do. The moment I was used to it again, the sun disappeared behind a bank of granite-coloured cloud. I shivered and had a vision of Sam, alone, swimming between decaying piles in inky waters. I shook myself and drank tea from a Thermos, replacing the image of Sam with thoughts of the evening's dinner, when I looked forward to the lack of responsibility that comes from being part of a group.

It's always a shock to the system, turning up at a party after a long, lean period of solitude. The fear that after all that time you just won't remember how to engage with more than one person at once. If you can manage to keep things flowing with just one person, you feel you're doing well. I tried to explain this to Stanley, as we drove in his van from Camden through the centre of London. Honking the van's horn at a group of travellers who'd managed to clamber on top of one of the mighty Trafalgar Square lions.

Under one of the Square's massive spot-lights, they looked like circus clowns riding the back of a giant cat.

We stopped at the off-licence on Acre Lane for beer and cheap red wine. The two Asian brothers who ran the place greeted Stanley with the warm recognition afforded to one of their best customers and then turned their attention back to the telly behind the counter. Stanley told me that last time they'd had a party, he and Marina had got caught up at the offy watching the Poll Tax riots on TV. It became the 'London's Burning' party that everyone remembered with the echo of a hangover and churning guts.

Stanley opened the front door of his house to intoxicating food fumes. Welcome to Brixton's home of vegetarian Indian delights, muttered Stanley, a committed eater of pasta and pizza. In the little kitchen, Marina was juggling coloured spices, the rich red ochre of cayenne pepper, the burnt sunflower gold of turmeric and the deep woody brown of dried cumin. I shut my eyes and I was in Charlie's kitchen in Balmain, sitting on a wooden bench and sipping tea while Nella talked about the Higher Arcana.

- Oh God, what paradise is this? I asked, giving Marina a birthday hug.

- Anyone who calls our kitchen paradise earns herself a margarita, no questions asked, said Marina, pouring me a tumbler of thick white liquid from a jug in the fridge.

- Mind if I watch? I asked, already settling into one of the garden chairs. I'll help if you'd like.

- No. You just relax, Soph, she said, her hair lustrous against the deep green velvet of her dress. I've got this routine down pat. Where's Stanley?

- The moment we walked through the front door he went

straight for the telephone, I said. Talking to his new woman ... seems really happy, doesn't he?

- Yes, said Marina, watching. That OK with you?

- What? That Stanley's got a woman?

- Well, you know ... you and him ...

- Marina, Stanley's not my type, I mumbled, realising I was drinking very fast. You know how it is.

- Just checking, she said, moving to stir the dahl and squeeze lemon into it. Let me guess ... you're into much older men who like to sit around in pubs all night and write all day?

I glared at her, feeling the hot rush of tequila in my veins, trying to work out whether she was attacking me, testing me, or just doing girl talk.

- Hey, she said. I don't care what sort of men you're into. I've been totally infatuated with writers myself. It's just that usually all it takes is a very brief conversation with them and not only can I no longer contemplate fucking them – but I can't even bear to read them!

- I sleep with them before I've read them. I can't read them after I've met them either!

- So who do you read? she asked, offering her cheek to Stanley as he came floating down the stairs.

- Here, let me get you a drink, I said, jumping up to go to the fridge, relieved at the interruption.

- Soph not workin? teased Stanley, all flirtatious goodwill and smug in the knowledge that he was the only one of us getting regular sex.

- She's going to entertain us while we work, said Marina, winking at me.

- Oh yeah? goaded Stanley. I've seen one of Soph's performances.

- She's going to tell us a story, Stanley.

- Which story? I asked, happy to feel an allegiance with her. Shall I tell you one of Sydney's urban myths?

- No, she said, ignoring Stanley's nod to the contrary. Tell us a real story ... tell us what you're doing in London.

- You want me to tell you what I'm doing in London? I repeated, unused to direct questions. I think you're the first person to ask me that in all these months.

- Marina has a real subtlety about her at times, said Stanley.

- Thanks, Stanley, said Marina. She's Australian, she appreciates frankness.

- Alright, alright, said Stanley. Do we get a story or not?

I poured myself another margarita from the jug I'd positioned beside me and panicked. I didn't want to lie to these two – to my two friends.

- I came to London to find my father, I said, and once those simple words were out, I wondered why I hadn't gone around telling the world. It's just that now I'm here I can't really bring myself to search!

- I thought you were with him when you got here, said Stanley, confusion clouding his face. Wasn't it your father you were staying with at that hotel?

- Er, no, I said, imagining you could actually watch friendship dissolve. It was such a sleazy story. I didn't want to tell you because I thought you'd be too disgusted to bother with me.

- But the story, Sophie, said Marina, smiling me on and looking incredulous at once.

- It goes like this, I said, starting haltingly at the beginning, at the real beginning when Zelda first came to London, glossing over plenty in between, and finishing up with me sitting in a bar, drinking with McKee and knowing I didn't have the first idea about how to find a father.

When I finished, they gaped at me.

- I know it's sordid, I said, pouring myself yet another drink and stopping mid-movement.

- No. No. We'll help you, said Marina, throwing an arm around my shoulders. We'll help you find him.

Stanley sat and stared at me, fiddling nervously with his empty glass. Looking away from me and studying the tiles, as if the answer lay there, wedged between them.

- You're upset with me Stanley, I said, moving away from Marina to crouch beside him. I'm sorry for lying to you.

- Hey, it's not that, he said, trying on a smile and pulling his eyes from where they'd stuck to the tiles. I'm just wondering what the fuck happens when you find this guy. I mean, what do you say?

Marina looked from me to Stanley dumbly and then at the food, as though trying to remember what she'd been doing.

- What do you say to him? Hi Dad, don't you recognise me? What have you been doing all my life? he taunted. And supposing you do work out how to break the news, how's he supposed to react? Do you really think he'll be pleased to see you?

- He's got to know the truth, said Marina, shifting her attention to the bowl of spinach she'd been washing. It's only right.

- He needs to know me, I said in my own defence. It's my duty to find him.

- Duty! said Stanley, holding his glass out for more of the tex-mex sludge. I'm just trying to put myself in his place; some woman you haven't so much as thought of for years and years has your kid, never tells you, and then suddenly this stranger comes at you out of the blue, calling you Daddy. I mean, let's face it, you're going to wonder what the hell she wants from you.

- You're being sexist, said Marina, tearing stalks from leaves the colour of her dress. You're assuming that he'll think that just because she's a young woman and he's an older man, she wants something from him ... money.

- That's not fair, said Stanley, sitting on the edge of his chair. The thing is, supposing I were adopted and went off to find my biological mother at age twenty, she'd be just as likely to suspect me of wanting something from her. That's the kind of world we live in.

- That's pretty bloody cowardly, said Marina, sharply. You're saying he'll be scared shitless and maybe Sophie should spare him.

- I'm not, he said, laughing nervously. I'm just saying she may not get much of a welcome, that's all.

- And then again, said Marina, she might.

I knew all of this, had thought it through dozens of times before. Had thrashed it out, worried over it, sweated over it, dreamt about it, but at the end of the day, I was prepared to take a chance. There had to be more to aspire to, emotionally, than what Zelda could provide. The unknowing would kill me if I let it, of that I was sure.

- It's all a bit academic, I sighed. At the rate I'm going, I'll never know what it feels like to have a father.

The other guests began to arrive, and I could hear the ebb and flow of conversation. From the upstairs bathroom window, I could see the mirror-image backs of the houses opposite. As in a room with mirrored walls, the image repeated itself over and over again, to the point where I could no longer identify the original, the real. I'd begun to feel that way with my search, I'd been following so many false leads it seemed I was doing it on purpose. It had got to the point where I could no longer tell whether my actions were genuine.

Lila told us to wear sexy lingerie and clothes that we could remove gradually. A bit of healthy lip was fine when dealing with the blokes, she said, but we really shouldn't show too much scorn towards the bouncers. Be cool about drugs, no matter what; don't ask to buy from them, but if they offer a free taste, don't say no because they'll think you're green. Don't just take your clothes off, said Jessie, caress yourselves, make it sensual.

When receiving this advice over a late Marlborough Street breakfast of mangoes and pancakes, Sam and I had laughed about what we pretended was a silly game. Filled with false bravado we'd pronounced that dealing with the blokes was no sweat at all, and that free drugs were just fine, too. I drank three cups of strong coffee in a row in a desperate bid to keep the energy level at fever pitch, and then worried about stripping with a full bladder. Smelling the fresh coffee and pancakes, Jake had left the work that he'd already been absorbed in for two hours, and wandered into the kitchen with a distracted expression on his face. For a few moments he sat with a cup of coffee balancing on his knee, waiting for a pancake like the rest of us. With a sudden focusing of his eyes on Lila, he tuned in to our conversation, sighed, and retreated to his small utopia where shapes and forms were pure.

In the house we were buoyant, high on some sisterly euphoria. Us against them. We're The Adventurers; we're going to use what we've got to screw money out of those bastards who leer at us in the street. We're gonna feel really good about this because it's us on top. It's going to be fun ... a laugh.

Outside, though, in the harsh, unsympathetic light of late morning, removed from the Marlborough Street hype, I started to feel like myself again. Like the person who treads gingerly and moves with a degree of reservation. Even Sam seemed suddenly quieter, and when she did speak, her voice was flat and diminutive. The bus we rode from Central Station to Kings Cross moved through the city streets too quickly. And these men on the bus, were they taking an early lunch, leaving the grey of their office to get a bit of titillation at the Cross?

We got off near the hospital, suddenly reluctant to get into this thing. Wanting to approach by foot with caution. There was little romance to be had at the southern end of Darlinghurst Road; tired blocks of red brick flats left over from the thirties, pizza and kebab joints with those plastic streamers in the doorways that ensured the flies stayed in once they got in, newsagents displaying glossy images of big-breasted women and pretty boys. I even caught Sam eyeing the office of the Commonwealth Employment Service, but dismissing it with a shrug of her lightly sunburnt shoulders.

As we sighted the saccharine glow of the Coca-Cola sign that marked the beginning of the Cross proper, the concept of what we were about to do, even as only a trial run, dazed me. And standing there, mesmerised by the shimmering immediacy of the neon sign, I fell back as if I'd been hit when a car pulled up in front of us with a blast of the horn. Horrified, I stared at the passenger door, preparing to flee.

- Hi, Zelda, said Sam, turning to roll her eyes at me and crouching down to speak through the window.

- Where are you two off to? Zelda asked, in that voice that said she was in a hurry but observing custom, regardless.

- Um, I said, leaning down to look at my mother, as if to make absolutely certain it was her. I didn't recognise your car. I thought you were some creep who was going to invite us for a ride.

- Going swimming at the Boy, said Sam, shaking her shoulder bag and gesturing towards Woolloomooloo and our favourite pool.

- It's alright for some, said Zelda, patting her briefcase on the seat beside her. No doubt Sophie will imagine someone's trying to pick her up at the Andrew Boy Charlton as well.

She sped off with another flourish of the horn as Sam and I gaped at each other. We clasped our hands together and laughed.

- That was a bit catty, said Sam. I guess she still hasn't recovered from your latest conquest.

- The guy wasn't even her boyfriend Sam, I said, unnerved enough to defend myself. He was just there for lunch one Sunday with a few other people. He called me and invited me out a few days later.

She just gave me that arched eyebrow look of mock knowing.

- What was wrong with accepting a dinner invitation? I continued. That was my first real date.

- That's pretty funny, said Sam, slapping my shoulder and pulling me across the road with her. Soph-the-seductress! First date at eighteen!

I didn't think it was funny, though. When I stopped to think about it I felt awkward about the number of guys I'd slept with in ratio to the number of intimate candle-lit dinners I'd had. The idea of a shared meal or two before the first fuck was becoming increasingly attractive to me.

Lila had told us that Fred would be expecting us, but when

we buzzed on the intercom from the exposed corner on Darlinghurst Road, the indolent voice asked us which Fred. I huddled close to the intercom, and said we'd come for an interview, but still the voice feigned ignorance.

- We're here for a trial. A demonstration, I said, thinking that a passer-by who overheard might imagine I was talking about a new cocktail blender.

The door clicked open and Sam put her shoulder into it lest it shut again in our faces. As we mounted the narrow staircase, decorated on either side with mirrored tiles, I almost wished it had.

At the top of the stairs we were greeted by a greasy-haired weasel wearing brown slacks, a beige shirt, a brown tie and brown hush puppies. I never could forgive a man for wearing beige. At once he conveyed the image of being both bored and agitated. He told us not to start until Fred came down.

Despite the fact that there was no natural light in the bar room, you could tell it was daytime. Somehow all those things you barely noticed in the heat and excitement of the night were glaringly apparent during the day, when the ugliest part of the bar, the punters, was absent. As I walked across the gold swirls on the carpet I felt the rubber soles of my boots stick again and again to all of those fluids that spill on the floor of such places. The stench of stale cigarettes was almost palpable, and the lime green laminated tables shouted at the burnt orange of the walls. The mirror ball that hung over the stage reminded me of every drunken night of my life and the short catwalk that stuck out from the stage into the room was like an afterthought; some bloke's fly with a bit of white crushed business shirt hanging out of it.

- Of course I make the decisions, said the weasel, gesturing that we should both turn around in front of him for a cursory glance at the merchandise.

- Tatt, he said, and pulled a notebook out of the front pocket of his shirt, scribbling the word quickly. Any others?

- Yes, we both said, slapping our hip-bones.

- Done this before? he said, gesturing for us to turn around again.

Yes. No. I said no, Sam said yes. It didn't matter because he wasn't listening or didn't care.

- Of course, we have booths. For peep-show, he said matter-of-fact. But I prefer to put the older, tireder girls in them. I'd start you off on the stage.

I looked at the stage, which was more of a raised platform, barely separate from the tables. I wanted to sit down on one of the nasty brown vinyl chairs and laugh, and say, Got you! We were only joking, but before I got around to that, the massive bulk of Fred appeared. His size 52 jeans let out an audible groan as he sat down in a seat right up where the stage met the catwalk. From a hefty brown paper bag he pulled out a triple-decker hamburger.

The weasel scuttled off behind the bar, and for one glorious moment I thought he was going to offer us a drink. Instead, he turned on the PA system and started fiddling with cassettes.

- First girl up, he said through a microphone from behind the bar.

- Can't we do it together? I asked, aware of how high and proper my voice sounded.

- Only if you do lezzo sex, he said again through the mike.

- Well, no, I said quietly, nodding at Sam and in the direction of the stage.

When she shook her head no, I mouthed Thanks Sam, and trying to look bored and casual as opposed to shit scared, I sauntered up the three steps on the right-hand side of the stage. Lila had said that you could never see much of the audience because of the lights, but Fred hadn't bothered with the lights so from where I stood, right at the back of the stage, I could see Sam and the two men with alarming clarity.

Abba's 'Dancing Queen' came over the PA, loud and crackly, and I stood and tapped my right foot, giggling quietly. After a few bars, the music stopped just as abruptly.

- What the fuck's wrong? barked the weasel from beside an enormous bottle of Amaretto. We haven't got all day.

- What? Was that the music? I asked, hovering in some no-man's land midway between laughter and tears, watching Sam with her face buried in her hands, shoulders shaking with suppressed laughter.

- That's the fucking music, said Fred, spitting a glob of fried onion onto the stage. What do you want, Princess? Fucking Joan Sutherland?

So there I was, shimmying away on this flimsy platform, fixing my gaze on some point on the wall and imagining I was someplace cool. Removing the flowing silk shirt was easy, almost as much fun as waving it around a bit like it was a feather boa and dropping it over the edge of the stage, away from Fred, as I imagined strippers do. Unbuttoning the close-fitting purple top involved more concentration and that was when I remembered to touch myself, to run my left hand up my thigh under my skirt and move my hips around as though I was really enjoying it. I had this terrible urge to look at Fred, to see how he was reacting, but found myself unable to wrench my gaze from that point on the wall.

Now, with my purple lace bra, skirt and boots on, I started

to feel ridiculous and had this dreadful need to pee. With hands that shook, I fumbled with the zip on the side of my skirt, and began to shimmy the thing down over my hips while I went on trying to move to the music. Stumbling a little as I stepped out of my skirt, I strode down the cat-walk, swaying to the music in my bra and pants as though I were a lingerie model. I stopped halfway down the walk and bent forward, swaying my arse in the air a little, thinking yeah, play it, play it. When I turned back to face the audience, or where the audience should have been, I slipped out of my bra with false modesty, and stood, hips gyrating, cupping each breast with a cold hand.

I hesitated then, knowing the song was drawing to a close, remembering Lila saying I had to go all the way, but hoping for a reprieve. Even running one of my hands up and down the inside of my thigh in the hope that this was enough. But no, one could never reveal enough. So again I turned, swaying my arse out into the room, and slowly rolling the lacy stuff down over my hips, down over my buttocks till I had the terrible, blood-chilling feeling that people could see my tiny red anus. Rolling the fabric up again, I turned to face them, and this time rolled my knickers down and stepped out of them in nearly one motion. Clutching the warm fabric to one breast, I danced a little on the spot, my face suddenly hot, and my cunt feeling the strange, part-humbling, part-liberating experience of being paraded before strangers.

WHEEL OF FORTUNE

Down four flights of tenement stairs and out on the street, I realise I've left my cards in a heap by the bed. I know there's no time to go back, yet setting out on such a mission without the cards seems symbolic. As I walk the four sweltering blocks to the subway station, my shirt is already threatening to stick to my back like a second skin, all the better to see me in, and I feel like giving up there and then. Instead, I think cool breeze, Sydney Harbour thoughts, and descend into the even steamier subway.

The F Train's carriage is air-conditioned, the coolest place in the city. I might ride it all day. Might spend the day emptying my bag of change, and then the dollar bills, instead of riding up the Hudson. Might know the city's beggars, homeless, and ill, rather than knowing him.

My arms are a golden, honey colour, touched by the sun of three cities in almost as many weeks. Zelda's arms are still pale, milky, and will remain protected from the sun that would leave her fair skin angry with freckles. My father's skin will be as dark as the forest, as gritty, as textured as the land itself. Suddenly I have an alarming vision of them together, Zelda and my father, and I am jealous.

I try to feel connected to this place, these people riding the subway in the city where he was born, but whom do I identify with? She could be kin, this old, bloated woman asleep in the plastic chair opposite, who could have been asleep in this carriage for days . . . or the mini-skirted business woman beside me whose skin is as flawless as the soft leather of her shoes. Better not to think. Better to watch the stations of downtown Manhattan flash by, to watch the ebb and flow of its people as they loom and recede, and leave me to myself.

The house groaned in its sleep as another north London street subsided. When I awoke it was in the coldest hour, just before dawn, but I knew it wasn't the cold that had disturbed me. The days were finally lengthening and the night had lost its malicious edge.

It was from a dream that I woke, with a jolt and a gasp. A dream about Sam and me, a dream of betrayal. In the dream, Sam and I spent hours coming down from a trip, lying on the futon mattress in her dimly lit Marlborough Street room. It is daytime, and her match-stick blinds slice the light into jagged strips that move before my smarting eyes. Next door the neighbours are fucking. Downstairs Jake is locked in his room working, giving us the silent treatment as we discuss our plans for the journey with growing excitement. Every now and then one of us begins to cry with exhaustion, with relief at the end of childhood that will surely come with the departure. Hours, perhaps days, pass in this fashion. Every so often one of us drags down to the kitchen for more vegemite toast and Fanta.

Suddenly the whole pace of the dream shifts. The light in Sam's bedroom has grown harsh and there are three violent raps on the door. Sam is somewhere between waking, sleeping and reliving her trip, but I am alive, alert. The taxi has arrived to take us to the airport; as I gather together my passport, ticket, and teddy-bear stuffed with money, I kick her inert body, and shout Sam, Sam, Sam. All the while I'm saying come on, we've got to go, get up, but she is either not stirring or laughing at me. Marina is driving the taxi, and tells me that I'll have to leave Sam behind. That it's vital that I catch this plane. I kneel, sobbing, at the foot of Sam's bed, pleading with her.

As the taxi pulls away from the house and accelerates towards the end of the street I howl Sam's name out the window, as though she may still come. At the first traffic light we stop at, up on Cleveland Street, Jake strolls up to the window and says If only you'd have asked me Soph ...

Watching for the first hint of day above London and trying to recall the whole dream, I began to feel an irrational annoyance. Impatient with the wait for dawn, the wait for day, and the wait for my own future, I flung myself out of bed with a thud that dislodged photos from the frame of the mirror. I scuttled downstairs to make tea, refusing to be haunted. I'd done what I had to do, what was right at the time. Sam could have come if she'd wanted to; but she'd chosen to stay at home to go on living her petty romances and to prolong her acid-induced adolescence.

Hearing Randolphe's feet on each creaking board upstairs, I crept back to my bed, unable to face a constitutional or his scrutinising gaze. On the bed I shuffled cards, finding small solace, wondering how many hours and days of my life I'd spent just so.

I rolled onto my back and stared at the ceiling with its regular moulded edges, and behind me at the top of the standing mirror with its upside down images of Sydney Harbour, of Sam, Jessie and Lila all dressed up to go out, of Jake bending over some sculpture that his body obscured, his naked torso grainy in the dimly lit black and white image, as though he too had acquired the dusty texture of one of his stone creations.

It had been months and months since I last had sex, and I slid my cold fingers down inside my leggings to see if I still felt anything. To see how hard it was to make myself come. With icy fingers and a body that had been curled in on itself for as long as I could remember, it was no simple task. I searched my memory for the last time I had had sex that I really enjoyed. Dick had been hairy, thick-waisted and insatiable in a heavy-handed way that had made me turn my back on him once we'd both had our roughly provoked orgasms. Like a card index that suddenly halts at the sought-after address, the replay taking place inside my head stopped with a jolt at Simon. Zelda's surfing Boy Wonder who rode his waves with a breathtaking sensitivity. The one who first put his tongue to my clitoris when I was already on the crest of my own wave. The one with the smooth, Golden Syrup coloured body.

With blood pumping in parts of my body that I'd forgotten about, I dragged myself to the telephone that threatened to ring forever, and curled myself into a high-backed armchair before finally picking up the receiver.

- Yes, I said, more over-ripe than I knew.

- Soph? Is that you? asked a voice down an echoing line whose accent convinced me I'd conjured the return of Simon.

- Who's that? I asked, feeling like a little girl caught with her fingers in the chocolate paper.

- It's your old mate Jake. Remember me?

- Jake? I said, thinking not of him but of Sam, distracted by the briny smell on my fingers.

- Am I interrupting something? he asked.

My head filled to high tide mark with images of his back, arched over some inanimate object that he would breathe life into, and the vast window behind him, opening onto the city's rear. The evening sky would be bluer than blue, bluer than anything your average Londoner had ever seen.

- Oh, you know, I said, shrugging off panic. Just the usual roll in a card stack.

- Yeah? Wish I was there, he said, jocular Jake.

- So do I, I said, more seriously.

- Yeah, well, I promised to call if . . .

- If what? What's happened? I asked, the weight of the night's dream pressing down hard on my fluttering belly.

- Don't panic. It's alright. Everything's going to be alright, he said gently. It's good news I think.

- What is? Where's Sammy?

- She's somewhere in northern Queensland . . . still with the same bloke. She's pregnant, Soph. She's gonna have a baby.

- What?

- A baby, he repeated, as if speaking to a child through a tin can connected to a piece of string.

- She doesn't want a child, she wants to party, I said. Has anybody tried to talk her out of this? Jesus Christ!

- Well, I certainly haven't, he said. She sounded so happy Soph.

Across the world, my silence roared.

- She said she'd been clean now for four weeks, ever since she started to think that just maybe.

- What did she say, exactly. To make you so sure? My mind reeled with shock but also registered just the faintest glimmer of excitement.

- She says she's finally worked out what to do with the next few years of her life, he said with a tone of voice and pitch that was pure Sammy. Says she's going to be a mother and do it really well. Stay clean, have the child and make herself a home somewhere.

- Is it still the Sanyassin? Is this *It* with him or what?

- I really don't know, Soph. I don't think she does either. I got the impression that he's a good bloke and all, and is all for the kid, but even if he weren't she'd do it anyway.

- I'm speechless, I said, using one of Zelda's phrases from my adolescence.

- So what's happening with you?

- Oh, I dunno Jake. I guess I'm just messing around, biding my time until something falls into place.

- Yeah?

- I've got a meeting with some woman at a publisher's this afternoon. I'm going to tell her some bullshit story about photo research so I can go through her files. It's pretty tenuous, but ...

- A lot less tenuous than sleeping your way around the world in search of some sort of truth, he said quietly.

- If I want your moral commentary I'll ask for it!

- Hey, come on, I worry about you. We all do.

- Well, for your information Jake, I've been celibate since a week after my arrival, I said, immediately wishing I'd kept my mouth shut.

- Sure, Soph. Look, I've got to go. I'm in the gallery and I'm supposed to be chasing up someone's bullshit offer of a London exhibition. Bye Soph, bye.

- But Jake, it's true, I said, knowing he'd already gone.

I left the house feeling half-dressed, unprepared for the big bluff I'd lined up for myself. Or that Marina and I had contrived between us. The quiet streets of Dartmouth Park hung frozen in the balance between winter and spring, with the tiny dawn-coloured blossoms that had just appeared looking as though they might bypass summer altogether, arrive at autumn without ever having reached their full splendour.

I marvelled at how slowly my blood seemed to move through my body as I shifted from foot to foot while waiting for the 134 opposite a brute of a pub; its turrets and flags reminded me of one of the Woolloomooloo Bay battleships. The washing line of drying beer towels on the roof every bit as jubilant as a string of coloured flags.

As a child I had been afraid to sit in the front seats at the top of the bus, convinced that the branch of a gum tree or a low-lying bridge would come crashing through those great grime-smeared windows. In London though, the only seats I was content with were those at the front on top. Sitting further back, I was drawn into the worlds of the other passengers, looking for a life, any other life to try on for size.

An early afternoon weekday and Camden, or what I glimpsed of it from the bus, had the look of a waking child. At the weekends traffic crawled slowly down only two of the road's four lanes. The other two would be clogged with glamorous types come from the south and the west in their street gear to indulge in a bit of Camden grime, sleaze and dreaming.

Driving south through Mornington Crescent, where the tube station was closed more often than it was open, I wondered whether that ghostland was paying the price of Camden Town's great affluence. Or whether it was really the other way around, and Camden Town with all its bustle and noise was the place that bore the most severe blight. Then over the spaghetti tangle of roads at Euston and into the more sedate realm of hospital buildings and colleges in Gower Street. Randolphe had told me about Bloomsbury and the Bells and the Woolfs, but driving down Gower Street, past its string of shabby B & Bs and one-star hotels, his description was of some other world.

The bus delivered me to a stop just above the square as the fraught-sounding woman at the publisher's had told me it would. I couldn't imagine Zelda telling anyone which bus to catch. If you didn't own a car in Sydney you were considered socially disabled, but the bus was as sacred to your average Londoner as the cow was to a Hindu.

There was still time to wander a little, and join the dots between the blue plaques that were worn proudly on the uniform facades of the Georgian town houses. Most of the names on the plaques meant nothing to me, and I felt vaguely ripped off. Cheated by the preposterous notion that Australia and England shared the same history.

I was uneasy approaching the Georgian block with its arched doorway and lead-light windows where Zelda would have come to work. Inside the front door, in a corridor that had been converted, rather unsuccessfully, into an office, an Australian woman a few years older than me asked if she could help. I had to put my hand to my mouth to stop myself pouring out the story like an undigested meal. Surely she would have understood? She, too, must have crossed the globe and come to this frigid city in search of something. Instead I casually told her I was there to see the woman with the extraordinary name: Marina's friend, Arraminta.

On the walls were black and white photos of authors, apparently famous, obviously esteemed. Despite the grandeur of the building, the place had an air of irrevocable decay, heightened by the jumble-sale appearance of the furniture in the wind-tunnel reception. The woman behind the desk huddled over her typewriter and shivered as she played and replayed the Dictaphone, finally saying, Fucking woman, much louder than she could have realised, and pulling the headphones off in disgust.

- Can't understand the bloody names, she said to me. Been here six months and I still don't know who's who or what's what! Only just worked out that the term vegetable, here, pertains to fried potato and limp lettuce.

- I know the feeling, I offered, eager for distraction. I finally realised that when I called a guy a spunk and everyone looked at me in disgust, it wasn't because they thought he was a Neanderthal or anything, but that here spunk means sperm!

- So, are you here for the job? she asked, testily, intent that I wasn't going to have it without sitting in that cold wind-tunnel of an office for months first.

- I didn't know there was one, I said, smiling, siding with her. I'm doing a research project on the development of the portrait in photography. Going around to a bunch of publishers to ferret through their photo files.

- Oh, she said, with a raised eyebrow, a bullshit detector that worked. So, where are you from?

- Sydney.

- I'm from Melbourne.

- Hm, I said, looking around the walls for inspiration, knowing neither of us would start on the Do-you-know-so-and-so game, and determined not to get into a slagging match about the merits of Sydney over Melbourne.

The first door in the hallway opened to the sound of ringing phones, and a voice, taut as a straining fishing line, saying, Tell her I'm not in.

- Sally, said a big-haired woman with a tight, quivering mouth. Do come in.

I sat, staring dumbly.

- Sally? the woman said again, speaking to me.

- Sophie, I said, apologetically. My name's Sophie.

- I'm Arraminta, she said, pronouncing each syllable as though convinced I was intellectually challenged by it.

- Hello Arraminta, I said, feeling hysterical and wanting to call her 'Ave a Mintie. Thanks for making the time to see me. I'm sure you must be very busy.

- It's a welcome break, you know? Not having to be on the phone hustling. And anyway, any friend of Marina's ...

She led me into a room where my first impression was of chaos. Six telephones were ringing, and two young women were hunched over desks, trying to carry out conversations over the din. The floor was awash with paper. Piles of manuscripts leaned against walls or teetered on desk-tops in unlikely towers. Where wall spaces weren't covered with bookshelves, a riot of promotional posters screamed their message from behind cracked glass panels. A dim blue throbbed from the room's one computer, and two typewriters hummed idly, half-typed letters lying like three-dimensional question marks.

Arraminta walked daintily through the rubble to a corner desk nestled by a window overlooking the square's garden. My boots kept sticking to stray pieces of paper – press releases, I noted – and I glanced around self-consciously to see if anyone cared. Where the tops of the scratched wooden desks weren't littered with books and paper, there were organic clusters of white plastic cups, half-filled with cold coffee or dust-topped red wine.

- Would you like some coffee, Sally? Arraminta asked, collapsing into the black leather chair that looked as though it belonged in an office of glass and chrome, not between splintering wooden desks and a chaos of books.

- It's Sophie, actually, I repeated, even more apologetic this time.

- Oh, I am sorry, she said, suddenly looking at me. It's been one of those days. Budgets you know?

Under her desk lay a sleek pair of stilettos at a crazy angle, one to the other, and I imagined her exchanging her scuffed loafers for these glamorous slippers when she went off to launch books. Stuck in a wall recess where most people wouldn't notice them was an assortment of postcards, some with rude slogans on them like Stanley's t-shirts, and others with black and white pictures of Paris and New York.

- God, is it four already? she asked, a mixture of panic and relief in her voice. Well then, it's time to open a bottle of wine. Glass of red, Sophie? Cup of red, I mean.

- Sure, why not? I said, marvelling at the foreign territory I'd landed myself in.

- Go to hell! she said, glaring at her phone when it rang, and then looking beseechingly at her colleagues, willing one of them to stop what they were doing and answer it.

- Probably just some little old lady ringing up for Marcel

Proust's number so she can invite him around for tea, she said glibly. I sensed she believed she'd said something funny.

- Oh. Does he only drink champagne, then? I asked.

- Hah! That's a good one! she said, guffawing to herself and turning to one of her colleagues. Does Marcel Proust drink champagne!

I bit my tongue and watched her reach into a deep drawer to pull out a bottle of wine. The corkscrew was in an orange plastic desk organiser that held pens, pencils, rubbers, paper clips and earrings.

- Mm, that's good, I said, tasting plastic, not wine.

- Left over from a party last week, she said, proud of her recycling talents.

- Fucking condescending slimy git! said one of the other women as she slammed down her receiver. Says he won't bloody well consider that interview unless I meet him at the Groucho tonight to discuss it.

- Never mind Jane, said Arraminta, apparently the one in charge. Here, have some wine. Don't worry, he'll pay. He always does.

- Oh, fucking great! Jane said, her voice low and angry, her face flushing as she slopped wine into the mug. I was going to stay home and cook David dinner. I haven't seen him for days!

- Now Sophie, Arraminta continued, wincing as her telephone started to ring again but visibly resolving to ignore it. What was it that you wanted? You're not here about the job.

- No, that's not why I'm here, I replied, glancing defensively at my boots and leggings. I'm a photographer. I'm doing some research on the history of the portrait in photography.

- Oh, how fascinating, she said, suddenly looking interested in her ringing phone again.

- So I'm going around to publishers looking at a two-year period, chosen at random, I told her, unable to look at her for fear we'd both laugh. I was hoping to see your catalogues for 1969 and 1970, then look at the photos of the authors you published in those two years.

- Oh, she said, twisting her mouth in either irritation or deep thought. I doubt we've even got any catalogues that old. Certainly going back five years ...

- It must be those two years for the purpose of my research, I repeated, inwardly cursing Marina for her assurance that this would work.

We sat in awkward silence, both inspecting the other's footwear as though part of some sort of integrity test. After she'd apologised profusely and answered two calls, the door opened and closed with a swish of paper and Jane came in, waving catalogues.

- One of our editors has been here forever, she said, handing me shabby booklets so unlike the multi-colour, high-gloss brochures that Zelda was producing now. She needs them back, but said by all means to go and chat to her if you need any help. She's very sweet.

- Thank you, I said, quaking at the thought of meeting a woman who would have worked with my mother, failing to notice the defiant glares that Arraminta and Jane shot each other.

- There you are, said Arraminta, and with one hand on her phone dismissed me. The photo files are down there. Jane will no doubt be able to assist you if you have any problems.

Before I could thank her, she was already speaking to someone she called John Darling and her voice had all but crystallised with its new-found tones of treacle. Clutching those booklets as though my life depended on them, this time I floated across the debris on the floor.

With my back to the filing cabinet that I was sure would reveal an image of my father, I sat on the floor to pore over those pages like some deranged literary groupie. I made a list of all the men's names for that two-year period. As I formed the characters of each name, nearly thirty of them in all, I thrilled at the prospect that one of them belonged to me. Or could have belonged to me if it weren't for Zelda. I'd always fostered the unformed fantasy that, had my father known about me, he would have wanted me so much more passionately than Zelda ever had.

And what a Pandora's Box of names it was; a list with such breadth of possibility that my stomach had began to flutter. French names, Italian names, Russian names. I pictured myself fur-hatted and walking the streets of Moscow, clutching a photograph and a phrase book. With a combination of sorrow and relief, I crossed six of the names off the list when the catalogues told me that the authors had died some years prior to publication. With those six went my Russian father, but not the possibility of further travel.

With the crumpled list in one hand, I stood to open the file drawer that began with A. Looking into that enormous cavern of bulging files, a voice in my head screamed, No, don't do it ... You don't want to know ...

The prospect of a lifetime's unknowing, however, of a lifetime's wondering, left me nauseous. If I had coerced myself into believing that without meeting my father I'd never be happy, then so be it. Search I would, search I must. When I reached the first file that corresponded to a name on the list, I placed it gingerly on the floor by my feet, unable yet to muster the courage to open it. The pile grew, until I had worked through all the drawers and my panic heightened when I realised I was four files short.

Sitting on the floor again, this time with my back to the room in some gesture that pleaded privacy, I opened the first of the files. Author number one looked to be very English upper middle class, dashing in a white-haired way, but must have been all of eighty at the time of the portrait. I put a cross beside his name on the list and shut the folder, pushed it to one side. Number two was far more Zelda's style; young, blond-haired, blue-eyed, a mixture of English Public School, Scandinavian fjords and Hitler Youth, and as I remembered from the catalogue, one of the Americans. He got a question mark beside his name, and his file was placed to my left, closer to my body than that of number one.

In what I thought was a rational process, I culled another five men from the list, mostly on the basis of age. Even with my pile of fourteen hopefuls, a wave of disappointment was rising in my stomach. What I had been most frightened of I became the most disheartened by. Secretly I had believed that I would open one of those files and see a face gazing up at me with my mouth, my nose, my forehead. A face that said without hesitation, I am your father. Instead I sat pouring over dim black and white images striving with mild desperation to come up with similarities, to recognise an expression, the line of a jaw, the fall of what meagre hair most of them displayed. And then to try and pick the sort of man Zelda would seduce.

When Arraminta left at six o'clock sharp, all gushy farewells, I was still poring over those fourteen files, frightened to reject a single contender. It didn't seem to matter how dark, or how fair, or how freckled, there was a glimmer of resemblance in each. And at half-past six, when the publicist whose name I hadn't heard and who therefore must have been the most junior got up to leave, I was still staring distractedly at images of fourteen different men. At quarter to seven, when Jane got up to open another bottle of wine, I'd begun to favour three of the men over the other eleven, for reasons I couldn't possibly have articulated, but then became dismayed to learn that all three of them had been living in London. I assumed this suggested they still lived in London, and that none of them could be the outdoorsman the Camden clairvoyant had alluded to.

- Sophie, said Jane, flat-voiced, exhausted at half-past seven, standing over me with her brow furrowed. Are you almost finished? I've got to go and meet this creep. I'll have to lock the door after me.

- Oh, alright, I said, sounding desperate and fumbling to get the files in order. Yes. I've seen enough now. Though a few of the files are missing.

- Did you find what you wanted? she asked, watching me put the files away, convincing me that she knew exactly what I was looking for.

- I may need some more information, I said, my back to her, a poor liar. I may end up deciding to send out brief questionnaires to those I include in the study. I might ask you for some addresses one day ... I'll have to see how it goes.

- We don't usually give out authors' addresses, she said, downing the red wine in her mug and grimacing. But seeing as you're Zelda's daughter, I'm sure it'd be fine.

- Who told you? I asked. I never said anything about Zelda.

- Hey, it's no big deal, she said, putting on her voluminous grey coat and black felt hat. I was at McKee's reading on Charing Cross Road. I saw you go off with him. I saw that piece in the paper, too.

- Nothing happened between us, I burbled, sounding for all the world as though something had.

- I know, I know, she said, coming up close so I could see the purple tinge from the wine on her lips and the purple indentations under her eyes from the work. McKee phoned and told me the same thing. Wanted us to sue the paper for slander. For slandering you, not him. He's a really decent guy.

- Yes, he is, I said, disproportionately moved by her words. Look, I'll leave you to get ready for your meeting. Thanks for your help. I hope I won't have to pester you again.

- Do pester me, she said, following me out the door. Don't be put off by Arraminta, she's a bit uptight. Comes with the job.

Outside in the tranquil, gracefully lit square, so untouched by the countless little dramas that had taken place on its wide flagstones over the years, once again I suppressed the urge to pour out my tale.

- Sure you don't want to come to the Groucho and have a drink with me on the old lech's account before he arrives? she asked, as I warmed to her in spite of myself.

- Um, no thanks, I said, moving away as I spoke as if to remove myself from temptation. I've been there before. It's not my favourite place.

I moved in a trance-like state into the garishly lit chatter of Tottenham Court Road and on every man I passed sat the face of one of those I'd been staring at for the past two hours. In order to combat an overriding sense of futility, I opted to just keep walking. To wander, to observe, to pass things by, and in this way to postpone the moment when I would lie on the floor in front of the fire in Randolphe's house and admit to myself that it was hopeless. To start the long, slow process of reknowing myself as a woman who would never have a father.

On our third night, Sam was on two girls before me. I'd only watched her the once, at the audition, and her painful, uncharacteristic shyness had disturbed me to the extent that I felt that I should be saving her, not encouraging her. This time, I could see the audience loved her coyness and matching school-girl costume.

That third night she came bursting into the dim corridor they called a change-room, clutching the dark, box-pleated tunic to her breasts just in time to help me into the side-zipping black leather jeans that were part of my costume. Because of my tattoos I played a butch biker. Once, inadvertently, I was the butch biker dyke when the manager sent one of the other girls out on stage to surprise me, to simper at my feet in terror, wearing some slip of clothing that I was supposed to tear from her body.

- Soph! Soph! shrieked Sam, decibels rising. You'll never guess who's here. You won't believe who's in the audience tonight.

- Rob Lowe, I said, trying to sound bored, but thinking, Oh fuck, oh fuck, it's Zelda. Go on, shock me. Tell me there's an attractive man out there tonight.

- Yes, there is, but not just any attractive man, she said, playing for a reaction to a silent house. It's Jake. Jake's in the audience. Sitting on his own drinking at a table off to the right of the stage.

Silence met her agitation as I fiddled with the zip of my jacket.

- That blonde waitress is hovering around, but he's ignoring her, she cajoled. Mean look on his face, too.

- So what? I said, thinking goddamn bastard, how dare he. What's the big deal? He's seen it all before ...

- Aren't you even a little bit nervous? she asked, puzzled, disappointed.

- Why the hell should I be? I won't even be able to see him. It's just another night, Sam.

Of course I was lying, but then I'd begun to suspect that Sam was lying to me about things too. So long as I swaggered out onto the stage and started swaying to the music right off, I'd be OK.

As I hit the pool of light, centre stage, all leather and zips reflecting the spotlights, I was gripped by an irrational anger. It seemed to me that Jake had crossed some undrawn line between friends, some line of decency. The filthy scowl I wore on my face as I strutted the stage only served to enhance the act. It was only after I'd flung down the leather cap, and was slowly unzipping my jacket to reveal the leather corset underneath that I allowed myself a glance off to the right. And sure enough, there he was, looking like he'd just knocked off work at Clyde's.

The music they gave me was Prince's 'Little Red Corvette', which seemed like a pretty dumb choice to me. It wasn't just that it was a little too fast and not exactly conducive to undoing zips, but it was about a car, and I was supposed to be a biker chick, for Christ's sake. The management reckoned the audience wasn't smart enough to make the connection. It was a song I liked myself, a song I would have danced to in another life with my clothes on at a club where the men danced too. A song I could move my pelvis to and pant along with. And that night I moved my pelvis with extra force, and removed my clothes with more menace, and waved my arse more tauntingly, and rubbed my tits and my pubic mound with wet-lipped, lascivious longing.

Off stage I sweated and panted like I'd been running fast through the angry night. Sam was waiting, and when our eyes met she started fanning her face and breathing loud.

- Oh, Soph, she said, her voice neutral. And to think, you

don't even care that he's here. I'm going to go and buy a drink to cool the poor boy down. See you out there.

We'd done our three sets for the evening and were technically free to go, but if certain customers made their need obvious enough, we were supposed to hang around and chat. Seething, I doused myself in cold water and scrubbed to remove the layers of makeup, the eyeliner, the base, and the nipple rouge. All I had to struggle into were my cut-offs and an oversized white shirt that I knotted at the front. Sometimes I wore long black knee socks, and with my tattoos hidden imagined that none of the bourbon-drinking punters and their wandering hands would recognise me.

Sam and Jake were laughing and drinking together, and his hand rested on her thigh. I nodded at them and ignored the enquiring looks of the fat-fingered yobbos as I breezed past. What dumb-fuck male manager had designed his strip club so the girls had to leave through the crowd of leering customers?

Out on Darlinghurst Road a taxi pulled up straight away, but before I could get in, Sam and Jake had each grabbed an elbow and were propelling me down the street that led to Clyde's. To the place where Jake parked the ute when he worked. All the artists Jake knew seemed to drive these same, beat-up utility trucks with a fine film of dust perpetually coating the front bench seat and tools rattling around on the floor as they took the corners too fast.

They'd decided that on that still and sultry night sleep was unlikely and I had to admit that the idea of a moonlit swim in Parsley Bay sounded pretty damn good. It was late enough that we didn't have to worry about offending the dog-walking residents with our skinny-dipping.

We crossed the grassy expanse of the clearing, surrounded

on three sides by trees. In the moonlight, the low-slung shark's net looked as fragile as a spider's web. The silken surface of the water looked impossibly benign. I stood on the sand in my boots as Jake and Sam shed their clothes fast, she turning to me with a nod of appreciation towards Jake's round white buttocks as he ran towards the sweetly seductive shallows.

I'd done my stripping for the night, and for the moment I just wanted to keep myself to myself. When the other two had swum out to the shark's net and were floating on their backs, offering their bodies to the moon, I finally dropped my clothes in a heap and slowly waded into the harbour. The water on my body was like the reassuring touch of a gentle lover. Smoothing away the hard surfaces and the anger. Washing away the swell of self-hatred that made me choke in surprise when it rose from time to time.

With smooth, sure strokes I swam out to my friends, loving them both, thinking, This moment is a gift.

- So, did you enjoy yourself tonight, Jake, I said, thinking, I could just reach out and touch you now, under the water. Did you have fun?

- Yeah, did you Jake? Sam asked, still floating on her back, still offering up her breasts and pubic triangle for the great lunar caress. Isn't Soph brilliant? Isn't she a natural? Bet you got hard, Jake. Bet you did.

- Yeah, Soph was alright. Soph was good, he said, swimming right up close so I could feel him disturbing the water near me. But she looked so mean. So angry. The sort of woman you'd go to bed with knowing she was going to hurt you. The sort of woman most men aren't game to proposition.

- What about me Jake? asked Sam, as close to shy as she got.

- You, Sammy, were exquisite. You're a born coquette. Coy and enigmatic ... as though you're nowhere near showing us all you've got.

We swam in to shore, Jake before us with sharp, water-slicing strokes. Sam and I hung back so we could watch as he struggled, wet arsed, into his jeans. Turning to me, Sam whispered that if I didn't want him she was sure she could find a use for a body like his. And I laughed, a non-committal, flippant laugh that was supposed to reveal nothing.

Chipper in his sheepskin coat and pork pie hat, the old man pointed first to the seagulls on the river and then to something closer in, something being carried along by the current. On the opposite embankment, traffic hummed day and night in front of a row of one of Chelsea's most exclusive mansion blocks. One of the more expensive addresses in London, where old and new money alike bought an unobscured view of the Thames, of Battersea Park, of the dazzling Peace Pagoda and of the Battersea Power Station. The two latter structures made up in idealism what they lacked in functionalism.

The man had wandered down towards the spun sugar form of the Albert Bridge, and I, moving towards the barrier between park and river, still couldn't identify what part of the city's unnameable flotsam and jetsam he had watched so avidly. On first glance a pale tree branch was a section of woman's thigh. A black plastic bag was all that could be seen of the dark overcoat worn by a man just drowned. A green, battered barge moored a hundred metres off shore lay low in the water under its mass of river detritus; bearing great tangles of drift-wood and branches that could have passed for bird's nests as easily as they could have been mistaken for great naturalist sculptures.

The barge was probably a floating rubbish tip, but I preferred to think of it as a sanctuary or a coffin for river birds. Or as an open-air doss house for drunks scraped from the Oxford Street pavements each evening ... a great, floating rat trap.

Further west, jutting out into the river like the unfinished sentence that gnawed away at you from your past lay the Garden Festival Pier. Another wharf, hovering over dark waters, but this one so insubstantial and with so few piles lodged in the depths that it gave me very little sense of the underwharf. The structure itself wasn't the problem, rather the fact that Sydney Harbour, not the Thames, was my dream landscape. I was a foreigner in London, trying to eke some sense of mystery from a landscape that was not my own. Trying to find beauty in what was, to me, brown sludge and a melancholic sky.

- Soph, Soph, called Stanley from the steps of the Pagoda.

I trotted off towards him, my gait uneven through trying not to disturb the banana cake that lay at the bottom of my bag. I clasped a narrow, square box to my right breast. Marina was throwing newly picked, blue flower heads into the lap of the east-facing Buddha. It was Marina who had phoned me that morning to invite me on their rites of spring picnic. The bi-annual house picnic, she'd called it.

A serious picnicker, Marina led us away from the Pagoda towards the Albert Bridge, telling us it was essential that we get as far away from the car park as we could. Away from the Chelsea mothers, who drove across the river to walk their toy dogs, who left their steaming turds on the grass just a cigarette butt's throw from where their mistresses parked their cars.

On top of the red plaid blanket, she spread the banquet of breads, cheeses, olives, salads and fruit. The cake and chocolate biscuits were carefully positioned, still in their bags, under a protective layer of jackets as though the sun might actually melt them. Bottles of fizzy water were opened, Stanley explaining that he didn't like to drink in the sun and me giggling at the thought of him baking and fermenting at a Marlborough Street gathering.

- It's nothing, I said, in response to his query. I was just thinking of the amount of beer that gets drunk at your average Sydney barbie. I doubt you'd stand the pace.

- You're homesick, said Marina, clearing away empty plastic bags to sit beside me on the rug. It's good to know where you're from . . . to carry that with you.

- But Marina, I said. I'm not sure that I have a home. When I lived there, Sydney didn't seem like home . . . neither of the places where I slept on a regular basis were mine to call home.

- But now that you're away, you can see that Sydney's your place, your spiritual home, she said, lying on her side on the rug and popping an olive into her cheek. I can tell by the way you talk about it.

- Next thing she'll be planning to leave us, sighed Stanley.

- I am. She is, Marina and I said at once.

- But I've told my friend with the photography gallery about you, said Stanley. I told her I may even have some photos to show her.

- And I was going to take you to Donegal, said Marina, wistful.

- I'm not leaving yet, there are still things to do. It's just that my best friend's pregnant and I really want to be there for the birth, you know? A restless silence descended.

- I'm sure I'll be back, I continued. With my sense of synchronicity, I'll probably discover as soon as I get home that my father's been living in London all along.

- What'll you do when you get those addresses? asked Marina.

- Dunno, I said, feeling the spider legs of panic on my body. In my head I keep composing this dumb letter: Dear Mr So and So, I am Zelda's daughter and I'm planning a special reunion for all of her ex-lovers. I've only made preliminary plans at this point, so date and place are still flexible. If you feel you should be invited, please drop me a line care of the following address.

Marina shrieked, but Stanley just scrutinised the contents of a plastic bowl.

- You two are so bloody transparent. You act as though you hate men, but what you need is a good fuck!

- Oh, Stanley, I groaned. You just assume that everyone wants what you've got.

- Soph and I've got our inner lives, laughed Marina.

- Yeah, inner lives, I chimed. We've got our art ... I've got my photos and Marina's got her reading. It's as good as art, the way she consumes and dissects books.

- Art! Get out of here, said Stanley, animated and moving to sit closer to us so he could act like he was confiding in me. She only reads dirty books ... she's a real wanker, Marina is!

- Grow up, Stanley! I said, putting as much venom in my voice as anyone could in languid, picnic mode. And you stop listening at keyholes!

Marina stared daggers of mock-betrayal at me and then started to giggle.

- And as for your photos, Soph ..., he went on. From what you've told me, there're some pretty racy snaps by your bed!

- You do realise, Stanley, that you've just snookered yourself, don't you? Marina said, cool, composed. You've just proved that we don't need men!

Marina and I fell on each other, laughing, wheezing, throwing back plastic cupfuls of fizzy drink.

- But Soph needs male models for her photos ... don't you Soph? he persisted.

- Are you volunteering, Stanley? I fired back.

- Uh, uh, he muttered, blushing all over his head as only someone with so little hair could.

- Don't worry you poor, shy thing, I said, handing him the box I'd brought with me. Why don't you see how sexually stimulating you find these?

I held my breath as Stanley and Marina perused one image after the other with reverence, all the while waiting for them to start chuckling and exchanging embarrassed glances.

- Jesus Christ, said Stanley, and looked up at me and smiled.

- You're a bloody genius, said Marina, serious now. But they're so sad, so melancholic.

For a moment the three of us grinned inanely at each other.

- Well, if you really like them then I do need you, Stanley, I told him, holding out my hand. I need you to help me arrange an exhibition before I completely lose my nerve.

As we walked back towards the river, Stanley talked with excitement about how impressed Loulou, at the gallery, would be with the photos. About how he was sure she'd agree to mount a small exhibition. About how I'd be discovered and how I'd be famous as the first Sydney, Brixton, Camden photographic celebrity. But even as he spoke, I watched a Qantas plane fly overhead, going east along the Thames from Heathrow.

In the late afternoon, I felt like one of those puffer fish that Sam and I used to leave out to dry in the sun. The idea was to rid the fish of all its poison, but really it was just a cruel way of killing it. You wound up later with a solid, spike-covered ball, good for hitting out into the bay with a cricket bat. All I was good for, once I'd had all my toxins sweated out of me, and my energy sucked by the stream of customers, was collapsing into the nearest body of water; unlike the puffer fish, I would be resurrected. Sophie as phoenix would rise from the salty waters of the Boy, the Olympic pool that jutted out over Woolloomooloo Bay, and without a flame in sight the catharsis was absolute.

Lying on the topmost concrete step by the pool, I looked out across the narrow stretch of bay to the fingerwharf. It was a relief to lie there, silent and brooding after so many hours of talk, of counselling that came from who knows where. I watched the lycra-swathed swimmers glide across the field of blue, their underwater forms shimmering, rippling. The light played through water on taut, tanned bodies following dark lines along the pale blue length of the tiled pool. I liked the way the salt dried on my skin, coating me in a fine crust, tart on my darting tongue. I liked the way the light reflected off the great body of brilliant water, making me close my eyes to block out the bustle of the summer afternoon pool. Behind closed eyes I let the underwharf creep, insidiously, into my head.

I was lying, half waking, half sleeping, when a warm, damp hand was laid on my calf. Opening my eyes, confused, not alarmed, I focused on a wraith-thin, wild-haired man in baggy khaki shorts. His right hand almost completely covered the serpent.

- So beautiful. So wise, he said, not opening his eyes. It's a symbol of great wisdom.

- I don't know about that, I said, closing my eyes, feeling

unthreatened, feeling that it was the most normal of lazy conversations to be having beside a public swimming pool.

- I speak the truth, he said, his voice unwavering, the slight pressure on my leg constant. Even though you walk alone, the wisdom of your ancestors goes with you.

When I opened my eyes again, although the pressure on my leg remained, the man was gone. I swung my legs around to sit on the edge of the step, to scan the bodies for his, but everywhere was sleek lycra and slicked back hair – no brush-headed hippy in sight. Goose bumps rose on my skin. What he'd said about the serpent was an echo of something I'd heard before. That the serpent coiled around The Hermit's staff on the ninth card of the Higher Arcana was also a symbol of great wisdom. It was the card that marked the shift between growing towards the world and growing in, towards yourself.

Around the corner from Marlborough Street I stopped at my favourite milk bar to buy five Golden Gaytimes and a big bottle of fizzy water.

The house was silent with only a faint, metallic grinding sound coming from Jake's room. Dumping all but two of the ice-creams in the freezer, I padded into Jake's room with the bottle of water and the Gaytimes. He was rubbing the curvy surface of a block of sandstone that he had told me was an abstract representation of Jessie and Lila. Unable to resist the fine skin on his curved back, I silently went to slide one of the ice-creams along his spine. The way he flinched made me recoil.

- Sorry, I said, moving to sit opposite him on a milk-crate so I didn't have to look at his back, fine as it was. Jesus! What happened?

His right eye glowed with its decoration of a great aubergine-coloured blister. An almost perfect black eye.

- I should have put this on your eye, I said, handing him the ice-cream, waiting. Jake?

- It's nothing. OK? he said, still not looking at me. I slipped when I was carrying this home yesterday. Fell down and hit my head on it.

Yeah Jake, I thought to myself, looking back and forth between his eye and the flawless slab of sandstone. I looked around the room with its charcoal sketches on the walls and lumps of rock and metal strewn about the floor. His things would look out of place in my cushioned bedroom. Indeed, the pile of my clothes, a bright, mirrored skirt flung across the old green armchair in the corner - looked out of place in his.

- Do I impose on you by spending so much time here? I asked, my voice not sounding like a voice I knew. I mean, it's not just that I treat this house like a second home, but I treat your room, your bed as though they were my own. It's not as if we're lovers ...

- Impose is a dumb word to use between friends, he said through a mouth full of ice-cream. I think you'd know it if I didn't want you here, Soph.

- I must scare away all your girlfriends.

- Have you seen any hanging around lately? he asked.

- Well, no.

- You're not scaring any away then.

There was silence between us, rare not for its lack of words but for its awkwardness. Part of the reason Jake and I could spend so much time together related to the ease of both our silences and our words.

- The weirdest thing happened at the pool this afternoon, I said, catching his left eye fixed on my serpent. I was lying in the sun, half asleep, when I opened my eyes to see this hippie guy with his hand on my tattoo.

I waited for the nod of wonder, or smile of encouragement that was not forthcoming.

- He told me the serpent represented innate wisdom ... that although I was alone in the world, I carried with me the wisdom of my ancestors.

- You really talk bullshit sometimes, Jake said, leaning over his rock again without meeting my eyes. You live in a fucking fantasy world.

- Is that what you think? I asked, winded. And if I do, what of it?

Silence again. Infuriating, untouchable silence.

- Why is it so different from the world you inhabit with all these lumps of rock and metal?

I sat, waiting for a response. Waiting for an indication that he'd even heard me. Nothing. I stood, took a vicious slug of water, and threw myself face down on the bed so I could lie and sulk in comfort. I could lie and seethe against Jake and breathe in the comforting smell of him on his pillows at the same time.

I woke at the clatter of the girls' return, confused to find myself asleep when it was still light outside. Jake, asleep beside me, lay facing me on his side, his arm outstretched as though he'd been just about to touch me before he fell asleep. Sitting up, moving quietly so as not to wake him, I slipped from the room, closing the door behind me.

Golden with the sun's parting rays, the kitchen retained the afternoon's warmth that had retreated from the thick-walled depths of the Victorian house. Sam and Jessie were rubbing moisturiser into their sunburnt breasts, and Lila, cancer conscious, pretended she hadn't burnt in the slightest and concentrated on cutting green vegetables for dinner. Of course, it was *her* nipples that peeled three days later.

- Hi Soph, said Sam, giving me a coconut smelling bare-chested hug. We saw you two asleep but didn't want to disturb you.

- You looked so post-coital, said Jessie, prolonging the moisturising process and looking, wet-lipped, in Lila's direction.

- Did you do it? Sam asked, holding a cold bottle up to her bright red nipple. Did you and Jake finally do it?

- How post-coital can you be fully clothed? I said, shaking my head. Anyway, where've you been? Looks like you've just come from an orgy.

We languished in the kitchen, all glowing shades of pink and red after a day in the sun. They'd been at Tamarama, sun-bathing topless and making a great show of periodically sluicing each other with creamy blockout.

- It's such a sexy place, said Jessie. You should try it. Might do wonders for your libido.

- According to Sammy, she doesn't need any help, said Jake, appearing on cue in the doorway. Ugh. Can't a man walk around in his own house without being accosted by naked breasts and libido?

- This is our house, said Jessie and Lila at once, grab-bing him, running creamy hands over his body. And no, a man can't.

- God, he said, swatting their hands away. A man just wants to drink a beer after a long day's work and look what he has to contend with.

- We're just not used to you looking so damn sexy, all black-eyed and butch, said Lila, laying a cold zucchini on the swollen eye-lid for a moment then turning to the sink.

- What are we eating? he asked, moving in beside Lila. Great. Half a market garden!

- You have to remove all the fat from your diets, said Lila on her favourite topic, waving a vegetable knife around and inadvertently flinging pale green slices onto the floor. Especially if you want to go on drinking.

- We do, we do, said Sam, downing her VB in one.

- As we get older our bodies just can't go on dealing with all the shit we've been pouring down our throats, Lila said, dazzling us with her knife skills, snarling at Jessie with her hand in a bag of corn chips. Jake, you're not exempt from this lecture . . . you're the least active of all of us. You don't dance and you don't fuck. You'll be piling on pudge before our very eyes.

Sam and I looked at each other and snickered. Lila could talk; she was short and Rubenesque where Jake was tall and lean. Fiercely protective of her gal, Jessie turned the chill stare of her turquoise eyes on us. How dare we laugh at Lila.

- Jake's work is very physical, I volunteered.

Jake was sitting half in and half out of the room; with his legs out in the yard, he leaned against the door frame. Mostly he looked away from us, out into the darkness.

After dinner, Sam and Jessie gobbled their ice-creams under Lila's unforgiving gaze. The combined effects of sun and alcohol had gone to our heads, and when we burst out of the house we half galloped, half staggered down the road to hail a taxi. With skin tomato-peel tight and fit to split, we headed for a party in Woolloomooloo. The night had a freshness to it that you could just about bite after the soporific heat of the day. Free of the heavy heat shackles, people we passed in the street moved with twice the speed of their daytime actions, gorging themselves on great gulps of crisp night air.

Down in the bay, we piled out at the quietest of the waterfront pubs, the one that hadn't been embellished with tubes of neon and plastic menus for seafood lunches. The Bells was exceptional for its air of unremarkability. It was the sort of pub where you could sit at the bar on a high stool attached to the ground and drink yourself into a stupor quite undisturbed if you were a bloke. If you were a woman, the stupefied cod beside you might periodically lean across to offer you a drink. As though you might not be capable of buying your own passage to oblivion.

Jake took up residency at the bar and we girls circled the pool table with tequilas and vodkas in hand. Before we'd even started the game of doubles, I knew Sam and I would lose. We lost to Jessie and Lila when we were drunk and they lost to us when we were either sober or on speed. Nevertheless, what we lacked in skill when tipsy, we made up for in bravado. Jessie and Lila were cool sharks at the pool table, while Sam and I were dags, cheering inanely when we did something right, pouting and disconsolate when we did something wrong. I played pool because I loved the feeling of chalked cue connecting with solid sphere of dense plastic, loved the clacking sound that the balls made when they hit each other square on, and loved the magic of sinking one every now and then. Sam played because she loved the theatre of it, and Jessie and Lila played to win.

By the time it was my round at the bar, Sam and I were getting wiped off the table and I no longer cared to watch. When I sought out Jake for commiseration, his stool was empty and his glass not quite full. I knew he'd gone, but I had to be sure. I leant against the door of the men's loos, and opening it with my bottom, called his name. In response I got some low-level abuse from one old-timer and a whiff of urine that scoured my nostrils. I told Sam to finish up and go on to the party without me; I knew where it was. I went out into the night in search of my friend.

I knew where *I'd* go in that part of the world to get away from things. Across the road loomed the fingerwharf in dark silhouette, and although the underwharf was invisible in the night, I could hear the slapping of the water against hundreds of rotting piles. I wondered if that bulky beast would sink into the harbour one day, burying its secrets beneath it, or whether it would be renovated and sanitised like some of the wharves in the west harbour.

I walked fast past the sewerage plant, not stopping to check, but sure I could see the low curve of the bag woman, asleep on the warm concrete of its roof. How had she, an unloved woman on the street, outlived Nella? I reached the dark, tree-lined steps I would have to climb, and remembered Nella's warnings about only going to the point by the road at night. Then I thought of the tough old bag lady, and sprinted up the steps.

Although I hadn't been there often since Nella's death, I knew the way to the point as well as I knew the dark path from Zelda's house to my rock. The moon hung low and buttery in the sky, illuminating the curves of the tarred path. And I wasn't sorry to be out of the pub, away from the clutching, clinging cigarette smoke and the sticky carpet that reminded me of the strip club. It was quiet out there, with sandstone and Moreton Bay Fig trees on one side and water slapping against the sea wall on the other. If someone came at me, down the sheer rock wall, or from behind, I could run to where Jake would be sitting in silence on the point.

But there was just me, hot skin stretched taut across my cheeks and shoulders, and the pale figure on the bench right at the point. It was one of those nights on the harbour when the sheer spectacle of the water itself replaced any urge to gaze at the bridge or to ogle the Opera House, or to stare, wide-eyed at the fairy land of white lights on the opposite shore. The light, it seemed, was in the water. The moon bled a crooked path out towards the Heads and all the light from the harbour foreshores danced slow and sexy on the water's surface.

- Hey, I said, sitting on the bench beside him and taking his cold hand in mine.

- Why did you follow me? he asked, his voice as lifeless as his hand, resting limp and sorry in my own.

- I missed you, I told him, moving his fingers to my lips for a moment and then holding his hand in my lap. I wanted to talk to you.

- Why?

- To understand.

- What's to understand?

- Do you want the questions chronologically or by subject? I snapped. I don't think you're very honest with me. Not in the way I'm honest with you.

- So? I'm just your confessor, he said blandly, taking his hand back and wedging it between the bench and his thigh. That doesn't mean I'll confess to you.

- Fuck you Jake, I said. You're the person who's the closest to me in the world right now. Please don't turn away from me.

And when I said that I knew it was true, that a distance had opened between Sam and me. A slight breeze stirred coloured chip bags on the grass.

- So, what do you want to know? he said, a flatness bordering on belligerence in his voice. If you were one of the others, you'd ask me why I wasn't fucking anyone, but seeing as it's you and

we've reached a stalemate on that one, you'll want to know who
I've been brawling with.

- I want to know why you lied to me this afternoon.
- Has anyone really close to you ever hit you?
- Sam hit me once, when she was really out of it, I admitted.
- And you didn't want anyone to know, did you? he asked,
but his voice was still dead flat. You just wanted to protect her,
to make it all better, didn't you?
- Something like that, yes, I said, remembering how in my
head I'd made a million excuses for her, and how we'd never
discussed it, just not seen each other for a few days.
- Last night, my father hit me, he said, matter-of-fact, as
though he were telling me his Dad had made him a cup of tea.
- I don't understand.
- What's to understand? He's just an ugly drunk, that's all.
- Don't be flippant, tell me what happened, I said, moving
to crouch in front of him so he had to look at me and feeling
the shudder when I put my hands on his knees.
- I went to see my Mum, like I do sometimes. Dropped in
with some flowers, and photos of that piece I just finished, he
told me, still managing to look out to sea and not at me. She
was looking really tired, you know? Told me Dad had been
having real trouble keeping work and drink separate. He just lost
a contract on a house ... been working on the plans for days.

Jake stood up then and walked away, down towards the
water, and continued speaking with his back to me.

- She kept saying she thought it was getting worse, that it
was a bit of a vicious circle, said Jake, his voice strained. Anyway,
she got a bit teary and that's when Dad came in.

His voice trailed away as the noise of a floating disco tainted
the night, all 70s pop and lurid, flashing lights.

- As soon as he saw her, he started to yell about how he's tired of her crying, how she makes him sick, he said between songs. Barely acknowledged me, just mumbled something about not listening to her stories. She started to say that we were both worried about him. Next thing I know, he picks her up and he's shaking her like a rag doll ... cursing her as though it was all her fault ... telling her she was turning me against him.

- And? I asked, wanting to go to him, but forcing myself to stay on the bench.

- That's when I finally moved in, pushed between them. He dropped her and turned, swinging his fist as he came towards me.

- I'm sorry, I said.

- For a moment, before he actually hit me, I saw pure hatred in his eyes, he said, stopping to take a few deep breaths, swallowing sobs. Mum and I were both on the floor, stunned. He just stormed out, smashing the glass in the front door behind him.

- And your mother? Where is she now?

- She's there at home. With him! he said, his voice cracking. She won't leave ... says she still loves him. She's just going to stay.

- Jake, I said, going to him and taking him in my arms as his body welcomed the sobs it had been blocking. I'm sorry. I'm so sorry.

For a few moments we just stood there, swaying on the uneven ground. Then his body stiffened again and he put a rough hand in my hair, holding my face up close to his.

- You feel really sorry for me now, don't you? he said, his voice bitter like I'd never heard it before. You wanna seduce me now? Make you feel better, having done your bit for the pathetic boy?

- Jake.

- Then you can go and wave your pussy at a whole room full of old men ... fuck the one who fits your fantasy.

I raised my hand to slap his face, but just held it there, unable to hit him and unable to pull away.

- See? he scorned. You feel so sorry for me you can't even hit me. And Soph, you should hit a bloke when he talks to you like that.

He pulled away then, turned his back and was gone, walking fast, disappearing in the shadows beside the road and not looking back.

In the white, porcelain splendour of Randolphe's bath tub I shaved my legs for the first time in months and examined the serpent. My rough skin absorbed moisturiser like butter on hot toast, and my legs assumed a chalky sheen. Even my nipples had cracked over the long winter and would have felt coarse to a lover's tongue.

When Randolphe called me to the telephone, he raised one eyebrow at my bare legs and tatty, Sydney cut-offs, or perhaps it was at the serpent.

Jane, from the publisher's office, began immediately to recount a conversation she'd had with the elderly editor about Zelda.

- I tried to explain to her about this study you're doing, though I'm not sure I quite understand it myself, she said, businesslike when we both knew that she was going out of her way. She said Zelda knew some of those writers you want to contact ... they'd probably be delighted to help you out.

- Really, I said, feigning surprise.

- Her writers were usually quite dedicated.

- Was this editor a friend of Zelda's? I asked.

Across the room, Randolphe sat in a rug-covered, overstuffed armchair, reading the paper and circling things with a vicious sweep of his red pen.

- She had a hell of a lot of respect for her, Jane said, awkward, trying to say the right thing. She's supposed to have been a brilliant editor but terrifying to work for.

She waited for me to protest, but I just played with the curls of plastic-coated wire.

- I'm not saying she was bad-tempered, just volatile. Passionate, you know?

- Yeah, I know, I said, uncomfortable in my treachery. She's still like that. Probably more grumpy than volatile now, though.

I copied down twelve addresses in three separate continents and the British Isles, as Jane dictated. For her it was a routine enquiry – for me it was something terrifying in its immediacy. Something that would force me to act.

With my eyes darting up and down the list till the room started to spin, it was difficult to take my leave of Jane without sounding like I was rushing off to be ill.

In the silence, loud after the babble of my conversation, again I scrolled my eyes over the list of addresses. France, Italy, Ireland, England, America, Australia. I placed asterisks beside those names, those addresses, that somehow resonated with me more deeply than the others. After five minutes, the only author without a mark beside his name was the one who lived in Perth.

As I sat at the table by the window, alternately staring at the page and at the pale sunlight on the shrubs outside, Randolphe rose and left the room. In the kitchen, the sound of crockery being moved around made me remember, with guilt, the mess

I'd left there the night before. Marina's excitement would be pure as a child's and Stanley would roll his eyes and stutter. Sam, in a high pitched voice, would advocate house calls for every one of them. Jake would mumble that I just didn't need a father.

Randolphe manoeuvred into the room with a frail precision, bearing a tray laden with fruit buns, butter, milk, and his best silver teapot.

- You know the way to my heart, I said, moving in to sit on the scratchy foot-stool by his chair. Did you and Nella drink pots of tea together?

- Only on a few occasions, he said, in the tone he always used to answer such wistful questions. I didn't grow up with her as you did. They moved to Australia when I was ten, leaving me here at boarding school.

- That's so unfair, I said, feeling my legs tense as they did when I was angry with Zelda.

- I wanted to speak to you about Nella, he said, pouring the tea. I wanted to tell you that I knew she was going to kill herself. She wrote to tell me a few weeks before.

I stared into my tea cup, searching for some appropriate response, but the pale, mud-coloured liquid was inscrutable.

- Why did you tell me that? I asked, wanting to block my ears.

- If you think Zelda's guilty of not preventing her death, then so am I, he said, his eyes sad. If that's why you've pushed Zelda away, then I deserve the same treatment.

- But you couldn't have done anything, I said, small voiced. You were all the way over here. You couldn't have convinced her that she'd be looked after ... could go on living for years and years.

- Why couldn't I? he asked. I could have flown to Sydney and taken responsibility, made a scene and insisted she let me see to everything. I chose not to.

- Why? I asked, wanting to scream at him that I didn't want to be having this conversation, that I didn't want to know.

- I respected her wishes, he said, almost apologetically. Because I loved her, and I didn't want her to suffer.

- That's the difference between you and Zelda, I said, my voice cold, sharp as broken glass. Zelda neither loved nor respected Nella.

- That's not true Sophie. When we were children she worshipped Nella.

- Crap! I said bitterly. She only worships herself.

- When Zelda was fifteen, she fought so bitterly with our father that they rarely spoke again, he said, watching me closely. On one of his trips back to Sydney, Zelda confronted him. Said he was making Nella miserable. Accused him of cheating on her.

- What did he say?

- He neither denied nor accepted her accusations. He slapped her across the face and told her how dare she speak to her father like that.

- What did she do? I asked, wondering just how long she'd been getting the last word.

- Slapped him back, he said, a twinkle in his eye. Told him he was too old and too ugly to play the gigolo.

- Really? I laughed, thinking, Alright Zelda.

- You know what I'm asking you? he said, gripping my hand in his so I could see where the veins were knotting the way Nella's had. What I'm asking for you to do for my sake, and for Nella's?

I shook my head.

- I'm asking you to give her another chance. To speak to her as an adult.

- Dolphi, I said, wanting to run from the room and from him and from my conscience, and to dance until I forgot who I was. I don't even know how to begin. It's been so long since we've talked.

- You'll think of something, he said, smiling, buttering a bun.

- She'll expect me to apologise.

- Perhaps it's better to focus on the future, he prompted. Perhaps you should ask her for advice. It's amazing how flattered people feel when asked for advice.

- I've never asked her for advice, I said, looking for a way out of the conversation and seeing the list by the telephone. I can't imagine that there's anything she knows that would be of much use to me.

- You'll think of something my dear, he repeated, passing me the plate with the buns. How much longer do we have?

- Six weeks, maybe, I said, thinking more that it was six weeks before I would see Zelda rather than six weeks with Randolphe.

- I don't quite know how I'll survive without you, he said.

- Don't tease, I said. You'll be relieved. The gas bill'll plummet, the kitchen'll be pristine, no more late-night creaking of the stairs, no bug-eyed dreg beside you on the heath.

- Exactly, he said. How will I survive?

I rose to sit on the arm of his chair and hugged him. I wasn't used to such openness from him and the warmth and sadness in his voice made me want to crush his whole body to mine.

- Come with me! I said, with such a flash of inspiration that I bumped the tea table and caused an excited clatter of crockery. Move to Sydney! You'd love it. You could live in Nella's flat.

We'd just kick out the tenants like that. You'd love it.

- Oh, child, he said. This is my home ... where I want to live out my days. I'm too old and too comfortable to go gallivanting around the world like a twenty-year-old.

- But Randolphe, you're not old. You've got more energy than me.

- I'm just a better actor, he said, pushing me away so he could pour more tea. I've had longer to practise.

THE STAR

Pushed along by a cushion of hot fetid air from the subway, I emerge sticky with my own sweat onto one of the marble walkways to Grand Central Station. I think about how the fingerwharf would have once been this way – all comings and goings and people and life.

And then I'm in the vast gaping space that's the biggest open concourse in the world. Having spent a lifetime preparing for this train trip, I could so easily miss it by standing agog, eyes fixed on the deep ocean blue of the ceiling's night sky one hundred odd feet above, trying to count each of those 2500 gold stars. The marble staircase that sweeps with such elegance from the concourse up to Vanderbilt Avenue also distracts, as does the bar on the terrace to the right. How delicious to sit and watch, separated from the world decisively by the low marble columns of the wall, a barrier that would define so well the space between voyeur and real people.

But I stand with the other commuters, staring at the board that confirms the town my father lives in does, in fact, exist.

I am gripped by an irrational, choking panic, convinced that something will go wrong; I've lost my ticket, the clocks on the concourse are slow and the train has left, I'll be hit by a lightning bout of dysentery and will stand, immobile on the concourse as my boots fill with my own shit that smells of terror. But none of these things happen, no-one comes along to surreptitiously slide a blade between my ribs, I am not arrested as an impostor, a pretender, a girl who thinks that perhaps she is someone.

The guard at the arch leading to the platform glances at my ticket and waves me on. I'd expected a struggle to get down the platform onto the train and into a seat, wanted a physical struggle, but the platform represents a calmer zone than my own mind. And I just go on telling myself to keep moving, to keep on. To sit on the left-hand side of the train so I can stare at the Hudson all the way.

In my mind's eye I glimpse him, my father. Dark eyes pierce me from the images on his book jacket, yet look inwards. He, going about his quiet, writerly life by the river that he loves.

The train weaves its way under Manhattan and emerges on the island's western shore, further uptown than I know. Out of the corner of my eye I see a drift-wood fire burning between the tracks, and brown, rag-clad people, clustering around the flames. As if the cold that wracked their bodies in the bitter winter months is still there, despite the day's oppressive *humidity. With a jolt, I understand the privileges Zelda has given me.*

Nights of stripping blurred one into the other. We'd leave the club around three, having drunk ourselves sober between sets as the night wore on.

What fascinated me about stripping was how quickly I got used to it. How quickly I shed the residual skin of modesty. What I couldn't get used to was being touched by men after the show. Being poked like a great peach, to check for ripeness. Having men run their hands over my arse as they would the curves of a Porsche they could never afford.

The moonlit swims were rare now, and normally it was just Sam and I, stumbling down the stairs and out into the street.

Despite the cool autumn drizzle on Darlinghurst Road, I told Sam I needed to walk. Needed the air. It was a week since Jake and I had discussed his father. A week since he'd walked away from me in the night.

- Honestly, I said, as we walked beneath the Coca-Cola sign at the Hyatt. I can't believe you were seriously considering that guy's offer.

- Why not? He wasn't particularly ugly or anything.

- That's got nothing to do with it.

- That's got everything to do with it.

- It doesn't matter who the guy is, or what he looks like, it's still prostitution. Would you really fuck someone you didn't know for fifty bucks?

- I'd probably try and charge more, she said, with such savvy I wanted to hit her. Depending on how good looking he was.

There was silence between us as we left the last red, glowing overflow from the Cross and moved into the more residential part of Darlinghurst. Even in the hub of inner-city partyland, most lights in the flats and terraces had been extinguished. The cars that drove up and down Darlinghurst Road at that hour of the morning were up to no bloody good.

- I think fucking someone you don't really like is just the same as fucking someone for money, only doing it for money's smarter, she said, baiting me. How many of the men you've fucked have you actually liked, Soph?

The drizzle was turning into rain and already my shirt was sticking to my shoulders and the denim on my thighs was heavy. Two out of ten, I thought, but I wasn't going to give her the satisfaction of telling her.

- Why are you so desperate for money all of a sudden? I asked, You're no great consumer. You buy as few clothes as I do.

- A girl's got to party, Soph, she said, a harder note in her voice. I'm hardly going to sit at home every night listening to you and Jake talk about life, art and the universe, am I? More to it than that.

- So, it's all going on drugs then, I goaded. You're buying lots of drugs.

- Not lots of drugs Sophie. Never lots of drugs. I respect my body. I only buy quality products and they cost money.

- Oh, so they do, I said, side-stepping a horde of newly released clubbers.

The crowd was all around us one moment, engulfing us in a cloud of cigarette smoke, cheap perfume and stale dance-floor sweat, and the next moment gone. Turning in unison into an all night café and leaving the street to us again.

- I know you're scared of drugs, she said, with the syrupy

Trust me voice of the family GP before he shoves in the speculum. It doesn't make you a dag or anything.

- Well, thanks Sam, that really reassures me, I said. Drugs mess with my head ... I can't give a real reading for days afterwards. The images on the cards don't connect with my intuition.

- Just because you can't handle it doesn't mean I can't, she said as we turned off Oxford Street and headed up into slumbering Surry Hills. You think you know all there is to know about me Soph, what with us practically growing up together, but I'm telling you, a lot of the time you're just guessing.

Her tone wasn't bitter, but her words revealed a true antipathy and made me stop, mid-stride. I watched my friend as she stopped, too, a couple of paces ahead, and turned to face me. She didn't laugh, she didn't make a silly joke and pretend, she just stood and stared me down, a gutter glint in her pale brown eyes. I faltered, wanting to give her an emotional kick in both shins.

- Race you home, I said instead, charging off up the road, kicking an empty strawberry Moove carton in front of me, and in my forced mirth, erasing our conversation from the clean slate of the early morning.

We arrived at the house, damp with sweat and drizzle, running the length of Marlborough Street in step. Tiptoeing down the darkened hallway, we tried to regulate our breath, as though the sin of deep breathing might wake the whole house. In the kitchen, we crammed pieces of carrot cake in our mouths and washed them down with apple juice, smiling at each other now, conspirators in the furtive sport of midnight feasting.

- You want to stay with me tonight? she asked.
- Um, might see if I can squeeze in with Jake, I said, thinking

both of the cockroaches and that it was probably time for a reconciliation.

Sam just shrugged and walked out of the room, leaving me to brush my teeth at the kitchen sink alone. In the hallway I took off my wet clothes so as not to disturb him, quietly pushed the door open and crept inside. Jake's breathing was inaudible. As my eyes adjusted to the dark, I saw that the bed was empty, and from the stairs I could hear Sam softly calling my name.

Upstairs we both crouched outside Jessie and Lila's door, holding our breath. From inside the room came sounds of movement; light, wet slapping sounds and uneven breathing. I could hear Lila saying, It's inside you now, I'm fucking you now, and then the sound of a deeper, male voice, moaning. Maybe in pain, maybe in pleasure. And then Jessie's voice saying no, no, not yet, not yet. Then the man's voice, Jake's voice, saying Oh God, I'm gonna come, I'm gonna . . .

Sam and I watched each other for a reaction as the sounds of sex subsided. Looking for traces of jealousy, of lust, or even of disgust.

- Have you seen how big the girls' dildo is? mouthed Sam, backing into her room and pushing the door to.

I hesitated there with my hand on the doorknob, my body shaking. But as soon as I heard movement in the room again, I turned and fled, stumbling on the landing and scrabbling about on the floor to pick up what I'd dropped. Partly dressing in the hallway, I only stopped for a moment in the street below to look up at the open french doors leading to the girls' bedroom, and to see the silhouette of someone standing at the curtains, a soft light flickering behind.

In the taxi that took me across the Bridge, my heart beat fast and my whole body tingled. A little voice inside my head called me a stupid bitch and said I should have walked right in. Another voice told me it was none of my business. The first voice said that it bloody well was. The second voice said Who cares, you're out of here! I just leaned back in the seat, asked the driver if he would please put on the radio, and watched the harbour spin by below me. With the sun rising over the eastern suburbs and 70s disco playing, I opened the window all the way, and in my dark sunglasses pretended I was a girl detective from Hawaii Five-O.

On the stark walls of a small gallery behind Brixton High Street, the warped, fractured images of Regent's Canal and the groups of kids that scuttled about its tow path brought north and south London together. It wasn't a single group of people I'd chosen to study, or the daily drama of the tow path with its runners, lovers and drunks; it was the canal itself, the play of shadow and light on the scum-topped water, the way that in places the buildings forming part of the canal wall appeared to cower at their proximity to the abyss. Above all though, it was the yawn I was obsessed with, the gaping emptiness in a city so filled up with itself. Sometimes the canal felt to me like the city's only possible zone for dreaming. The only quiet, watery place for melancholia, or for an intimate lovers' stroll. A place for suicide, for murder, and for sex.

In one night, I hung the twenty-seven shots, all mounted, none framed. The process itself distanced me from the work in a way that the developing hadn't, made me feel less like I was hanging up flaps of my own flesh for public inspection. It made me able to bear the concept of not being able to screen the images from hostile eyes. Stanley and Loulou had started helping at seven, after Loulou had spent hours during the day in her darkroom working to a deadline. At eight-thirty she went home, full of encouragement, leaving the imprint of her bear-hug on both of our bodies. At nine-thirty Stanley went out for a pizza and came back with steaming tubs of soul food from a café by the recreation centre, which burnt my mouth and made my nose run. At two, I pushed him out into the cool of night, telling him not to wait up for me.

It wasn't that there were still photos to be hung, rather there were photos to be re-arranged. Shuffling; mixing and re-mixing the images until I could finally read the story. Like turning a kaleidoscope ever so slightly to one side or the other, each adjustment produced a whole new effect. I experimented with sequences of light and dark, of activity and stillness, and then emptiness, the void, gradually dissolving into bustle, light and action. By four I'd come up with single-word titles for each image, to write with bold strokes on the tiny cards Loulou had left for me. By five, I'd decided to leave the cards blank.

After another hour just sitting, legs crossed on the parquet floor, absorbing the feel of a room filled with my own photographs, I began to relax. To uncoil, and lose my resistence. To like the idea, finally, of strangers looking at my work. Of strangers passing comment, perhaps even purchasing an image that had previously inhabited my dream landscape. Of course, I'd stripped for strangers, and had sex with near strangers, but those were surface acts. Acts that involved a woman's body, any woman's body, and from which I could coolly distance myself.

Outside, buses and cars on Brixton High Street were already aiming themselves at the West End. As I walked through the sleep numbed back streets, I thought of Randolphe, striding out on Parliament Hill. I tried to transpose an image of him onto the early morning foreshores of Sydney Harbour. What would he wear in that context, in the heat? I couldn't imagine what he'd substitute for the red wine and cigars of his journalist's club, or for the reticent company of the women with whom he conducted his most proper relationships. Nor could I see him at the beach, pale legs glowing like strips of white neon tubing. I could imagine only too well though, his disappointment, his despair over not being able to find a quiet, gentleman's pub in which to sit and read. I suspected that he was right. He was too old for it. He would be lost in translation rather than flourish in it.

Ripe for sleep, I sat on the top of a bus that took me across Clapham Common, where my eyes were soothed by the fresh, green havoc of summer leaves. I was carried level with first-floor flats, past windows part-opened. Pale curtains, being sucked outside in the morning breeze. Carried past kitchens where half-dressed women who lived above shops reached listlessly for the switch of the electric kettle.

Crossing the Chelsea Bridge in the early morning begged comparisons I'd promised myself not to make between Sydney Harbour and the Thames. Twisting backwards in my seat I watched the four massive chimneys of the Battersea Power Station, trying to imagine the great balloons of steam that must have once spewed from the monster's nostrils. The building was more sleeping dragon than derelict shell. I imagined that one day it would stir to life again, to belch its smoke and flame out over the Thames. To sully genteel Chelsea with a vengeance.

By the time I was sitting on the smaller bus, heading north from Oxford Circus against the traffic, the outside world had begun to blur. With my eyes closed, the rhythm of the bus dictated the pace of canal images that flashed before my eyes. And every now and then there'd be a foreign image, a wild card, a black and white glimpse of the underwharf, of the water through the trees from my rock, or of the heavy, silt-loaded banks of the Thames.

In his kitchen, Randolphe was sipping tea over the pink pages of the *Financial Times*. He tutted at me when I told him I'd been up all night at the gallery, but I heard the excitement in his voice when he announced how long we'd need to get to Brixton by bus that evening. Randolphe was a great believer in being able to see where you've come from and where you're going to, and as a consequence rarely used the Underground. I kissed him on the cheek, dislodging crumbs of toast, and stumbled off to bed, lulled by the sure, halting rhythm of all the buses I'd ever ridden.

I'd intended to rise, and to linger over the cards, to calm and reassure myself, but found that I didn't need to. Found that once I'd woken, had lain in the bath singing Blondie songs that bounced back at me off the white tiled walls, had dressed in the purple fabric that no longer reminded me of Dick, and had shaken my whole head of hair around so it would dry before we left, there was neither time nor inclination for the cards. Downstairs, Randolphe mixed bloody marys and picked at the smart purple tie I'd given him, the one he only ever wore out with me.

- You do look lovely, yes, you do, he said, casting an eye over me that, as usual, declined to look as far as my boots. Are you sure I shouldn't be wearing a dinner jacket?

- Dolphi, we're going to Brixton, I said, giggling at the prospect of the dinner jacket on the bus. This gallery's about as close to the street as anything but the gutter could be. You'll be the only one there wearing a suit ... it's no Groucho Club!

- I don't want to let you down my dear, he said, taking polite sips from his glass and pretending not to notice the way I tossed mine back. Why don't you wear this for luck ... Nella would have wanted you to have it.

From his jacket pocket he took a tiny velvet box. I held it in both hands, vaguely afraid of it. In it lay a ring adorned with a large, water smooth chunk of lapis lazuli, its colour in places rich and in others pale. The lapis sat cradled in a finely wrought, lacy silver base, cold beside the unexpected warmth of the stone.

- It's beautiful, I whispered, slipping the ring onto my second finger and feeling the immediate reassurance of its weight, its perfect fit. Was it Nella's?

- It was, he said. It was the first gift my father gave her. The first time he told her he loved her.

- Hmpf, I snorted. That didn't last long, did it?

- Maybe it did, maybe it didn't, he said, pouring more of the vodka and tomato juice. As she told it, they were once terribly in love.

- When did she give it to you?

He went to speak, then moved over to the window where the light of the early evening danced with the night.

- Oh, she just sent it to me one day, not even registered post, he mused. Thought it might encourage me to find a good woman ...

- And so? I prompted. Didn't you ever meet anyone worthy of it?

- Not until I met you, he said, squeezing my hand. I'm not a courageous man. Love is not for the fainthearted.

On my second long bus trip of the day I sat upstairs with Randolphe, and together we watched the wilting, relaxed look of the city after what had been for London, a hot day. The West End seemed softer in those summer months, with workers looking vaguely foolish in their relative states of undress, unused to exposing arms, legs, pink flesh that had been burnt in the park at lunch-time.

Crossing the Thames for the second time, this time nearer to Whitehall and the South Bank, again I mourned the river's inaccessibility, its forbidding banks that offered only syphilitic rats and sucking mud to the would-be wader. I mourned the possibility of walking a breezy shore in the heat and the magical privilege of watching the moon bleed a long trail over an expanse of open water. I mourned Sydney Harbour.

Brixton hummed, with music pumping from open car windows. Bare-limbed people boogeyed on down the road, nursing open cans of Red Stripe beer. Children stayed out playing in the streets 'til after nine, and then fell into bed, exhausted, to sleep under a single cotton sheet with the breeze and the music from someone else's party pushing at a dusty curtain.

I took Dolphi's arm as we crossed the High Street, my dress damp at my armpits and at my thighs. I felt the heat emanating from his black sleeve and smiled at his sense of protocol. As we strolled down the lane towards the gallery, feigning nonchalance, Randolphe kept saying Well, well, well.

Before we reached the corner I heard Pogues music cavorting in the heat. Stanley's choice. He said the Pogues were synonymous with Camden, with the canal, that they would help evoke the right atmosphere. Really, I knew he was just one hell of a Pogues fan, and that the music made him feel happy, reckless. The sound of talk and of laughter also greeted us, but of this I was suspicious. I wouldn't have put it past Stanley to decide that this, too, was a way of evoking atmosphere, a taped version of the real thing.

Turning to look through the door and the windows that faced

out onto the street involved such a conscious effort on my part that Randolphe, feeling my reticence, slipped his arm around my waist. It would be one or the other, I was thinking, an empty, photograph-filled space, or a room crammed with all the people I'd ever halfway known.

The room looked much smaller than it had when I was alone there in the morning, and my first impression when I faced it head on was that it was another room. A place that had nothing to do with me. At first glance I recognised none of the chic people sipping bottled beer, engaging fixedly with each other, not with the photographs. Randolphe pushed me forward, into the smoky chatter and smiled like a child when Stanley shook his hand and then filled it with a bottle of Mexican beer. As things settled into some sort of focus I saw that I did, in fact, recognise a few of the people. That Stanley's awkward charm had convinced everyone I'd met in London to come and stand in that room for half an hour, in order to sip beer for nothing and humour me.

Grinning inanely, despite my cynicism, I looked on while Marina came to kiss me and lead Randolphe off around the walls to see something of Camden that he might not already know. And, there was me, not smoking, not drinking, not talking to anyone; a fly on the wall. But suddenly it was Sophie this and Sophie that, hands clutching at my wrists and elbows, pressing cold clammy bottles upon me and hot dry kisses on my cheeks. When the brave few had attempted to discuss the photos, rather than just saying Wonderful Darling, instead of shaking with dread I shook with excitement. Having my photos discussed as though they were something more than a hobby left over from childhood made my head spin. For the first time in years I'd done something I was halfway happy with.

Funny how in an evening when so much of import, of heart-felt sincerity, is spoken you can remember almost none of it. You can remember the sensation of being bathed in goodwill, a feeling akin to lying by the pool and feeling the salt dry spotty on your skin, but you just can't remember the words.

I recall Randolphe beaming from ear to ear, wandering around between groups with his jacket off. Chatting to 'the young people'. I recall him coming up to me shortly after we'd arrived to tell me with pained sincerity that it was the women in our family who'd ended up with all the real talent. Later he and Stanley moved outside to smoke cigars, as though both celebrating a difficult birth.

I recall Loulou introducing me to a photographer's agent, a woman who pressed her slick grey card into my hand and stood so close to me to talk that I could see her pale scalp through the bleached-blonde bristles of her hair. And I recall Stanley taking me off in a corner to insist I drink a miniature bottle of mescal, worm and all, before moving down the road to the serious dance zone of the Fridge.

- I'm so very, very proud of you, Randolphe said, clutching both my hands with bone crushing strength before he went out to find a taxi. If only Zelda could have been here ...

I found myself agreeing with him, yes, if only Zelda could have been there. If only the other half of my world could have been there, those from that place I called home.

And in my state of alcohol and pleasure-induced euphoria, I wasn't out to debase myself. To do something mean and tough-arsed, or to play the slut at my own party. I was just out to have fun. To dance with my friends, and tell them all how much I loved them, and to hear them saying Don't go Soph, Stay with us, Don't go. And to know that I was going, going home.

For most of the day thunder had been bouncing off the harbour foreshores in a parody of Zelda's wrath. It wasn't that she was angry when I finally told her I was leaving. In fact, her reaction amounted to little more than a shrug and a teetering trip to the drinks cabinet. It was in the weeks between my announcement and actual departure that she'd worn her shroud of fury whenever she was at home. None of this anger was directed at me; it seemed to diffuse in the atmosphere and hang on every wall of the house.

She'd been ranting about the inefficiency of her assistant, which I read as the fellow's reluctance to engage with her in extra-curricular activities. She'd been fuming about the reviewers' negative consensus over a novel that she'd chosen to champion herself; that of a former lover, I assumed. And every now and then, she'd rant about London, in an abstract way, about what a dirty, crowded, cold, prejudiced city it was. This last series of outbursts was the most confusing, as Nella had told me that Zelda had blossomed in London, that she'd been transformed from an angry young woman to an inspired fury in a matter of years.

The thunder storm came the day before my departure. Padding around in the morning, barefoot, I chuckled in wicked delight as Zelda swept out of the house before the storm had broken, wearing fawn suede shoes and a great, billowing copper silk outfit, all clacking beads and Opium. She hadn't smelt the rain in the air, or heard the furious calls of the birds before the storm, or even caught a glimpse of the great black mass of clouds gathering in the south-east, just offshore. How she'd have hated seeing those soft shoes ruined and her shimmering silk swathe splattered with rain and clinging to her stockinged thighs.

There were a thousand and one things for me to be doing

that day, to prepare myself, but most of it I spent curled in an armchair pulled right up to the wall of sliding glass doors, watching the ravages, the dark intensity, of that last storm. Watching the way the fog came down to slowly veil the opposite shore, and eventually, to erase the whole bay, leaving me alone on the edge of the world with only a few bending trees for company. They quivered against the force of the driving walls of rain that came in along the harbour from the Pacific.

Sam had called to say that she couldn't bear to leave the house, but did I want to go over to Marlborough Street instead. Seeing as I'd be there in the evening for the farewell dinner, anyway, I said No, No, I have so much to do, but I'll book the taxi early. When she said, That's fine then, so easily, I wondered whether she wanted me there at all. I imagined her holed up at Marlborough Street, smoking joints with the girls.

So there I sat, watching, inhaling the storm. It had broken around eleven, turning what had been a crisp, bright morning into torrid half-night. When the rain came down so hard I could no longer see the trees out beyond the deck, I dropped my robe on the chair and skipped naked onto the wooden slats of the deck to dance, arms outstretched, in the jubilant rain. A dance that said Yeah, fuck yeah, I'm outta here!

The drive to Marlborough Street had all the qualities of a trip through murky sludge in a space capsule. I breathed in time to the womp, womp, womp of the windscreen wipers, clutching a plastic bag containing five chilled bottles of Zelda's posh champagne.

I was wearing one of my clinging, spangled Indian skirts for the last time, with a black bra top under my leather jacket. In the cab I left the jacket zipped up to the neck and still felt the flesh that covered my rib-cage prickle. My hair was damp and frizzy around my face and my cold fingers curled in on themselves in the overlong sleeves.

Hesitating at the front door, I wondered, for just a moment, if I should knock and wait to be shown inside. The hallway was dark and the house still, the smell of garlic the only sign of life. The soft light in the lounge room came from four tall candles.

Jake sat alone, hunched over, the piece of soapstone he was working on the table in front of him. He was rubbing it, strong-fingered, with a soft polishing cloth. He didn't look up until I moved to stand close to him, where he could smell the wet leather of my jacket and I could smell the vague, sandalwood tang on his skin.

- What is it? I asked, placing my hand tentatively at the back of his neck, on the knobby bone at the top of the spinal column.

- It's for you, he said, turning towards me, where bent over as I was I could almost brush his cheek with my lips.

- Thank you, I said, holding the stone in my hand, his fingers not ready to release it, I hovering between moving right away and moving forward, into him.

The front door slammed and the loud chatter and harsh laughter of the girls came rushing to engulf us. Followed close behind by Jessie and Lila themselves.

- Where's Sammy? I asked, standing to kiss them both and slipping the stone into my pocket, still warm from the hours it had spent in Jake's hands.

- She's just popped upstairs to do something, said Jessie, looking away from me. She'll be down in a minute.

- Why aren't you two drinking? demanded Lila, moving into a bustling kitchen momentum. Take one of those bottles and go and settle in the lounge while Jess and I finish the dinner. Don't worry Jake, you're off the hook now.

- He's made this wild paella, said Jessie, pushing us both through the door, Jake with the bottle and me with the glasses.

Sitting in the lounge room in a long skirt and sipping champagne demurely was the most formal thing I'd ever done in that house. Even with Jake wearing his usual dusty jeans and thin, white t-shirt that showed curve of his back. I sat in one of the massive thirties crimson flock armchairs and pulled the carving out of my pocket. The stone was warm with my own heat now. As I examined it, Jake turned to flip through the pile of records, unable to sit and watch as I scrutinised his work. It was a small, fist-sized carving of two people, curled together in sleep, or in rest, or just in a warm, close embrace. There was nothing sexual about it; in the pale grey stone, the two figures could have been twins, lying together, spoon to spoon, in the womb. The curve of paler colour in the stone ran right along the sweep of the outside figure's body.

- Jake, I love it, I said, holding the small carving to my lips.

The Cocteau Twins started to play, but still Jake fiddled with the records.

- I might go and change, said Jake, taking a swig from his drink.

An awkwardness had grown between us that barred me from his room. Since his father had hit him, he and I had learnt to dance a wide berth around each other. I might as well have hit him myself, for all the guilt I felt towards him and his own cool denial of our former intimacy. In fact, after a summer spent sleeping almost exclusively at Marlborough Street, close to the music and the parties and the night, I'd spent most of the winter sleeping on my own in my bed at Zelda's.

From upstairs I heard Sam's door open and her stumbling footsteps as she rushed down the stairs calling my name. When she came to hug me, I saw how crumpled she looked, and yet how filled with nervous energy. Speed, I thought, but later she told me she'd shot coke and I acted as though she was just telling stories.

- Soph, Soph, she said. Tell me you're not really going away tomorrow. Tell me you're not really leaving.

- Sammy, I said, squashed by the weight of her body and her need as she sat half on the arm of the chair and half in my lap. You know I've got to go. You know I've got to find my father.

- You don't need him ... it's us you need, she said, pressing my face into her damp shirt as Jake came back. Don't leave me on my own.

- What about me? asked Jake, mock hurt in his voice as he sat opposite us on the even larger crimson sofa. Don't I count? Don't I look after you? Don't I sit up with you at night when you can't sleep? Don't I ply you with tea when you need it most?

- It's not the same, she wailed, sitting up suddenly and speaking fast. You ask her to stay Jake. If you tell her you'll miss her she'll stay, for sure. Tell her you want her to stay.

- She knows that none of us want her to leave, he said to Sam, not to me.

- That's not the same Jake, she said, on the verge of something ugly, broken. Tell her what you told me the other night.

- Oh go back to bed Sam, he said, getting up to pace the room, and returning to the pile of records. You're really losing it, you know?

I was hurt on Sam's behalf, but trapped, unable to protest her case. A witness to a domestic argument that I, only a fringe-dweller in the house, had no right to intrude on. It was then that I noticed that Jake had dressed for dinner, wore clean, close fitting black jeans, a belt with silver studs, and a wing collared shirt with its sleeves hacked off. There was no tie at his throat, but all the buttons were present and done up.

- Lookin' suave Jake, I said. Do you have a date later?

- You don't seriously think I'd go out on the night of your farewell dinner do you? he said, scowling at me. Just thought I'd dress for the occasion. Didn't realise I'd be the only one.

Sam wore ripped jeans and a big khaki army shirt that I'd left in her room one day. Her hair was a mass of tight braids. Her bare feet were black as the street. When Jessie and Lila called us, Sam disappeared upstairs again.

In the kitchen we sat around the candle-lit table eating hot corn chips slathered in a fiery guacamole. We were waiting for Sam, to open another bottle of champagne, and to complete the picture. Prince played on the ghetto-blaster, drowning out the melancholy of the Cocteaus, the rain, and the tension from the other room.

Sam came clattering into the kitchen in the school tunic and hat she wore on stage, her hair wet from a three second shower.

- Going to work? asked Jessie, pulling at the top of the tunic.

- Nah, this was all I had that wasn't in a ball on the floor, she said. And then, proudly, I stole it.

- Why? I asked. Aren't you going back?

- Course I'm going back, she said, draining her glass and burping. D'you think I wouldn't have the nerve to go alone? The only reason I stole this was so they'll let me wear your leathers.

- Why the hell would you want to do that? I asked, despairing at the prospect of Sam going, night after night, to the strip club, alone.

- Because I'm fed up with playing the silly young thing! Fed up with acting coy and harmless, she said, sounding sad and harmless. I want to be the tough girl. You don't have a monopoly on that.

'Little Red Corvette' came on and Sam got up; for one awful moment I thought she was going to show us exactly what it was she was made of.

- I'd like to make a toast to my best friend, she said, shaky-voiced. And to her trip into the unknown to find her father.

- To Soph, the girls said together, while Jake just drank.

In spite of Jake's efforts to create the perfect paella, the level of interest in food was at an all time low. The meal, and the table itself, served only as the means to draw us together for an hour, after that, it was the drink. The champagne ran dry at about the same time as our pretence at eating, and that was when the first of the vodka bottles was chiselled out of the over-iced freezer, and when Jake excavated some J.D. from the cupboard under the sink. The remains of the dinner were appropriated by tortoiseshell Gough from over the back fence, his adversary, Malcolm, having faded back to the weatherboard grey he came from.

With fingers pressed to each other's backs so we could feel the other's bone, could almost press through to the other's lungs, Sam and I whirled around the lounge too fast for the electro beat of the music. Too fast in a room full of candles and too fast to retain any semblance of control. If I'd been watching, I would have said we were duelling, not dancing. That we were pushing each other to see who'd back down first, to see which one cared the least, whether one's love was truer than the other's. Distances between chairs, walls and tables became incalculable, and as often as we waltzed, we tumbled: into the sofa, into the empty fireplace, into the low coffee table pushed back against the wall that left a great, purple welt on Sam's shin, for her to cry over when I was gone.

With a more benign, sexual energy, Jessie and Lila moved around the room, their pelvises and foreheads pressed against each other's. Avoiding Sam and me as if by radar. My imminent separation from Sam was imbued with all the guilt and remorse of a lover's break-up, and yet, without the context of that formal relationship, we could find no words to voice anger or betrayal.

When Sam collapsed in a heap in the armchair, closing her eyes and humming to herself, I moved to sit on the fourth step of the wooden staircase that descended into the room. Just above sat Jake, his knees wide apart, hunched over on himself. He swigged J.D., and I swigged vodka, and we both watched a dance that came as close to the act of sex as anyone can get while fully dressed and standing upright. I watched Lila trace an invisible line with her tongue from Jessie's chin down to her left nipple.

- Why've you been avoiding me? he asked, moving down a step so I could feel the cool denim of his jeans against my clammy back.

I pushed out a hard laugh, watching Jessie move so she was dancing with both her legs wrapped around one of Lila's.

- Why did you abandon me? he asked through clenched teeth, cold hands on my rib-cage just beneath my breasts.

My guts churned at the words that should have come from my mouth. He was the one who'd abandoned me. The one who kept his life all to himself and scorned my own.

- You lied to me, I said, thinking if only he'd put his hands on my breasts instead of my ribs as I watched the way Lila's head arched back as Jessie moved. About being celibate.

- How many times did you listen at their door? he asked coldly, deflecting the blow I'd aimed at him back on to my own body. Were you jealous?

- Jealous! Hah! I muttered, shivering as one of his hands did move to my breast. Jealous of your status as toy boy to two women who love each other! You're just like all the other guys.

- Oh, I am, am I? he said, his voice very low, catching in his throat, his fingers finding my nipple under the black lace.

- Dream on, I said, pushing his hand away and standing, scowling in Sam's direction.

As I swaggered over to Sam's inert form and the room warped and buckled around me, making me feel like someone in one of my own photos, I thought to myself, Calm, calm. Don't let me lose my temper on my last night. It was with a fraught, forced gentleness that I held her shoulder and shook her, begging her to get up and dance again. Telling her it would be our last dance.

- She's out for the count, said Jessie, catching me by the arm and drawing me to them. We will be too, soon. This is goodbye, Soph.

For a moment, the three of us stood swaying, clutching each other, repeating the words, Look after yourself, look after each other, until they kissed a cheek each, swept past Jake on the stairs and disappeared.

Again I stood by Sam, shaking her, telling her she had to dance. Ignoring Jake where he sat on the stairs and watched me through the carved wooden bars.

- Maybe you'll dance with me now, he said in a soft voice. Dance with me, Soph.

Not even glancing in his direction I snorted, and went on trying to raise Sam. Then I heard his footsteps, and the creaking of the steps, and upstairs, a door, the girls' door, opened and closed. Standing and letting go of Sam, I turned to the emptiness.

- Jake, I whispered, as though he was just up on the landing, or about to come out of the bathroom. Please don't just leave me. Without saying good-bye. Please.

But the house was silent, save Sam's laboured breaths. Tears and despair came and went in silence. I stood in the Marlborough Street lounge room for what I was sure was the last time and surveyed the night's wreckage; the empty bottles, the tipped over glasses going sticky in the night, record sleeves scattered about the floor, candles burnt down low, Sam's crumpled-in-on-itself body, and I wondered whether I dared leave, and if I did, whether there could be any such thing as return.

I clung to the belief that nothing could make my skin sing the way the salt water at the pool in Woolloomooloo Bay did. That is until I swam for the first time in one of the dark, deep, delicious freshwater ponds on Hampstead Heath. My summer-damp skin was rank with the grime of the tube, the West End, dozens of buses, hundreds of cars and thousands of cigarettes. That feeling of being smeared with the hung-over breath of a whole city left me the moment my pointed fingers, then the arc of my body, met the water. Only a short walk from Randolphe's, the Women's Pond became my sanctuary, refuge from the still-aired closeness of the lab where I developed photos in Camden. And from the heat haze that shimmered on the road in front of the buses I wilted in, and the heat that rose in angry waves from the raw concrete of the Brixton footpaths.

On my last afternoon in London, Marina and I lay on our towels on the grassy slope above the pond, with the tops of our one-piece cossies rolled down. Between swims Marina interrogated me about Sydney and its people, as though she were making the journey with me. With as little nostalgic longing and as much honesty as I could muster, I described them each to her in turn, with Zelda as an afterthought, in the list of people who awaited me. Not that they anticipated my arrival. I hadn't spoken to Jake for months, not since he'd phoned to tell me the news about Sam. She and I had exchanged postcards in a haphazard sort of way, always out of sync. She would send me a card from somewhere in the Northern Territory, and I'd write to her care of Marlborough Street. I was convinced that she could have no sense at all of the new life I was about to leave.

By the quiet London pond, Sydney and its blasé, party-lined shores seemed terminally distant. Departure was such a difficult concept, despite the fact that I'd already confirmed my seat on the flight, and that my London life was packed away, for the most part. Early that morning, Randolphe and I had gossiped over the baking of quiche and making of dips for the 'drinks party' that he insisted on holding for me that evening.

- I'm definitely coming to visit, Marina repeated. I might even consider emigrating. Once I get some cash together.

- But Marina, I said, mocking, teasing. You can't even raise the money for a bus ticket to Donegal let alone four hundred quid for a flight to Sydney. Six if you want a return!

- That's just logistics, she scoffed, rolling onto her stomach to expose the fine skin on her back to the sun, a back devoid of the galaxy of moles and freckles that gave my own its national identity. The thing is, will they like me? Your friends? Or will they confuse me for a Pom and take the piss?

- You've got as much chance as being taken for a Pom as I do! Anyway, the country's bloody full of Irish. You'll meet more there than you do here, I told her, watching the beads of sweat form tiny, spherical islands between my breasts like mercury leaking from a thermometer. They'll like you just fine Marina. Like I do.

On the far side of the pond where a fringe of trees screened us from the prying eyes of passers-by, one of the life guards swayed in her row-boat and waved an oar about maliciously, shooing away a group of blokes hanging on the fence in the hope of glimpsing some firm female flesh. She threatened them with arrest if they didn't bugger off, but they just laughed. Called her a bitch-dyke, said they didn't want to see naked lesbians for all the money in the world.

As the shadows lengthened, and the grassy slope took on more the quality of a lawn dotted with bodies rather than smeared with them, I willed time to stop. I lay on my stomach pretending to be asleep so Marina would stop talking and asked myself whether it was really time to leave. Whether I wasn't perhaps acting prematurely because I'd been homesick, and because I fancied I could be of some use to Sam.

I still hadn't found my father. I'd desisted the moment I was in possession of that list, as though that page held his essence but I hadn't quite identified him yet. At least I had no further desire to hang around book launches like a tart in search of a trick. Waiting for someone to come along and trigger that predatorial response in me. The image of Dick, whenever it crept into my mind's eye, made me want to hurl myself into the nearest body of water. To once again have the print of his hands washed from my skin.

Beside me, Marina shivered and stood to put on her clothes in a hopping dance. The bravest of the day's swimmers breast-stroked the length of the pond alongside a family of brown-bodied, green-headed ducks. I caught my breath at the sudden vision of loss that opened up before me. When you start to live your life in two places, you're forever leaving something behind. Destined, always, to be missing something. To be longing for someone.

The trees surrounding the Women's Pond left it with nearly an hour less sunlight than the other ponds. We walked around the greater expanse of the Men's Pond, where swimmers still cut its surface and sunbathers lay on the banks trying to tempt the last of the sun's rays with their immaculate bodies. The hollow wooden thud from the unseen shuttlecock courts carried across the water, punctuated by cheers and curses from behind the high timber fence. Randolphe had made the four-season shuttlecock tournament sound like some secret Masonic rite from which women were strictly, irrevocably excluded. He'd mumbled something about men feeling too inhibited to swear in front of women. Paff. If Sam were there with me we would have stormed the joint, our mouths like putrid drains, gushing with all the four letter words we'd ever heard.

In the morning there wouldn't even be time for Randolphe and I to make a final heath circuit. He estimated that we must leave the house by six-thirty to reach Heathrow in time. If we'd planned to take the bus, it would have meant leaving forty-five minutes earlier. Stanley and Dolphi had argued, politely, about which of them should accompany me. Dolphi, endowed with the family's own strain of obstinacy, won. There was no question about me going to the airport alone. I'd teased Dolphi about how he felt obliged to monitor my behaviour till the last, to minimise the chance of my meeting another Dick.

- Soph, Marina said as we were met by a wall of quiche-baking fumes in Randolphe's hallway, isn't this father enough?

I had to travel all the way to London to have any notion of home. I'd thought London comprised some vital part of my upbringing, like learning to talk, or read, or dress myself. But the only thing that living in London taught me, same as a dozen northern hemisphere cities could have, was that it wasn't my place and that my place suited me a whole lot better.

To say that I landed at Kingsford Smith Airport and gave a sigh that encompassed the whole harbour would be an abject lie, but I liked the image. On my arrival in Sydney I was so filled with trepidation that I could barely breathe. The panic had set in after the stop in Singapore, where I'd changed Sterling into Singapore dollars and tried phoning both Marlborough Street and Jake's studio. Nobody home and I wouldn't leave a message. What to say? I'm coming? That wasn't why I'd called. I'd phoned because I wanted to hear a voice that would anchor me to the place I was going to and relieve the ache that wracked my body after saying good-bye to Dolphi.

Foremost in my mind was the notion that now I really wanted it, I wouldn't fit in Sydney either. I'd be like some emotional refugee, inhabiting the territory of someone else's magnanimous hospitality. I'd be forced to shuttle back and forth across the world, hoping that somewhere something would click.

My heart raced as I wheeled my trolley into the arrivals hall and I had to force my eyes to only sweep the wall of people awaiting their loved ones. I knew there was no-one there for me, but looked twice at the dirty-blond head of one guy and at the mass of red, piled up hair on a woman much older than Zelda.

It seemed that no-one arrived at that airport without someone to meet them, whether it was a lover or a tour guide. I rode the near-empty Airport Express back into the city.

On the expressway, the sun came out from behind the tiniest

wisp of a cloud and I was dazzled by a light so strong that I could only face it with my eyes closed. I'd started to think of the summer sky above London as blue, but on that bus that took me through Sydney's southern suburbs, I relearnt the colour blue. The sky over Sydney on that crisp spring day was a shade halfway between the deepest and palest of the striations in my lapis lazuli.

It was when we drove past the shell of the old Resch's brewery and I had a sudden flash of the Battersea Power Station that the first twinge of excitement stirred in my belly. Familiar territory up ahead. Pubs I'd drunk in with Sam. Clubs I'd been disgorged from just as the light of dawn turned us all into sweaty Halloween pumpkins with great, black gaping eyes and mouths hanging open in thirst. Down those side streets lay houses where people I knew lived. We passed restaurants where women I knew from the club scene waited table.

How inelegant and how apt, I thought, as I half dragged and half wheeled my great lumbering case across Elizabeth Street. But that method of arrival was eminently preferable to being ejected outside somebody's house by Zelda's latest assistant. I couldn't resist nipping into the milk bar to buy myself a banana Paddle-Pop, and to be greeted by Stavros as though it were only last week that he'd seen me. How ya doon? Nice, nice girl, he'd said. And then, because I hadn't bought ice-creams for all of them, I sat on my case on the corner of Elizabeth and Marlborough Streets, to scoff my Paddle-Pop like a greedy, furtive child. Not that I cared who saw me, half expecting one of them to come wandering along only to stop and double up with mocking, welcoming laughter. There's Soph, been all the way to London and back and all she bloody well wants is a banana Paddle-Pop.

This time I did knock. You have to after so long, making bets with myself as to who would answer the door. If it were a heavily pregnant Sam, how on earth would I hug her? If it were Jake, how on earth would I not?

But it was neither. It was a woman with dreadlocks the colour of my ring, the paler blues.

- Yes, she said, unimpressed at the sight of someone who didn't have as many earrings as her.

- Who are you? I stuttered, inexplicably on the verge of tears.

- Name's Bella. I live in the front room, she told me, gesturing towards Jake's door. And who are you?

- Soph. Sophie, I said, my tone flatter than the runway I hadn't kissed. Friend of Sam. And of Jessie, Lila and Jake.

- Sam? she said, lifting her floating top to fiddle with her belly ring. She the one having a baby?

- Yeah. Where is she?

- Having the baby, she said, as though I was a complete moron. Barely seen the girls for days. You'd think they were the fucking midwives or something.

- Which hospital? I barked, as though I too were the midwife, late again.

- Dunno, she said, bored. Crown Street? Paddington? Nah. Yeah. Paddington. That's the one.

I pushed past her into the lounge room, telling her I was leaving my case, not to worry, it was OK. Not to panic. Not to panic.

Out on Elizabeth Street I panicked. For one terrible moment, I couldn't for the life of me remember how to get to Paddington. All the buses were going the wrong way, and how long would they take? But suddenly I remembered where I was, and hailed a taxi like the Sydney girl I was.

Rushing through the car park I pulled up short at the sight

of Jake's ute. Wanting to go and sit on that dusty bench seat, run my hands over the cold, hard tools on its floor and rest my forehead on the steering wheel. But there was Sam to think of. At the reception I had to say her name three times before they understood and told me her room number and that visiting didn't start for another ten minutes.

- So, she's not giving birth then?

- Er, no. I don't think so, said the sister, looking at her file again and giving me the opportunity to dart past her down the corridor.

I raced around, counting rooms, expecting to be stopped, expecting not to find it, expecting the worst. But in front of me, suddenly, loomed the open door of Sam's ward. Breathing heavily, I stood against the wall outside the door, thinking, Thank god, I'm in time, thank god. Bracing myself, I stuck my head around the door to see, oh-my-god, Sam breastfeeding.

- Oh my god! I said, and resumed my position outside the room by the door until Sam's shrieks of Soph, Soph, Soph, brought me more slowly into the room.

She was in a ward of four, and two of the other babies on the teat were crying as a result of Sam's squawks. Neither of us cared. None of the three of us.

- Sammy, you've got boobs, was the first thing I said to her as I gingerly positioned myself a foot from the bed.

- Soph, for God's sake give us a kiss!

As I went to kiss her flushed cheek, for the first time I saw the screwed up, prune-face of her little boy. The tears came flowing down my cheeks and continued down to roll off the tip of Sam's nose. But the kid didn't care, he just went on sucking and yanked at my hair as it brushed his apricot sized fist.

- You had a baby without me, I said, crying now into her

cropped head of bleached hair. I wanted to be here. I thought I'd be in time. I'm so proud of you.

- A week premature, but look at the size of him, said Sam, tugging at my jacket so I could see him and not her scalp. Sophie, meet my son Starr. He's three days old.

- Three days! I said, this news prompting a fresh flood of howling. But where's the father? Where's your bloke?

- Shot through a month ago. I told him he had to shape up if he wanted to be the father of my child. He chose to ship out.

- Jesus Sammy, she still cries like a baby, said Jake from the doorway.

- And you've still got a lip on you, I said, the hair on the back of my neck standing on end, turning gingerly and rubbing my eyes with tight fists before being crushed in a big-armed bear hug.

- Hi Soph, Hi Jake, we said into each other's necks, breathing each other in before pulling apart, to stand, grinning inanely on either side of Sam's bed.

- I'm really sorry about your bloke Sammy, I said, watching her moving the tiny cat's arse of a mouth from one nipple to the other. Maybe he'll be back. Once he sees you and Starr he'll be bound to stay.

- Soph, she said, as though speaking to a confused child. Don't you see? I don't want him. I don't love him. Thought I did, but what I really loved was the idea of a child. I wanted a baby, not a husband.

- But, but, aren't you afraid? I stammered, looking to Jake for support. Bringing him up alone I mean. Aren't you scared to be a single mother?

- Soph, Zelda did just fine with you, and all she had was Nella for support, she said, smiling a warm, open-faced smile of trust. I've got my mother, and I've got you guys. How could I possibly go wrong?

- Some feminist you are Soph, teased Jake. Don't you know that fathers become redundant as soon as they've ejaculated?

- I don't know shit, I said, laying my blue-ringed hand on the golden dome of Starr's head. You'll both have to be very patient with me.

THE WORLD

Now the train runs beside a strip of parkland that divides the city from the river, keeping the two beasts artificially separate, as though the water-engorged bodies that swirl in the river do not belong to the city. As though the city's manic intensity has nothing to do with the way the river holds the narrow strip of land suspended between its bowed legs. The Hudson River is the right leg of a mighty brown woman who stands pressing her left leg, the Harlem River, in close. The narrow clump of land is the child that her straining legs won't ever allow to escape.

It doesn't occur to me even for a moment that I might not like him. I am already so taken in by him, by the concept of him. If he were a drunk, I'd forgive him, or a sleazy, big-handed womaniser, I'd forgive him. Even if he confessed to me that he *was a coward, had always known he'd had a daughter but was afraid, I'd forgive him. The only thing I could not forgive him, I am convinced, is his disinterest. If he isn't as intrigued by the concept of a daughter as I am by the concept of a father, I am sure I will shrivel up and die.*

As the train slinks north towards him, towards the apex of the island, my head fills with the words he used to describe this river. To describe the northern-most reach of the city's derelict parkland known as Spuyten Duyvil: the devil that spits in the eye of those who refuse to take the city's underlife, its threat, with the seriousness it commands.

And as the train crosses, clickety-clack, clickety-clack, over the bridge that connects the island at its northern-most point to the Bronx, to upstate New York, to the mainland, to the mid-west, and to the western frontier, I think, Here I come. Ready or not Daddy, ready or not.

Arranging to have lunch with Zelda did not involve speaking to her. A phonecall to her assistant could be made, he would suggest a window in her diary and call back to confirm once he'd consulted with her.

I was filled with sullen paranoia. I'd bump into Zelda on the street for sure. Taken by surprise, I would be unable even to engage in a civil conversation. Unable to present my calm, mature, sophisticated self. Unable to convey anything of how very altered I felt.

It was Sam who'd understood, almost immediately, my predicament. She'd said I was in Limbo. I wasn't home, wasn't away. The unfinished business wouldn't let me rest. It seemed that since I'd been gone, what with her own travels, her relationship, her straightening out, and finally motherhood, Sam had become the wisest person I knew. The only one whose words made any sense to me. The only one, apparently, who gave a damn.

She'd made peace with her mother, and I could do the same, she was sure. She and her mother were on the same team now, not consumed with rage, one for the other. Together they'd taken the lease on the small flat in the red brick building where Sam and Starr would live when they left hospital. She was the one Sam had gone to when her bloke had walked, the one she'd sat with doing her sums, working out just how tight it would be, living on a single mother's pension.

- So what happens when Starr turns around one day and asks the big questions about his Daddy? Wants to know his Daddy? I'd asked her. What then?

- I'll tell him it's Jake! she laughed.

- Why would you tell him that? my voice neutral, dead calm.

- Only joking Soph. 'Course I won't tell him that. Jake'll be surrogate father anyway. He loves kids, she said, lightly. I'll tell him his father's name. Tell him he can meet him when he's older, if he wants ...

- And what if he wants access to Starr? What if he comes back?

- There's no coming back, she said, more decisive than I'd ever known her. I won't stop him from seeing Starr, it's not my right, is it? But there's no way I'd let him move in with us. Not into my home.

At Marlborough Street, an eerie silence had descended over the house. I was absent in my own way, never really having arrived. Perhaps that's what you got from slinking in on the Airport Express unannounced. For not holding the obligatory home-coming do, prodigal daughter routine and all.

I was unsure of what I'd left and what I'd come to. One foot placed unsteadily in each city, threatening to tumble if both feet weren't permitted to stand together.

On the morning I was off to meet her, I'd so wanted to phone Randolphe. I needed to hear him repeat those warm words he'd used in speaking of my own mother. Wanted to hear again the tale of how she'd stood up to her father, of how she'd brought such a loss upon herself. I'd turned, instead, to the cards, but shuffling them, the images blurred before my eyes.

If it had been later in the year, and warmer, I would have gone down to the Boy to swim before lunch. To see the knot of tension in my stomach float away on the ripples caused by my own stroking arms. To lie in the breeze and watch the salt dry leopard spots on my pale skin.

Instead, I put on my own underwear and the charcoal tube dress I'd flown away in, piled my hair up on my head, donned a pair of dark glasses, and set off an hour early to walk the back streets to the Cross. I figured that if I left early, it would prevent me from sitting by the phone, waiting for her to call and cancel. I left the lapis lazuli behind, anxious about upsetting her. Ascribing her with emotions!

The act of walking through familiar streets helped me forget my destination. My panic eased as I strolled, by habit, the same route Sam and I had taken on all of those very early mornings. I walked past rows of Victorian terraces that could have been in the next street from Stanley's, or in any south London street, if it weren't for their balconies, hooded with elegant corrugated iron shells, tarted up with twists of flaky, iron lace. The Surry Hills backyards were inhabited by indolent cats and antagonistic currawongs, while the Brixton backyards provided pens for crazed pit bull terriers. In Sydney, the people wore an expectant look on their faces, that waiting-for-a-balmy-summer-night curl to their lips. While in London, they were already gritting their teeth and remembering, all too soon, how to hunch their shoulders against the ravenous autumn wind.

I'd wanted to meet her on my turf, so I'd suggested a restaurant down the lazy end of Victoria Street.

Unthinking, I walked all the way to the door of the strip club. What I was struck by there, standing outside that inconspicuous black door, was that I felt almost nothing. And then I felt relief, a great, cool, liquid wave that told me it was over. That some angry kernel, the hard inner core where the spleen came from, had been shed along the way. That I couldn't find it again if I tried.

Even with my meandering trek around the Cross, down side streets tinged with the sherbet lime of new leaves, past Clyde's where Jake may or may not have been at work, down Macleay Street so I could stand at a safe distance and look at Nella's old building, and then past clusters of sidewalk coffee drinkers, I still reached the restaurant fifteen minutes early. Planning to sit by an open window overlooking the street, guzzling mineral water to calm my nerves.

I walked up the few steps from the street into the lush, leafy interior and told the moustachioed maitre d' my name. Ah yes. Your sister has already arrived. For years Sam and I had waited in vain for someone to call us sisters; and now the first time I'd been taken as someone's sister, it was as Zelda's.

At least I had something to occupy my mind in the interminable seconds it took me to cross the floor to the table by a french window that looked out into a narrow garden, and past it onto the street. She would have seen me arrive, known already that our hair was done in the same style and that I'd made some effort to dress myself. Maybe she would also have seen that I wasn't angry, that I'd been wringing my hands in terror and plucking at the fabric of my dress where it rode up at the thigh.

- You really look well, I said, swallowing the other words I'd been rehearsing about how *good* it was of her to make time to see me.

I knocked the leg of the table with my boot and sat down with a thud. Looking to her to carry on where I'd started.

- And you look radiant, she said, with a high, strained voice that sounded as though it had been forced through a colander. Your hair looks lovely.

- Oh, I said, raising a damp hand to it, knowing, without touching it, that it would be messier than hers. He thought we were sisters.

And then we both pushed out tense little laughs, until they were real, silly, semi-hysterical laughs and we were laughing together for the first time in years. Maybe the first time since Nella's death.

- Nella used to pretend she was my sister, she said, right on cue, claiming my Nella for her own. She did it to rile me . . . knew how I hated it.

- I don't mind, I said, trying not to, almost flattered to be identified with the handsome woman opposite me in her tan suede jodhpurs, cream silk shirt and russet-coloured tie, loose at the neck. In London I met someone you used to know who said we were just the same.

- Who? she asked, abrupt, then more tempered. What was his name?

- Some publisher, I told her, not asking her how she knew it would be a man. I met him at a party.

Our waiter wore black 501s, black RM Williams riding boots, a white starched apron, and a white cotton t-shirt. His beach-blond hair made me think of Jake, just like every third man I saw in Sydney. The bleached hair on the back of his honey-coloured hands caught the light as he took our fussy order.

- Randolphe phoned me the night he went to your exhibition, she told me. If I'd have known I'd have flown over for it. I'd have liked to have been there.

- It was nothing, I said, my knuckles white, gripping the cold glass and in danger of crushing it. It didn't warrant flying all that way.

- I could have made it a work trip, she said easily.

- Oh, yeah. Well, that would have been different. You could have dropped by before a launch dinner or something, I said, catching myself after the damage had been done, wishing I'd worn Nella's ring and be damned.

- I missed you Sophia, she said, reaching across the table to put her cool hand on my wrist. The house was quiet as death.

I stared at the rising bubbles in my glass, the way they clung to the lemon slice like sperm to an egg. Goddamn it. There was a lump in my throat the size of the chunky white bread roll that I hadn't yet touched.

- Dolphi told me about the fight you had with your father, I said looking at the table, trying even harder. I never knew.

- I called him Dolphi when we were children, she said, her voice warm as the top layer of sand at the beach. I'm so glad that you two liked each other. It would've made Nella so happy.

- Why don't you invite him for a holiday? I said, swimming for dry land. Tell him he's got to let you return the hospitality. Tell him he's got to see Sydney before he, before . . .

- Maybe I will, she said smiling to herself. Maybe I'll tell him

I need my own dose of his special, soothing therapy.

Heartened because neither of us had stormed out, I reached for the crumpled wad of paper folded into my bag. I'd rewritten the list that morning, but the paper still looked as though I'd carried it around in my fist for a week. The names had been crushed up against my heart forever, or so it seemed.

- I wanted to show you this list, I forced myself to say, fast, so it came out like one long word.

I pushed the wad across the smooth wooden surface and gazed out the window at the people drifting down Victoria Street on one caffeine high. I couldn't bear to watch the way she would look at the crumpled paper disdainfully, and open it, cringing, as though it might contain a ball of spat out pink chewing gum. Holding my breath, I was sure her scowl would be audible.

For a few minutes she was silent and the beating of my heart echoed around the bare walls of the restaurant. Broadcasting my anxiety. And then she laughed, a warm, low, syrupy laugh. A laugh of delight.

- God Soph, she said. You can't imagine how unappealing half the men on that list actually were.

- Oh, I said, daring to look across the table to take in her smile. Is he on it?

- Third from the bottom.

- What? crowd noise from nowhere suddenly filling my ears and invading my head, chaos-induced confusion. What?

- There, she said, turning the page to face me and pointing at a name that I couldn't read, but that I knew anyway, because it was the third last name on a list I knew backwards, forwards, anyway. I was going to give this to you.

From under her chair she dragged a brown paper carrier bag with string handles. But all I could do was stare dumbly, from my cherished list to her softly smiling face. Her remembering face.

- They're his books, or the less esoteric of them, she told me in a language I'd forgotten how to speak. His letters are there too.

I just opened and closed my mouth, looking towards the distant waiter for help.

- I don't see why you shouldn't read them, she continued. You're old enough. You'll understand him, I'm sure. He was angry.

- But, but ...

- Why? she said, turning her face to the outside world, struggling with the words herself. I've been so frightened of losing you completely.

Was that the hardest thing she'd ever said?

- I ended up knowing I had more chance of losing you by not telling you who he was than by telling you, she said. You've reached an age now where you're strong enough to take him or leave him.

- Oh.

- He's a charismatic man, she said in a tone I tried to read as wistful. I didn't want you to meet him when there was a chance of your being overwhelmed by him. I know you'll like him Soph. Assuming that you want to meet him. It's his old address on those letters. Now he lives ...

- In upstate New York, I said, a child, all wonderment, learning to speak. I've got his address.

- I loved him, she said, oblivious to the waiter who was briskly arranging the table to accommodate the bowls of gazpacho. I loved him so much I nearly scared myself mute ... would have drunk myself into a big, black hole when I came back here if it wasn't for you, making me ill every time I tried it.

As I stared into my soup, a sweet, slow exhaustion came over me. The exhaustion of the traveller who has just caught sight of home, off around the next bend in the road.

- Tell me honestly, I said, forcing her to meet my gaze for once. Did you never regret leaving him? Coming here and not telling him anything?

- Huh, she said, taking her first, easy sip of white wine. You know I'm not one to sit around and have regrets. I made the right decisions then.

She took in my quizzical expression, and faltered, as though doubting herself.

- Yeah, it hurt like hell. Hurt worse than seeing Nella suffer, she said, going for the wine again. But it was the right decision. If it had happened five years later, I might have made a very different choice.

We ate our soup in silence, a weary, comfortable quiet, and I swallowed all the dozens of questions that kept clamouring to reach my tongue. I wanted to know my father for myself, not to know him through Zelda. I wanted to hear his words, read his thoughts and make up my own mind, wanted my own understanding of this man who I'd already invented and re-invented for myself so many times I lost count. And anyway, I wanted to tell Zelda about London, and about Dolphi, and taking photos, and Sammy's baby, and about the plans that were slowly jelling in my head for my own, brilliant career. I wanted to make absolutely certain that as I now knew who my father was, she knew who her daughter was.

As the words danced in my head, the words that would tell her about her daughter, fill in the gaps that the years had widened, I watched the warmth slide from her face. Following her gaze across the breezy, lemon-sherbet-feeling room, I saw a table of people laughing. Was one of them Zane? Even as I bungled into a rave about Sammy and Starr, Zelda was looking at her watch and preparing herself once again for her own tough world.

Among the books given me by Zelda was a return ticket to New York – what she called birthright. The departure date was only ten days after our meeting, but I saw no reason why it should not be so. I moved through those Fruit Tingle fresh days like a sleep-walker, frightened to turn my head left or right lest I distract myself. The image of him from his book jackets filled my mind – it was the face in my head when I fell asleep at night and when I awoke in the early morning. It was the face that filled the half-truth between sleeping and waking.

With the ease that only comes when things are rushing towards an endpoint, my arrangements flew together to form a brilliant mosaic. I blundered into a magazine editor's office where a bemused, be-waistcoated man agreed to consider using the photographs I took of my father, never calling him father, upon my return. Yes, I could use the name of the magazine, but I should not consider, not even for a moment, billing them for my expenses. Later when I learnt of the man's friendship with Zelda, it made me laugh, not spit. Sydney was Zelda's city, after all. Then it was a matter of faxing the New York office of his publisher on fancy letterhead that Jake helped me design. Like clockwork, the response came back. Photo session granted. Author's residence on the Hudson River. PM. Will be met at train. Please provide New York contact details.

Waiting two weeks, ten days, a week, a matter of days before meeting him seemed an impossibility. Part of me wanted to get him on the phone, there and then. Let the whole story come out in a great, desperate torrent. To hear his delight. His excitement. His insistence that I come immediately. That we fly to a point halfway between. But who did I think I was kidding? People were suspicious. Defensive, furtive, untrusting, cynical. Always on guard against someone who might conceivably want something from them. And why should a famous author be any different? Why should he not be worse?

And so the bright-skied days rolled by, one into the next. My social life revolved around Sam making up for the lost year. Really for the last two years, taking into account the Sydney year when we failed to communicate. I imagined that little Starr, silent audience to our duet, would one day recite back to us our whole, grubby history. Our ramblings were punctuated by visits from Jessie and Lila, or from a haggard, haunted-looking Jake who was putting a show together. Through him I met a New York sculptress, relieved to hand over the keys of her loft to someone who came with the recommendation of the golden boy. Relieved that her home wouldn't be empty and vulnerable. That her cat wouldn't have to rely on the neighbour's goodwill.

I spent two afternoons reading cards by the fountain in the Cross, but my heart and soul remained absent. The readings weighed like a chore and I felt guilty for accepting money for such paltry offerings. At times I was seized by the fear that the cards, one day, would no longer speak to me ... a rebuff from Nella herself.

Sam and Starr had moved from the hospital to their two-bedroomed unit on the edge of the inner-city where I would go, ostensibly to help out. I spent hours gawping at the two of them. Marvelling at their silent communication. At the way

Sammy reacted to Starr's faintest murmer. The way she knew just when to feed him, just how much, and just how big a burp would follow. The way she massaged his pale, jelly-wobble skin to smooth away his irritability. To make sure he knew just how loved he really was.

When the day before my departure dawned, I was filled with a relief that overtook the house and half the street outside. I felt like a fifty-metre freestyle sprinter trying to swim a length without coming up for air. There was nothing in my life but the moment when my fingertips would hit the tiles, and when I could breathe again. When I could lift my head out of the water, ears ringing, and take a good look around to see the place I'd willed myself to. Where I could finally look down at my body and assess its needs. Where I could stop and listen to the voices in my head. Where I could stop.

I'd isolated myself from all but Sam and Starr. Distraction was simply not permitted. I took no photos, just a few snaps of Starr with Sam's Instamatic, at her request. I didn't go out of my way to avoid Jessie and Lila, but they had their pre-occupations and I had mine. Marlborough Street, without Sam and Jake, had no heart. I didn't avoid Jake; I just didn't see him. His visits to Sam's unit took place in the early morning. He'd come at the start of his day and watch over Starr for an hour while Sam languished in the bath, or stole another hour's sleep, or raced out to the shops. He had a way with the child that both Sam's mother and I lacked. Sam and I put it down to his musky scent, we reckoned Starr could sense his presence, was soothed by it. Lulled by the whispers about the world that Jake filled Starr's tiny ears with.

I planned to slip away early in the morning as quietly and as inauspiciously as I'd arrived. Spending the day before with Sammy and Starr, and retreating to Marlborough Street in the evening, to sit, chair pulled up to the open back door, Gough an inert blob at my feet, and continue reading my father's novels.

At six, I was preparing to leave Sam's place, to ride the bus home in time for the show of fading light, when she unceremoniously dumped the sleeping Starr in my lap and told me I wasn't to move. She had a phonecall to make. Her face all mischievous delight, she dragged the phone into her room and shut the door behind her. For a moment I was filled with dread. Please god, don't let her be buying drugs for us. Don't let her start ... but then she was back, all enigmatic smiles, and I was pushed into the bathroom and ordered to freshen up. Handed a low-cut, clinging, cobalt blue dress that Sam had worn before her cleavage frightened even herself.

- Come on Sammy, what the fuck are you up to? I pleaded, emerging from the bathroom with hair down over my shoulders and half my bosom exposed. Is this some sort of practical joke?

- No. It's just some sort of surprise, she said hugging me. You've had such a quiet, serious time since you've been back. I was scared you'd leave thinking Sydney had lost its sexy swagger ... that you'd never come home.

- For god's sake Sam, tell me what's going on, I demanded, scowling at her. Tell me or I'll leave now.

And I was thinking sex clubs and ecstasy parties and I don't know what else. Feeling like I was stuck on an hallucinogenic merry-go-round that I'd have to die to leave.

- It's a blind date Soph! she said, her voice registering its highest octave yet, quivering with excitement, as I was supposed to be. You're going on a blind date.

- Jesus Christ Sammy, I said, standing there, needing to pee, clutching at the shimmery fabric at my thighs. Why?

- Soph, don't be such a bore, she said, bossy, annoyed. Did you completely forget how to have fun in London? When was the last time a guy put his tongue in your mouth? Or anywhere else on your person?

- Great, I whined. You've booked me a male escort and instructed him to service me. What makes you so sure I'll be vaguely attracted to this mystery stud of yours?

- You forget who you're talking to Soph, she said, coquettish, running her finger over my smooth calf. You forget that I know you almost as well as you know yourself, only I'm more honest.

- Listen Sammy, call it off, I said. I don't want this.

- Soph, spend an hour with him. For me. If you don't like him, leave after that. Just an hour, she pleaded, running her finger on up my thigh. God you're a tart Soph! You still don't know the western custom of underwear.

- I do sometimes. I would have tonight if I'd known. It's just that I'm a fresh air kind of gal.

And that was when the soft knock on the door came and I fled with Starr into his room. Low mumbling reached me from the hall, and then footsteps across the lounge coming to the door, and a pair of cowboy boots.

- Hi Soph, said Jake, smiling down at Starr and me, smirking at the way Starr was trying to squeeze milk from a handful of breast-flesh with a sharp-nailed fist.

- Oh, fucking great, I said, scowling at him. You're in on this too. What am I? Everyone's favourite charity?

- I wonder why it is that every time I walk into a room you're either hissing and spitting or crying? he said in a tone designed to provoke. Are you coming or what? Or are you going to stay in hiding for the term of your natural life?

- Not much chance of that with friends like you and Sammy,

I said, kissing Starr's forehead and handing him to Sam. Might at least get a ride home out of it.

Sam pressed herself into me in a hug that miraculously left Starr rounded and intact between us. I grudgingly agreed to phone her from the airport in the morning and followed Jake out into the close of day.

I sat, sullen, pressed against the passenger door, squirming so the vinyl of the seat wouldn't attach itself, with all its urban grime, to my naked thighs. It was the first time I'd been in the ute since my return and I begrudgingly took in its comfortable, tarnished interior. I thought of it as Jake's home. He shoved a Soul II Soul tape into the deck, its wires hanging down like so many intestines. The music only made me scowl further, a scowl I wore on my whole body; it reminded me of Brixton, and the place that had just taken on the glow that Sydney once promised.

- So, where are you taking me? I asked, blasé as the city itself, as we passed the turn-off we would have taken if we were going to Marlborough Street. Don't tell me ... you're taking me to one of those ritzy hotels in the Cross?

- Yeah, that's it, he said, inscrutable as a closed door. Shut up and you'll see.

We drove through Whitlam Square, along the tame perimeter of Sydney's own Hyde Park and turned off behind the cathedral on the road to the art gallery, the Domain and to Mrs Macquarie's Chair. And that's when I started to feel awkward, not just vinyl on flesh uncomfortable. Had visions of myself flying from the car, skirt dancing wildly behind me in the breeze as I fled at the first opportunity afforded by a red light. But there were no red lights and I'd become convinced I was paralysed from the waist down on account of being stuck to the seat. I wasn't afraid ... it wasn't that. I was just unprepared.

As Jake pulled into a park right out near the point, he killed the music and we watched the last of the day's tour buses fill and move off towards the Cross.

- You haven't been down here since you've been back, have you? he asked, more gently. What're you hiding from? You loved it here. This point, the bay ... they were your places ...

I nodded dumbly and shrugged, struggling against the barely perceptible pull of the underwharf. And then I dived from the car, running, sure footed, down the bitumen path to the point. Clambering onto the low sandstone wall, to stand, face into the wind, like some unlikely, booted figurehead, with skirt billowing out behind, forming a double bridal train with my hair. And there it was before me, the dusk harbour that I'd deprived myself of, that I'd not even permitted myself to contemplate. And there was a buttery moon, rising from the unseen certainty of the ocean, just above the Dover Heights headland to the east. It was then, and only then, that I took my great gulps of homecoming air. It was then that I let myself embrace the vision I'd so pined for through the London winter.

- Not going to lose you that easily, he said behind me, one hand creeping around my waist, the other clutching a plastic bag.

- Sleazy bastard, I said, slapping the hand away, turning to face the park.

- Don't be pissed off, Soph. It's not a joke. I wanted this to be a real date – if you'll have me.

I leaned forward and held my head in my hands, so he couldn't see that all the blood in my body had rushed to my face.

- Ah, I said, trying to force something more coherent from my open mouth. I'm so sorry Jake. I feel very stupid ... mean ... Sorry.

- No, I'm sorry, he said sheepish, looking away but moving to sit beside me on the sandstone. It was a dumb idea. Really dumb.

- No! It was a lovely idea, I said, taking his cold fingers in mine and moving them to my lips. It was a very sweet thing to do. The most sweet, touching thing ever.

- Come on, he said, pulling his hand away and standing. I'll drive you home.

- No. You're my date for the evening, not my chauffeur. What's in the bag?

- Just some champagne, he said into his shoulder. Nothing really.

- You sure know how to impress a girl, I said, grabbing his hand and dragging him behind me. I know just the spot for a bit of illicit champagne guzzling.

And so I led him along the path below the Moreton Bay fig trees that skirted Woolloomooloo Bay. Past the pool, down the steps beside the sewerage plant, along a second path beside the water, back in the direction from which we had come. Where the path ran out there was a tainted sliver of oily sand and then only water. And beyond the water, part of it, was the underwharf.

Still clutching his hand, I lowered myself onto another sandstone wall and pulled him down beside me. There we faced the sparsely lit length of wharf and it seemed to me that the underwharf had provoked every strong emotion that had ever writhed inside me. Mainly though, the gaping void, the inky dark represented fear above all else. It was down at the bay that I'd felt the first stirrings of Nella's loss and turned from them. It was down, opposite the fingerwharf, I'd first seen Sam pass out from some fantastic milkshake of speed and vodka. And it was the underwharf that snarled inside my head each time I'd gone to the strip club, or fucked a man because I was angry.

With one hand and both thighs, Jake prised the cork from the bottle and poured the fizzy, golden stuff into two paper cups just before the wind could carry them away in their emptiness.

- What are we drinking to? I asked, slumped over his hand that I had entrapped in my lap, all thick-skinned and callused.

- Your real homecoming?

- Your exhibition?

- That you'll miss, he said, as though he didn't care.

- I might not miss it, I said, not looking him in the eye. I might even be back for opening night.

- I'd like that Soph, but you've got to do what you've got to do, he said blandly, so I was unsure of his support. As if someone like you is only going to spend a week in a city like New York. As if you're going to meet your father and just walk away.

- I might surprise you, I said, staring right at it, the underwharf, which in the darkness bled into the rest of the Bay. I might take one look at him and decide that's all I need. Might not even speak to him.

- Well, I like surprises Soph, he said, now bringing my fingers to his lips.

We sat and drank in a silence that meandered between the complicit and the awkward. Limbo, I kept thinking. It's Limbo. I'm waiting for something to happen, but nothing will ever happen. I'll slip from Limbo to the underwharf and never come out the other side. Never know why Jake and I are sitting here, unable to move forwards or back. Never know what it's like to look into my father's face and have him recognise me.

- I never spied on you Jake, I said. With the girls I mean. I just heard something outside the door once, that's all. Do you believe me?

- Of course, he said, looking at me sideways, a grin smeared over something darker. I'm almost offended that you didn't ... Come on, then. I've got some food at the studio. I'd really like you to see some of the pieces for the show.

And when we went to stand, on the narrow wall, our bodies turned into each other of their own accord, as bodies do. With all of me pressed up against all of him. The kiss that nearly knocked us clean off the wall and into the harbour lasted longer than any fifty-metre sprint ever had. His thigh between my legs became an extension of my own desire. Where my hands held his back under the jacket, I could feel my own heart, beating right through his chest. And where his own hand hesitated, under my skirt at the top of the thigh, my skin melded with his work-rough fingers.

- Ah, I croaked, pulling myself away and towards the water. I'm frightened Jake.

- Of me? he asked, his face folding in on itself. Of me?

- No. Of us.

Dazed, like a witness to a murder, I let myself be led away. We walked the path around the bay with hands gripping the flesh just above each other's hip-bones, legs moving in one fluid motion. In the ute, we sat in a fine mesh of silence, still holding hands, him reaching over with his right hand to change gears when it couldn't be avoided. Neither willing to break contact lest we forget how to connect again. I wondered if this was how Zelda had felt when she was with my father and if this was why she had run. Whether she, Zelda-the-fierce, Zelda-the-brave, was as frightened as I was by my own imminent loss of self.

The back streets of Ultimo were gaping, empty chasms, where lovers could fuck in the shadows watched only by cockroaches. The ugly concrete stairwell in the deserted warehouse forced our bodies together again. Pressed up against the rough, damp wall with Jake's hips crushed against mine, my cunt grew heavy with desire. If he hadn't hauled me up the stairs after him, I would have sunk down, calling him to me, demanding that he show me his velvet tongue right there in that functional grey space.

But when we burst into the studio, feet ringing on the white concrete floor, and I saw the table set for dinner by the window, something in me softened. Something drew me back to myself, gave me enough distance to permit me to drop his hand. To walk to the table and light the candles and to take in the wall of lights that was the city's western face. I prowled the room, running my hands over the planes and curves of the work he'd done while I was away, as he did things at the stove in the corner. I crouched beside his futon, down the other end of the vast room, and raised a pillow to my face to inhale. I took in this monk's life of his and respected it, marvelled at how fragile it was and wondered that I was there at all.

From behind, he steered me to a massive work table, strewn with sheets of paper bearing the rough, charcoal scratches of his drawings. He rifled in a pile, extracting three sketches of a leather-clad woman in various degrees of undress. The woman was me, stripping for the crowd, sneering, hard and angry. But beautiful? Had he made me beautiful?

- Me.

- Is it? he asked, mouth close to my ear, hands on my buttocks. Are you sure?

- We'll just have to wait and see, I said, moving away from him to sit at the table.

Wondering when to speak the words that were racing around my body. Wondering when the words of love would come tumbling from my mouth to crowd the vast space with their need.

Can you understand a man from having some sense of the landscape that he's chosen for his own ... What do the half-wild banks of the Hudson say about my father? And that vast body of water itself that masquerades as a river?

The Amtrak carriage's air-conditioning is so ferocious I am reminded of the polar reaches of Randolphe's bathroom and of London itself. I am conscious of my silk shirt having dried crusty where it was previously wet with sweat. The growls from inside me, from my belly, draw me back from the river. Cause me to take comfort in the protected world of the carriage where I feel safe, anonymous.

The old Sophie would have gone to her father with a mixture of lover's sperm and cunt-juice perfuming her skin, forming a hard second layer where there was once salt. The old Sophie would have made sure the serpent was at the ready, not hidden, and chosen leather, not silk. The old Sophie might even have been plotting their mutual debasement. Or rehearsing a tale about Zelda with which to shock, to wound. The old Sophie would babble at him like a maniac, watching from outside herself as her mouth caught splinters from her own words.

But instead, the landscape blurs as I try to replay the plots of the four novels I've just read. Try and spot the clue that has so far eluded me. Try and imagine how a man, who must have already had a deep sense of the spiritual, of the contemplative, could have become involved with a hell-cat like Zelda. How he could have loved her.

There's another voice in my head that I try to ignore. It says that he knew about me. It says he was relieved that she up and left. That even though he may have loved her, he was too much of a coward to follow her across the world, to confront her. Too much of a coward to need to know the truth.

Now, in the shallows by the tracks, among the reeds and the driftwood, ducks float high and healthy, where further downstream anything that hit the water was dead-meat. They waggle their fine, thick tails as they dive for fish, and I see him in the reeds, lying low with his newly oiled rifle, shooting at the rich copper feathers but losing his prize to the river. To the underwharf. But it's not him, is it? It's a character from one of his novels, another of the reinvented fathers, this one man of the gun, not of the word.

I tell myself again to be prepared for that question, that very obvious question; What do you want from me? What do I want from you, Father? Father, I don't know. A few minutes out of his station, if Amtrak runs to schedule, a few minutes from him, and I still can't answer that goddamn question.

I slump against the glass. I know I'm not strong enough to weather his disinterest, despite the years I've squandered preparing myself. A denial, I am convinced, will crush me. I, creature of skin as thin and brittle as a sparrow's egg. I, skin so thin I am crying still for the men huddled around the fire under the north-western skirt of the city. Crying still for Randolphe, alone, for Zelda, alone, for Nella, alone. For Jake, at the airport, certain that I won't return to him.

What right do I have, I ask myself again, to blunder into this man's world? A world that's likely to be every bit as fragile as my own. What risk is there of wounding a fifty-year-old man, whose bones will take longer to knit back together than my own? Of forcing him to look back on his life, to assess, again, its worth.

Already I have seen a house, there another, which signals the approach of the town where he lives. A house that may or may not be his. May be where he sits, desk drawn close to the window to write, watching the river, startled again and always, by the blur of a train in the landscape. Where he rebuilds the world with his pen, according to his own specifications. Where he dreams of some Shangri-la. Of Sydney Harbour where a woman he once loved lives.

As the town is indeed upon us, I eye the lever of the emergency brake. Eye the toilet cubicle I would flee to if it weren't already occupied. Imagining myself locked inside, hands rammed in my pockets so they couldn't scrabble at the door at the last minute. Me spying through a ventilation shaft at a man, destined never to know his daughter. He would be none the wiser. He would still be alone.

As the train slows, so does my heartbeat. My whole life, the whole of my pre-rehearsed life story, could fill the space between beats. The station itself comes into view, the beginning of a long, empty platform, from which I recoil, as though spat at. Not there, not there, I repeat to myself. Bastard's stood me up. Piss weak, coward of a man.

But before the train even stops, I can see the tall, lean body of a man who stands, straight as a pine tree, waiting for the blow that is sure to knock his body to the ground. Without realising it, I, too, am standing, now pressed against the glass, leaving an imprint of my short, sharp panic breaths on the window in front of me. And he turns his tanned, wrinkled face towards my carriage, a face that speaks to me of the earth, the hills and a world beyond the cities that I have not yet learnt. And in that face I see nothing of my own, but I claim it, regardless.

And just when I am sure he won't, he sees me. Sees my face, my hands on the glass, my absolute trust, absolute terror, and gives a barely perceptible nod of recognition. An inclination of the head, and a vague, bewildered smile through crooked lips that says more to me than all the words in his novels read back to back. He moves, deliberately, to the other side of the glass, to lay a hand, his right hand, against the window below mine.